A MATTER OF COURAGE

Hong Kong Nights, Book Two

J.C. Long

Published by
NineStar Press
PO Box 91792
Albuquerque, New Mexico, 87199
www.ninestarpress.com

Print ISBN #978-1-947139-77-0
Cover by Natasha Snow
Edited by Sam Lamb

Winston Chang has spent much of his young life admiring the Dragons who have kept his area safe and fought off the gangs that would bring violence to their area. Now that he's an adult, he wants nothing more than to join the Dragons and live up to those standards.

The opportunity presents itself when his passion and knowledge of cars is just what the Dragons need. One of their own has been killed and his death seems linked to his involvement with the illegal racing scene known as the Dark Streets. Winston is needed to infiltrate the scene and find out who is responsible and why.

Steel has always been Winston's best friend, and Winston has always been there to get him out of trouble. Just as the stress in Winston's life reaches its peak, the relationship between Winston and Steel begins to change in ways neither of them expected.

Will Winston and Steel be able to find the courage to face not only the unknown killer stalking the Dark Streets racers but also their growing feelings?

Acknowledgements

I want to thank the team at NineStar Press for believing in this story and bringing the world of Hong Kong Nights to life. The entire team is a joy to work with. Special thanks need to go to my editor, Sam Lamb, who does a fantastic job making my stories shine. This is our fifth project together, and I hope we have many, many more!

Prologue

THE NIGHT WAS split by the sound of squealing tires and burning rubber. It was four in the morning, and the streets near Stanley Market were all but abandoned. The few people out and about were fishermen or people setting out for the local fish market in hopes of getting there early enough to get the best catches of the day.

That meant few witnesses for the cars involved in the illegal street race that went speeding through the market, drifting around sharp turns. One after another they came, some drivers more skillful than others.

In the middle of the pack was a silver Ford Mustang; it came through the turn less smoothly than some of the other cars, an imperfect drift that caused it to nearly spin out. Behind the wheel was Min Fa, twenty-seven with a boyish face and an adrenaline addiction.

Min twisted the wheel just right, maintaining control as he lifted his foot off the brake to correct his shitty drift. It caused him to lose speed, and two cars passed him, but he could make up for it. A spinout would have put him even more behind, probably cost him the race.

If his count was right, he was in fifth place now. He could come back from that. He was naïve enough—and brash enough—to think that he could still win. He hadn't won any of the other four races he'd competed in, yet, but he did better each time. He was mastering the techniques of racing, slowly. His drifting was still off, but each time he did it, he improved. Soon he would be doing it like a pro, and then he'd be raking in the money.

He had a plan, a good one, if you asked him. Let the other racers focus on winning. He would focus on learning, and when the time was right and the pot was big enough, he'd speed out to the front of the pack and get himself a win. It was the perfect plan.

Min was on edge, because this race had them speeding through some rather tight turns and busy streets. At least there weren't many people outside at that time. He pressed his foot down harder on the accelerator, picking up enough speed to pass the car ahead of him for fourth position.

All he needed to do was maintain that position and he'd advance in the ranks, qualifying for the next race. Min could almost *taste* the glory that would come to the Dragons when he won big. They might even promote him from foot soldier to red pole. He just needed Wei Tseng to see he had value, that he could be useful.

The prize money didn't hurt, either.

The big races could bring in as much as a million dollars, easy. Min thought about all the good he could do with that money. He could take care of his little brother, get him a place to live that wasn't a small, one-bedroom apartment. Pay for him to go to a good school, have the nice things he deserved. Maybe even pay for their mother to get clean.

That one was a stretch and he knew it, but when you had big bucks, you could dream big.

Min was surprised when he managed to surpass the third-place driver after he turned too sharply, crashing into a light pole and knocking it down. He maintained that position all the way to the finish line, much to his surprise, and the surprise of his competitors.

What surprised Min even more was that first place belonged not to the man everyone called Tiny, but another racer he didn't know. Tiny wasn't even in second. Min hopped out of his car and walked to the second-place driver—a woman named Mimi. The two had spoken from time to time, and she was nice enough to him that he didn't feel uncomfortable approaching her.

"Yo, Mimi, where's Tiny? I ain't never seen him land in less than second place before."

Mimi regarded him with an expressionless face. "Dunno. Tiny didn't hit the starting line today."

"What? He never misses the Stanley Market ride." Min frowned, wondering if Tiny was sick. Well, if he was, then it just worked out well for him. Allowed someone else the chance to win some cash for once.

Coming in third didn't earn him nothing but an invitation to the next heat—which he got from one of the muscle-bound men wearing sunglasses in the middle of the night. That in hand, Min hopped into his car and made his way home.

By the time he reached his apartment building in the Eastern District of the island city of Hong Kong, he was exhausted, and the sun was beginning to cast its light across the sky. Min would need to wake Yao up for school soon, after making sure his useless mother hadn't brought anyone home with her, if she was at home at all. Once he got Yao off, he could sleep for a few hours before heading in to work. Someone had to make money for the family, and it wasn't his mother, that was for sure.

Min was almost at the door to the apartment building when he heard the footsteps behind him. He couldn't say why, but something made him turn around. As he did, he saw the glint of light off the barrel of the gun and then the gun went off.

One

WINSTON CHANG AWOKE with a splitting headache, a mouth that tasted like rubbing alcohol, and the feeling that he was on a boat out at sea during a storm. His stomach flip-flopped just from opening his eyes, and he let out a pitiful groan. He closed his eyes again and gritted his teeth to fight back the nausea that washed over him at the smell of his own breath.

What the fuck did I do last night?

He waited until the bout of nausea passed and slowly opened his eyes once more. He was happy to find he could open them without making himself puke; it was progress. He stared up at the ceiling, confused. It wasn't the ceiling of his room. His ceiling didn't have those weird little texture-bumps all over it.

The next thing Winston noticed was the sound of someone else snoring. He turned his head to the side, wincing at the stab of pain the movement caused. His best friend, who liked to be called Steel, was lying facedown on the bed next to him, head turned facing his direction. Steel was still lost in sleep, snoring every so often.

Winston couldn't face him long; Steel's breath also reeked of cheap booze and poor decisions.

Staring back up at the ceiling, he tried to remember something, anything, from the night before. He and Steel had gone to a bar, that much he remembered—like he remembered it being Steel's idea, because it was always Steel's idea. The place was a dive, dimly lit, stinking of smoke and booze and sweat. At some point in the night, they'd been approached by a group of people who asked them to join their group. Winston had been hesitant, wanting to get in early, though he couldn't recall why he'd kept insisting they leave. Steel had convinced him to stay, as always. Winston never could tell Steel no.

He vaguely recalled stumbling back to Steel's apartment, which was near the club, unable to drive home, barely able to walk up the single flight of stairs to Steel's apartment. At one point, he had thrown up, though he couldn't remember when, and everything after that was a complete blur.

Grunting, he sat up, and immediately buried his head in his hands to fight the swelling nausea that threatened to empty the contents of his stomach. Once he had it under control, he turned toward Steel. The way the sheet fell, Winston couldn't tell if Steel was dressed.

He looked down quickly, lifting the sheet off his own form. He was naked and sporting quite the morning wood despite his hangover. It was funny the things the body did.

Why the fuck am I naked?

He glanced at the clock. It was nearly nine in the morning. He searched around him, finding no sign of his cell phone or clothes. He turned, shaking Steel's shoulder roughly. "Dude, where're my clothes? Dude!" He shook harder, and Steel finally stirred long enough to roll onto his back, muttering something unintelligible.

Seeing Steel lying like that made Winston's pulse quicken. He raked his eyes over his friend's sleeping body, admiring the musculature. Steel wasn't a gym bunny, but his body was lean from a rougher-than-average childhood, whipcord muscles standing out with his arms stretched over his head. The room was chilly—Steel always slept with his air conditioner on—and his nipples were stiff buds. The sheet pulled down just enough for Winston to see that he was wearing his typical boxers.

Everything about Steel drew him in. He'd known Steel since he was ten years old—almost eleven years, now. For pretty much the entirety of that friendship, Winston had been in love with him. Something he'd been unable to shake. Most of the time, he didn't think he wanted to—and then other times, Steel drove him crazy, and not just in a sexual way.

Winston couldn't help his eyes traveling down to the dragon tattoo on Steel's calf—his leg was sticking out of the sheet—and his admiration was interrupted by a jolt of envy. Winston longed to have one of those tattoos himself, the mark of the Dragons, the gang—for lack of a better word—that ran the Eastern District. The underworld of Hong Kong, both the island city itself and the New Territories on the Mainland, was run by gangs, competing against one another and struggling to gain power.

The Dragons, though, they were different. They didn't rule through fear, drugs, or terror, but by protecting and serving the community. Wei, the leader of the Dragons, didn't allow drugs to be sold in the Eastern District, and he didn't demand protection money from the people; he protected them because it was a duty he'd taken upon himself.

It was a duty Winston wanted to take up, too.

He reached out to touch Steel's chest and stopped himself, instead slapping Steel's stomach—though it might not have been safer to go near his friend's lower body.

Steel jerked awake, swatting at Winston, who knew his friend well enough to move quickly out of reach. "What the hell, man?"

"Where are my clothes?"

Steel flopped back on the bed, closing his eyes tightly. Winston sympathized with what he must have been feeling at that moment, and he was thankful his nausea was mostly gone, leaving him with just the headache.

"Dude, my clothes?"

Steel inhaled and exhaled slowly several times before answering. "You don't remember? You puked all over them last night, so they're in the wash."

So that was when he threw up. That question was answered. "Okay, so how did I manage to get them off?"

Steel chuckled despite how much pain his head must be in. "You didn't. You just tugged at the shirt like a baby, and I finally got you undressed. Dick stiffed right up when I took off those little boy briefs, too. How long has it been since you got some action, Winston?"

The sound of his phone ringing jarred Winston, and he peered around for it, finding it on the bedside table next to him. He grabbed it and saw that it was Conroy Wong, Wei's right-hand man in the Dragons.

"Hey, Conroy." He hoped he didn't sound too hungover. Conroy didn't disapprove of drinking—the opposite, actually; he drank like a tank and never in his life seemed to have a hangover—but if he knew Winston had one, he would take great pleasure in torturing him in as many ways as he possibly could. "What's up?"

"Yo, where the fuck are you, man?"

Dread coiled in Winston's stomach; he didn't like it when Conroy sounded angry at him. "What's wrong?"

"Nothing's wrong. Just wanted to make sure your punk ass was up. A few of my boys told me you and Steel were out drinking 'til dawn. How ya feelin'?"

"I'm fine," Winston lied. "Absolutely no problem."

"Good, then you won't mind hoppin' in your car and driving to the airport," said Conroy cheerfully. Winston guessed if he could see him at that moment, he'd have that smug little smile on his face that drove Winston crazy. "The boss is busy right now, and Noah will be arriving this afternoon. Wei refuses to let him just ride public transportation like a normal person, especially since—"

"Since the subway will take him through Twisted Viper territory," Winston finished. He understood Wei's concern; their recent run-ins with the Twisted Vipers had been far less than friendly, and temperatures were getting even colder, fast. Considering Noah was at the heart of that unfriendly encounter, Wei's concern was completely justified.

"What time is he getting in?"

"Just after noon."

"Damn it. That means I need to get going now."

"Get on it." Conroy hung up with that.

"What did Conroy want?" Steel asked. He was now sitting up in bed, looking relatively healthier. Winston felt a bit of resentment at his quick recovery.

"Asked me to ride out to the airport to get Noah. Wei's busy."

"Oh, is Noah coming back from America today?"

"I guess so." Winston started out of the bed but stopped. "What the fuck am I going to wear?"

Two

"THANKS FOR PICKING me up," Noah Potter said on the way back from the airport. "I was hoping Wei would come, though."

Steel grinned at Noah over his shoulder. "Hoping for a chance to give him a little road head?" He laughed at the way Noah blushed. He'd never met a person who blushed as easily as Noah. It was fun teasing the guy.

"Maybe I was hoping for someone prettier than you to look at," Noah shot back, despite his blush. He'd been around them enough to catch on and even return their good-natured jabs.

Steel wouldn't say it, but he'd grown to like Noah's company in the short time the *gweilo* had been among the Dragons. He was handsome, funny, self-sufficient, and he made Wei happy, which was a bonus for everyone involved; an unhappy Wei was not fun to work with.

Steel settled back in his seat as Winston pulled the car onto the main highway, picking up speed as they went. He rolled his window down and stuck his arm out so he could enjoy the rush of air. It was nearing the end of September, and the weather was still uncomfortably warm, but it was getting better. Slowly.

The three of them were quiet, Winston focused on driving and Noah probably thinking about whatever dirty things he wanted to do with Wei when they were alone.

Steel took the opportunity to study Winston from the corner of his eye. It was a habit he'd fallen into a long time ago, back when he'd first started to discover his own sexual appetites. Winston was an attractive guy with a youthful face and big, brown puppy-dog eyes. He kept his hair shaggy, almost hanging into his eyes, despite his mother's constant badgering about trimming it down. Steel desperately hoped he didn't.

From the backseat came what almost sounded like a chuckle, and Steel's eyes flicked to the rearview mirror. Noah met his eyes and smirked. Steel frowned. What was he smirking at? He was embarrassed to be caught with his eyes on Winston, but he couldn't help himself sometimes. Winston meant a lot to him, for a lot of reasons, not the least of which was how Winston was always there for him from the first day they met.

It was a memory that Steel revisited a lot, his first run-in with Winston Chang. It was the middle of the night, with a torrential storm in the middle of summer, just a few days after Christmas. Steel was fourteen, running from a man he'd tried to pickpocket. The man turned out to be more dangerous than Steel anticipated, and he needed to escape. The quickest way to do so was to slip inside somewhere. He found an apartment building and began to climb its fire escape until he found a window flung open against the heat. He slipped inside without thinking. He found himself in Winston's bedroom.

A ten-year-old Winston awoke at his entrance and stared at him for a moment, eyes wide, but not with fear, with curiosity. He must have seen something in Steel's eyes, because he motioned for him to stay quiet and left the room. He returned a few minutes later with some snacks he offered to Steel. It was such a simple gesture, but from that moment on, Steel owed Winston a debt he could never repay, as far as he was concerned.

The sound of Winston honking the horn jarred Steel from his thoughts and brought him back to the present. "Dude, where do you get your road rage from?"

"*Ong lan gau.*" Winston scowled at him. He grinned in return. One of the things he found most pleasurable in life was annoying the shit out of Winston.

"Do you kiss your mother with that mouth?"

In the backseat, Noah snorted. "He probably learned that from her."

"True."

"You know, Noah, I'm glad you're back," Winston said, speeding around a car that seemed to be going too slow for his liking.

"Oh? Why's that?"

"'Cause maybe now Wei will stop being such a *ga tsan*. Once he gives you the D, he'll cheer up again."

Noah rolled his eyes, but Steel caught the small grin on his face. Yeah, he was looking forward to their reunion, too, no doubt about it. Steel couldn't blame him; it had been a while since he'd gotten any, too. He'd been working on it while at the club, but Winston went and got thoroughly trashed and Steel needed to look after him. He'd lined up a pretty easy lay, but Winston would always come first.

Steel's phone rang, then, and he dug it out of his pocket. "It's Wei," he said. He didn't need the rearview mirror to see Noah perk up. Knowing better than to keep the boss of the Dragons waiting, Steel answered the phone.

"He—"

"Steel," Wei interrupted, his voice in that no-nonsense tone that never meant anything good. "Tell Winston I need you guys at the shop."

"Can do, boss—but why did you call me and not him?"

Wei snorted. "You seen how he drives? No way I'm adding talking on the phone to it while he has Noah in the car."

Made sense; even Steel couldn't really come up with a nice thing to say about Winston's driving. He was reckless, disregarded speed limits and personal safety. "But how did you know I'd be with him?"

Another snort. "Don't ask dumb-ass questions, Steel. When are you not with him? Just get here."

"Will do." Steel hung up. "Looks like we're taking a detour, bro. Wei needs us at the coffee shop."

Winston caught Noah's attention in the rearview mirror, wriggling his eyebrows suggestively. "I guess he can't wait to see you, Noah." Steel suddenly braced himself against the door of the car as Winston jerked the wheel, taking them around a truck that honked several times. The driver flipped them off. "If we get there alive, anyway."

Three

WINSTON GOT A bad feeling the moment he brought his car—a 1974 Chevrolet Chevelle Laguna, which he'd restored himself—to a screeching stop in front of his mother's coffee shop, Coffee by Constance. There was a black sedan parked in front of it, gleaming as if it had just been washed and waxed where it stood. Black sedans were never a good sign.

"You can just leave your luggage in the trunk," Steel was saying to Noah, but Winston ignored them, heading inside the coffee shop.

As always, the smell of rich, dark coffee and sweet pastries that permeated the air met him as he entered. His sister was behind the counter. Winston saw so much of his mother in her: the round face, the bangs, the sharp, sometimes too-knowing eyes. That face was troubled today, turning even more so when she looked up and saw Winston there.

Winston stopped, narrowing his eyes suspiciously. "What's wrong?"

"Nothing's wrong," Shelby said too quickly, dropping her eyes to the counter, which she began to clean even though it was already spotless.

"Something's wrong," Winston insisted, stepping up to the counter and leaning toward Shelby. She was seventeen and a very open and easy to read young woman. The expression on her face stirred uneasy feelings in his stomach, like little insects flapping their wings. "What is it? Wei called and had us come here, so there's something going on."

Shelby pursed her lips in a way that reminded Winston far too much of their mother. It was her sign that she wasn't going to budge. He knew better than to try to get any more out of her. He doubted the villains in a spy flick would be able to torture information out of her with any success.

"Shelby!" Steel came in the door behind Winston, as boisterous and loud as ever. Shelby smiled at him, as happy to see him as she was her own brother.

"Steel, hey! Noah!" Shelby perked up when she saw Noah. She'd distrusted the American at first, especially when he had become lovers with Wei, who had been the object of her teenage affections for a while. She'd warmed up to him, though, when she realized how happy he made Wei and how impossible her own feelings for the Dragons' leader were anyway.

"I think Shelby was hoping you wouldn't make it back," Winston commented.

"Shut up, Winston," Shelby almost screeched, leaning over the counter to slap his arm. "That's not true, Noah. It's not."

"Don't worry. I don't believe him," Noah assured Shelby.

"Wei upstairs?" Winston asked, making his way back toward the kitchen.

"Yeah, he is. He, Mom, and Conroy, and—"

"Great, great." Winston brushed her words away and went back into the kitchen.

The back courtyard of the coffee shop was the only way to access a set of metal stairs leading up to a second-story apartment above the coffee shop. Constance owned it, too, and loaned it out to Wei and the Dragons as a viable meeting place. Winston figured Wei paid rent on it, but he didn't know how much or when, and Constance had no intention of telling him, either.

"Hey, Wei, I brought you a present," Winston called as he opened the door, a big smile on his face. The smile froze when he saw inside. The room was the way it always was—a television in the corner, a beat-up couch, a poker table surrounded by chairs. It was the people inside that caught Winston's attention. It wasn't only Wei, Conroy, and Constance, but another figure, one that Winston hated seeing.

Allen Hong, his uncle.

Winston practically felt his blood boiling as he took in Hong's face; he was pleased to see it paled a little bit, at least. Standing next to each other, Winston could see the resemblance between his mother and her younger brother. At forty-one years old, Constance was still beautiful, her face that of a woman in her mid-thirties, at most. Her frame was slight, her eyes the same deep brown as Shelby's. Hong was a taller, slightly broader-shouldered version of his sister. There was not a strand of hair out of place on his head, and he wore a suit, like most inspectors for the Hong Kong Police Department.

"What the hell is he doing here?" Winston demanded. He barely felt the pain of his nails biting into the palms of his hands as he clenched his fists. He heard the other two enter the room behind him, but his entire focus was on Allen Hong.

"Good to see you, too, Winston," Hong said, a bit of exasperation clear in his voice.

"Do you not get when you're not wanted here?" Winston advanced toward Hong, but his mother stepped between them.

"Do I need to remind you who owns this place?" Constance snapped, her cheeks reddening. "You don't get a say in who goes where until you pay the bills, you understand?"

"After everything this *puk gai* has done—"

"Winston." The single word came from Wei, and it was spoken in a normal tone, but it had an immediate effect. Winston's jaw snapped closed, though he still glared at his uncle. He knew he was getting close to crossing a line with Wei, and he didn't want to do that. Wei already thought he was too childish to join the Dragons; he didn't want to give him more evidence of that.

"Guess it's like I never left," Noah remarked from the door.

"Sorry, Noah, there's a little business I need to take care of first," Wei apologized, his voice gentling slightly as he addressed his lover.

"What kind of business?" Steel asked, coming up to stand next to Winston.

Winston felt Steel's hand on the middle of his back, between his shoulders. That small pressure allowed him to relax, letting his shoulders sag and his fists unclench. He was grateful for Steel's presence there; he was the only one who could get through Winston's rage, and he did it without ever needing to speak.

"Dragons kind," said Conroy from where he sat on the arm of the couch, arms crossed over his chest. Winston was always jealous of Conroy's movie-star looks—his facial structure, his muscular body, his constantly perfect hair—it all made him seem like he'd strolled in off the pages of a celebrity magazine, not like he ran in the streets with a gang.

Next to Conroy, Wei was almost average, but he was handsome in a hard way. He had a magnetism, an unmistakable aura of power that drew people to him. It was easy for Winston to see what attracted Shelby—and Noah—to him, and what made him an effective leader. Wei inspired loyalty in the Dragons, and that was more than any of the other gangs, like the Twisted Vipers, could say. Winston wanted to be part of that, part of the Dragons, more than anything, and he would do whatever it took to show Wei that he was ready. He burned for Wei's approval; there was no one in his life he respected more, except for his mother.

Then his eyes fell on his uncle again, and rage churned in his stomach like molten lava in a volcano.

"I still don't see what that has to do with him," Winston said savagely.

Hong opened his mouth to say something, but Wei shook his head firmly and he fell silent. Wei turned to Winston. "You still haven't learned to control yourself yet. You still walk around like an entitled brat. You keep saying you're ready to be a Dragon? You can't even get out of your feelings!"

The anger in his stomach mixed with shame. "I am ready, Wei," he said, hating how tight his throat had become. "I'm ready to be a Dragon!"

"No, you're not," Constance objected.

"Mom, I'll be twenty-one in a month. You can't keep protecting me forever."

"You're my son!" said Constance fiercely.

"But I'm a man, now!"

"Enough," Wei snapped, drawing their attention back to him. "I've told you before, Constance, that you can't keep him out forever. Winston, you keep saying you're ready, and I'm going to give you a chance to prove it."

Four

WINSTON BLINKED. "What? Really?" He couldn't believe he'd heard Wei correctly. This was the moment he'd been waiting five years for. He wanted this more than anything. Just the thought of it had his heart racing, his pulse jumping with anticipation.

Conroy let out a bark of laughter. "I think he's gonna wet himself from excitement, boss."

"Don't call me that," Wei said, but the admonition was hollow; it was a dance the two of them had performed countless times and would continue to. "All right, Winston, I'll give you your chance."

Constance threw her hands up and stomped toward the door. Noah, who was standing awkwardly in front of it, stepped aside so she could exit.

"That is one unhappy woman," Steel commented. Winston elbowed him hard in the side. "Ow. What? I'm just saying. Constance looked pissed."

"She'll get over it," Winston said, mind not on his mother but on trying to imagine whatever task it was Wei had in mind for him to prove his usefulness to the Dragons.

"I'll go talk to her," Noah offered, and Wei nodded at him. Winston gave Noah a friendly wave farewell. He recognized Noah's subtle way of excusing himself from Dragon business so he didn't have to be dismissed. The white guy caught on quick. Probably one of the reasons Wei decided to keep him around.

"What is it you want me to do, Wei? I'm so ready for this."

"You better be sure," said Wei, seriously. "This isn't going to be easy."

Winston didn't know if he liked the sound of that, but Wei could ask him to do anything and he'd do it. Jump off a bridge? No problem. Light himself on fire? Where's the match? He yearned to be a Dragon—it was his rightful place, his way of honoring his father. The man died helping Wei secure the Eastern District from the Nine Stars, the gang who'd terrorized the territory before the Dragons rose up and took them down five years ago. It only made sense for Winston to join the group of people who were actually protecting the place his father fought so hard to free.

"Anything, Wei. Anything."

"You say that now," Conroy chimed in, but Wei glared, shutting him up.

"Okay, Winston. Your particular expertise is going to come in handy on something that Hong just brought to me."

Winston bit back a retort, knowing it would fuck up any chance of Wei trusting him. He wasn't able to resist glaring at Hong, though.

"Yesterday morning a body was found outside an apartment building near the border between Tai Tam Tuk and the Eastern District," Hong said, taking a photo out of his pocket and passing it to Winston.

Winston took it and studied the face of the man—young, probably not much older than himself, if he had to guess. He was handsome, in a way, but also appeared hollowed out, worn down by something other than time. His cheeks were shallow pits, his eyes somewhat sunken in, dazed.

"He looks familiar," Winston said after a moment, though he couldn't place him.

"He should. He's one of ours."

Winston turned to Wei. "This guy is a Dragon?" He shouldn't be so surprised; the group of people he was so familiar with were what the triads called red poles, lieutenants reporting to the leader, or dragonhead—a title Wei flat-out refused to claim—but there would be lots of grunts, or foot soldiers, to help protect the territory. The Eastern District was large, and the Dragons' territory expanded to damn near half of Hong Kong Island; no way Wei and the tight-knit red poles alone could control it. But this guy, he didn't strike Winston as the Dragon type.

In response to his blurted doubt, Hong handed him another photo, this one of the man's leg: there was a dragon tattoo spiraling around his ankle.

"His name was Min Fa," Hong went on. "Right now all we know about his death is he was shot outside the building—single bullet to the head, execution style."

"Was it robbery?" Steel asked, crowding in over Winston's shoulder to see the picture. Winston felt the warmth of Steel's breath on his neck and cheek, and a shiver passed through him.

"Nothing was taken."

"So someone targeted him because he was a Dragon," Winston surmised, doing his best to shift his position so that there was a little more distance between himself and Steel without drawing attention to it.

"We can't say that yet." Hong pulled out two more photos. "Both of these men were shot similarly in the last few weeks. It took place in different areas of the city, so it didn't get connected right away."

Winston studied the first photo, a tattoo-covered guy with big gauges in his ears, probably closer to thirty than to Winston's age. "That's a man named Myung-jin Park, Korean-born, moved here a couple years ago. He was found shot in Victoria Harbor."

The second picture was of an older man, a big, burly dude, his age hard to tell from the photo. "This guy is Iquey Chen, AKA Tiny. He was found shot in Hok Tsui. Both with the same kind of gun used to shoot Min, both shot around the same time of day—somewhere between three in the morning and dawn."

"They all have a connection," Wei added significantly.

"Right. They are all known to be involved in the Dark Streets races."

Winston let out a low whistle.

"Sounds like our car freak knows what that is," Conroy said.

Winston snorted. He couldn't think of anyone in Hong Kong who hadn't heard of the Dark Streets. It was an illegal street-racing operation that had come together in the last few months, really gaining fame recently when the money involved for the winner in the higher heats reached astronomical numbers.

"Of course he knows what it is," Steel said, patting Winston on the shoulder twice. Both touches sent tiny bursts of fire through Winston. "You thinking these deaths are because of their involvement in the Dark Streets?"

"Too early to tell," Conroy said. "That's where you come in."

"I don't know about using Winston," Hong said carefully.

Winston bristled. Who the hell did Hong think he was, trying to determine what he could or could not do? "That's not your call, Hong." Winston said sharply. He felt a surge of victory as Hong flinched at the way his name had been spat back at him.

"I don't like it either," Wei said, sounding like he also didn't like agreeing with Hong. "But we don't have any other choice."

"Why the hell hasn't Hong Kong PD closed the races down?" Steel demanded. "Roadblocks, something?"

"We've tried." The only thing that showed Hong's frustration with this was a sudden intensity in his eyes. "We've set up roadblocks, but there's no way to predict where they'll hold the next race, and it's never in the same place twice. Whoever is organizing these races always seems to know where the roadblocks will be."

"I've told you before Dang is dirty," Wei growled. Superintendent Dang was the head of the Eastern District precinct of the Hong Kong PD, and he was on the payroll of the Twisted Vipers.

"And I told you I've got to find proof," Hong returned evenly.

Winston looked between the two of them. They were both alpha males, and this struggle of theirs seemed almost inevitable. It was hard to believe he had memories of the two of them as friends. Before Hong became a traitor.

"What do you want me to do?" Winston asked.

"You're our resident car expert," said Wei, "so I need you to infiltrate the Dark Streets and find out what you can about these murders, and about who's running the show. Something like this going on in the streets, it's a threat. Let the people behind it get too much power and they start getting ideas."

"That sounds dangerous," Steel said, frowning.

"He's joining the Dragons, not the fuckin' boy scouts," Conroy snapped. "Since when do we do shit that ain't dangerous?"

Winston didn't even need to think about it. He didn't care if it was dangerous—actually, part of him was thinking the more dangerous the better. No way could anyone question his value if he took this on. Infiltrating an illegal street-racing circuit? Sounded like fun.

"I'm in."

Five

"YOU'RE REALLY FUCKING stupid," Steel repeated as he and Winston arrived outside the apartment that had been Min Fa's home. He couldn't explain why he was so furious, but he was, and since he wasn't one to bottle things up inside, he decided to make sure Winston knew it.

"So you've said," Winston muttered, ducking his shoulders under the insult. "What did you expect me to do? Tell Wei 'Uh, no thanks, sounds dangerous'? Are you out of your fucking mind? You know how long I've wanted this, man. No fucking way I'm missing this opportunity."

Steel did know how much Winston wanted it, and that was part of the problem. Winston was so determined to prove himself, to prove he was as good a man as his father, and Steel was afraid he'd end up doing something not just a little stupid but supremely stupid in the pursuit of that goal.

"Yeah, yeah, so make sure you're alive to enjoy it, all right?"

"No promises," Winston replied, stepping out of the car. Steel let out a hiss of frustration and followed him.

They both paused in front of the cordoned-off bloodstain on the sidewalk, the physical reminder of Min Fa's death. Steel wondered for a moment how the family must have felt coming home to see that symbol of what was once there but now wasn't.

Someone should really wash that off.

"You coming?" Winston called from inside the door of the apartment.

Steel took another moment to survey the rust-colored stain before following Winston inside.

"Wei said Min's apartment was two-eleven."

Winston and Steel took the stairs two at a time, examining numbers on the door to see which direction of the hall they needed to go down. They found door two-eleven smack-dab in the middle of the hall on the left-hand side.

They both stood there in front of the door, trading expectant looks, waiting for the other person to knock. "Go on," Winston said insistently.

"What? Me? No way. I'm not knocking on the door of the grieving family! You do it."

"It's just a door, Steel. Knock."

"If it's just a door, then you knock. This is your job from Wei; I'm just tagging along out of boredom." Winston grimaced, and Steel knew he had him. "Come on. Cheer up! This is your big chance to prove your worth and all that good stuff, right?"

Winston nodded reluctantly and took several deep breaths, seeming to ready himself. Just as Winston raised his hand to knock, Steel rapped his knuckles against the door three times in rapid succession.

"What?" he asked innocently in reply to Winston's dagger-like glare. "You know I can't resist fucking around with you." There was something damn near irresistible about Winston when he had that look on his face, something that made Steel just want to lean in and—

The sound of footsteps behind the door interrupted that line of thinking—and probably for the better; he wasn't wearing the best pants to pop an erection in.

A moment later, the door swung open and any thought of a sexual nature he might have had vanished. Standing there, pouty-faced, was a little boy, seven years old or so. He was small, with a buzz cut that only served to make his ears stand out and his head look bigger. His clothes were food-stained and too big for him, and his shirt had a big hole in it right under the left arm. He clutched a toy of some kind protectively.

Steel swallowed hard against a tight lump that formed in his throat. Looking at the kid's face, it was obvious this was Min's little brother. It was difficult to fight back the swell of memories that threatened to crest his defenses and wash over him, especially looking into those eyes. They reminded Steel a lot of his own eyes at roughly the same age, full of suspicion and loss and despair. He also saw a flicker of something else in there, though: hope.

Steel crouched down on one knee, bringing himself to the little boy's eye level. "Hey there, *daih dai*," he said gently. "Is this Min's house?" The little boy nodded cautiously. Someone had instilled the right ideas into him, taught him to be careful of strangers. They probably should have taught him not to open the door, too, but it was a good thing they didn't.

"What's your name, little guy?"

"Yao."

Steel smiled kindly. "Yao. That's a good name, a strong name. What's that you've got there?" Yao hesitated for a moment before showing Steel the toy he carried tucked under his arm: a Teenage Mutant Ninja Turtle.

"This is awesome! You like Raphael?"

Yao nodded.

"Me too. He's my favorite." He leaned forward like he was confiding a secret, pointing his thumb at Winston. "This guy here likes Leonardo." He rolled his eyes dramatically, showing what he thought of that, and Yao giggled.

"My name is Steel, and this here is my buddy Winston. We're friends of Min. Do you think it would be okay if we came inside real quick? Min had something important of ours that we need."

Yao studied Steel intently, as if gauging whether or not he could be trusted. Finally he turned and let them inside. The apartment was small and dirty. The sink piled up with dishes, the floor in desperate need of sweeping. Every piece of furniture looked ancient. There was a futon laid out on the ground next to the couch, which had a sheet and pillow on it. Steel assumed that Min and Yao slept there. The television was on some cartoon or other. There was an opened door that led to the tiny bathroom, probably equally dirty. There was a door next to the bathroom, shut, that must have led to the apartment's single bedroom. Along the wall was an old-fashioned wardrobe that was dirty and scarred, missing one handle and chinks from the wood.

Steel frowned as he surveyed his surroundings. This is where this poor kid lived? This was the life the gods consigned Yao to? It was unfair—but then again, when was life fair for anyone? Steel knew firsthand exactly how unfair life was to a young child. He saw a lot of himself in Yao.

"Yo, Steel?" Winston nudged Steel's shoulder gently, and he jerked, surprised. "Where is your head at, man?"

"Sorry, was just thinking." Steel touched Winston's shoulder apologetically. He was struck by the sudden longing to linger, to rub and caress, but settled for a quick squeeze. "Let's look around and see if we can find the phone."

Before they left the shop, Wei'd instructed them to find a burner phone that would be among Min's things. "It's how they communicate the times and locations of the Dark Streets races. I have no idea how someone gets their start in the races, where they get the phones, but once they have them, this is how it's done."

"If whoever did this was part of Dark Streets, how do you know they didn't get the phone when they shot him?" Winston had asked.

"They're not allowed to have the phones on them in case they are arrested during the races. It'll be at Min's house, somewhere. That's your way in."

Steel crossed the room to the closed door. As his hand reached for the doorknob, Yao lunged for him, grabbing his leg and shaking his head, real fear flashing in his eyes. "What's back here?" Steel asked kindly, wondering what it was that was causing so much fear.

"Daddy?"

Yao shook his head.

"Mommy?"

A hesitant nod answered him.

"Do you know where your brother kept his things?"

Yao took Steel's hand and walked him to the wardrobe. At Yao's encouraging nod, Steel opened the doors. There were sheets and things, but mostly clothes stuffed inside. The majority of the clothes were for Yao; there wasn't much that a grown man like Min would wear. Yao pulled his hand free of Steel's and tugged open the bottommost drawer of the wardrobe, revealing the few meager articles of clothing that Min had possessed. Right on top of the clothes was a foldable black burner phone.

Steel picked it up and tossed it over to Winston. He regretted it the moment he did; Winston's nickname when they were playing with the neighborhood kids was *Zhou*, clumsy. Winston fumbled to get a grip on the phone, but it slid between his fingers, clattering to the floor.

"What the hell are you doing out there, you little shit?"

Yao clutched tightly at Steel's leg again, body trembling at the voice. Someone moved around behind the closed door before it was yanked open, a woman in her forties and dressed in clothes as dirty as Yao's stood there. The odor of alcohol and something else filtered into the front room from the bedroom, and Steel wrinkled his nose.

"Who the fuck are you?" the woman demanded, her words slurred and her eyes unfocused. Steel clenched his fist tightly. She was a drug addict, just like his mom had been; he could see it clearly. A quick look at her arm revealed the telltale track marks. She was getting high and passing out in her bedroom rather than taking care of her young son. Did she even know Min was dead?

"We're friends of Min's," Winston said hurriedly, picking up the phone and stuffing it into his pocket. "He asked us to come—"

"Min is dead," Steel spat. The woman forced herself to meet Steel's eyes, focusing on his words and trying to comprehend past the haze of her high. Steel gently pulled away from Yao, walking toward the woman. He revealed the dragon tattoo on his calf to her and saw her eyes widen in understanding.

"We're with the Dragons, lady. You should know Wei Tseng doesn't like drug dealers in his territory."

"I don't buy here," she said, afraid. "You tell him I don't buy here and I don't—I don't sell it."

"I don't give a fuck whether or not you do," Steel said. His voice was taut with the anger he was struggling to restrain. "Your son is dead; you've got no one else to take care of this little boy here. I'm going to make sure some money gets around to you, because Min was one of us, and Dragons take care of their own. I want you to understand this, though." He pitched his voice low, so only she could hear him. "I will be coming by to check up on him. You better not spend a single fucking dime of this money on drugs. It goes to him—to food and clothes for him. You understand me?"

She nodded quickly. Her stale breath, reeked of booze and bad hygiene, coming rapidly.

"Don't doubt me. I keep my word. If I catch one hint of drugs in this house again, if I get the slightest idea this boy's being neglected, I will make you suffer."

Steel turned back to Yao. "Is it okay if I come back and visit you, *daih dai*?"

Yao nodded slowly, still not speaking. His big brown eyes said everything Steel needed to hear, though.

"Good. See you soon, little man." Steel ruffled Yao's hair and went to the door, motioning Winston to follow him. "Oh, and lady, get this place cleaned up. It fucking stinks."

The acid of anger and memory burned in his stomach long after the scent of that apartment faded. Steel could only stare out the car window, Yao's face etched into his mind.

Six

WINSTON KNEW HE was in for a battle the moment he walked into his mother's apartment and found her sitting in her recliner, holding a glass of wine. Constance only drank during the day when she was mad. He needed to step carefully; he knew from experience that the slightest thing would trigger her temper at this stage.

"Hey, *Mah Ma*," he said, keeping his voice as casual as he could.

"Sit down." Constance jerked her head toward the sofa next to the recliner.

"Actually, I've got some things I—"

"Sit. Down."

Winston heaved a put-upon sigh. There was no point in resisting and starting a fight, so he did as she asked, settling on the comfortable microfiber sofa and watching his mother expectantly. When Constance didn't say anything, Winston decided to head her off at the pass and hopefully avoid an argument.

"*Mah Ma*, I know you don't want me to get involved with the Dragons because you think it's dangerous, but—"

"You're exactly right, but that's not what I want to talk to you about."

Winston blinked. "It's not?"

"No." Constance took a deep breath, and nervousness tightened in Winston's gut. He'd never seen his mother act this way before. "I want to talk to you about your uncle."

Winston could not control the way his mouth morphed into a sneer or the tension that entered him at the mention of Allen Hong. "That *puk gai* is not my uncle," he snarled.

"I've told you before I don't want you talking about him like that." Constance's words came out like the crack of a whip, and Winston could recognize her now. In her anger, Constance was a force to be reckoned with. He'd even seen Wei back down from her when she got like this. "I won't have it in my house, do you hear me? You say what you want outside these walls to impress Wei and the Dragons, fine. I know I can't stop you. But here? My wishes will be respected."

"He's the reason I don't have a father!" Winston shouted, jumping to his feet.

"Your uncle had nothing to do with your father's death! He wasn't a cop then—he didn't become a cop until much later!"

Winston shook his head. He couldn't believe the way his mother could rationalize it in her mind. "It doesn't matter! He joined the same group of people who murdered my father—he betrayed everyone after what you all went through—"

"Get out of your hurt feelings!" Constance shouted, her face flushed with anger. "Allen chose a different path than Wei did—that's not a crime! Wei doesn't have all the answers, Winston. Wei isn't always right!"

The words echoed in the silence of the apartment. Winston was stunned. In the five years since the war with the Nine Stars, Winston had never once heard his mother speak of Wei in a way that was even remotely negative.

"This is my fault," Constance went on, trembling. "I can't do anything about Wei's issues with Allen, that's between them, but I let you nurture this grudge, and that's on me. But I've had enough of it, Winston. If this is how you're going to act, then I was right. You're not ready to join the Dragons."

"That's not your call," Winston said, almost tauntingly.

"No," Constance conceded. "I guess it's not." She shook her head, something like pity in her eyes, stabbing into Winston's heart. "One day, Winston, you're going to realize that family—true family—isn't something that can be so easily thrown away."

She turned her back to him, then, making for the kitchen. She paused long enough to look back at him over her shoulder, and Winston realized what it was he saw in her eyes that hurt so much.

Disappointment.

Seven

STEEL WAS WELL aware of the eyes on him as he carefully aimed his shot, bent over the pool table at a slight angle. His opponent was sort of sneering, as if daring him to find a shot to make. The thin, greasy-haired man had done a good job with defense; there wasn't any blatantly obvious move for Steel to take. The guy clearly didn't know Steel if he was feeling confident.

Steel never went for the obvious shot.

Sighting along the cue, he saw the shot he wanted to take. The right side pocket was a clump of four balls, one of them the eight ball and one of them his own. The other two were stripes belonging to Greasy. The eight ball was perilously close to the edge, and tapping it in the wrong place would send it tumbling into the pocket and cost him the game and one hundred dollars.

Steel wasn't about to lose one hundred dollars.

"Three ball, side pocket," he announced, drawing the stick back and striking the cue ball. It rolled into the side, bouncing away toward the pocket that Steel wanted. He watched it, silently encouraging it to hit in the right place. And it did; it struck the wall while barely nudging the three ball, sending it inching forward enough to lose balance and fall into the hole while also making the eight ball roll forward a little, in turn making it difficult for Greasy to land a shot in that particular pocket.

He grinned, less at the chorus of curses that rose up from Greasy and his buddies and more at the appreciative eyes that lingered on him from some of the women—and men—in the pool hall. Despite the smile, he wasn't enjoying himself near as much as he usually would. There was a lot of shit on his mind.

First and foremost was how Winston was about to go put himself in danger in the Dark Streets races. He understood the logic of it. Wei needed eyes in there, and the Dragons he trusted most were too high profile; the organizers of the race, whoever they were, would never let them in, and few people knew cars the way Winston did. None of that changed the fact that his best friend was about to go throw himself in harm's way.

Beyond that, the face of that kid, Yao Fa, kept popping into his head. He couldn't get the kid's intense stare out of his mind. He knew it was ridiculous, but he couldn't help feeling like it was his fault, like he'd failed that kid somehow. He didn't even know about him before today, though, nor had he ever met his brother, Min. Steel didn't interact much with the grunts, since Wei used him as muscle when he needed it.

But that kid... Steel saw too much of himself in him. He knew what it was like to have the drug-addicted mother putting her high over the wellbeing of her child. His young life had been a string of strange people coming home with his mother to join in, or else his mother disappearing for days at a time while she lay strung-out in some crack house or back alley.

Steel forced thoughts of little Yao out of his head, concentrating on Greasy lining up a bad shot he knew would cost him the game. "I wouldn't take that shot if I were you," he cautioned, but Greasy just sneered at him.

"What, because you don't want me to win?"

"No, because I don't want the game to be over so quickly."

Greasy just rolled his eyes, smirked, and took the shot. Steel watched the cue ball do exactly what he thought it would. Greasy struck the ball at a bad angle, sending it spinning off in a way he didn't intend. Instead of hitting the nine ball like he wanted, he struck the eight, sending it into the side pocket.

"I told you," Steel said cheerfully, collecting the money he and Greasy both placed on the side of the table.

"You know, no one likes a smartass." Steel turned to see who the comment came from and was surprised to see Noah standing there. Plenty of eyes were on him; he was probably the first white guy to come into this pool hall in its history.

"What are you doing here, White Boy?" Steel asked, tossing his cue stick over to someone else for them to play a round. He had a feeling Noah wasn't paying him a social visit.

"I came to find you. There's something I need to tell you."

"Is this official or unofficial?"

"I'm here, so what do you think?"

Steel nodded his understanding. Wei probably didn't want to draw any more attention to Steel than necessary, and coming himself would have still drawn more attention than sending in a foreigner. He motioned Noah to follow him and led him to the far corner where there was a vending machine dispensing bandages, gloves, pain relievers, and other things that might come in handy in a pool hall.

Steel took money out of his wallet, sliding it into the machine in case anyone was watching them. "What is it you wanted to say?"

Noah hesitated a moment and Steel knew he probably wasn't going to like it. "Look, Winston is great—you know I think that—but I'm worried. We're worried," he added meaningfully, and Steel knew the other person in that was Wei. Wei respected Winston enough not to come directly, but sent Noah out, which meant if word got back to Winston, it could look like just Noah being nervous and not like Wei doubted his abilities. Goddamn, the man was smart.

"I'm worried too," Steel confessed. "Winston's about to run off half-cocked into a situation we don't know shit about. Add in the fact it has something to do with racing when Winston already drives like a maniac...well, you get the picture."

Noah nodded. "That's why I'm here. We—I—want you to stick close to Winston during this thing. Three people have turned up dead, and we don't know if it's because of this race or not. We don't want Winston to be the fourth."

"I understand," Steel said quietly. He didn't need Wei's instructions for this particular matter, anyway. No way in hell he was going to let Winston go running off into danger without him. They had each other's backs, always. And if anyone tried to hurt Winston, well, they would have to go through him first.

Noah nodded and turned to walk away, Steel not following. When he was halfway across the room, Noah turned and called back to Steel loud enough for everyone to hear, "You have two days to get my money!"

Smart bastard. Steel almost grinned. "You'll have your fucking money, *gweilo!*"

A chorus of rough laughs met his words, and Noah nodded ever so subtly before stepping out of the pool hall.

One of the men who'd been watching his match with Greasy sauntered up to Steel at the vending machine. "Fucking gweilo think they own everything, don't they?"

"Yeah," Steel said, adopting a heavy scowl. "Fuck him."

"Or," the stranger said, leaning close to Steel's ear, lowering his voice, "you could fuck me."

Steel's eyebrows shot up—as did his dick—at the brazen proposal. "You know what? Sounds good to me."

The guy grinned and made his way out of the pool hall. Curious and hoping no one noticed the bulge in his pants, Steel followed suit. Outside, the guy ducked into the alley between the pool hall and the building next to it, an old dry cleaning shop. The alley continued until it wrapped around behind the pool hall, out of sight of the street.

"Right here?" Steel asked, glancing around.

"Why not?" The guy fell to his knees, hands going to the button of Steel's pants. Steel didn't resist as his pants were tugged open and pushed down to his knees. The guy slipped his hand inside the slit of Steel's boxers, tugging his cock and balls out through the opening and exposing them to the air. Steel's cock was thick and veiny; even fully erect it pointed at a ninety-degree angle, not straight up.

The guy let out a hum of appreciation and wrapped his lips around the head, flicking his tongue against the slit. Steel hissed in pleasure as the warm mouth closed around him, slowly sucking more in. Steel shuffled a bit so he could lean against the side of the pool hall and enjoy the blow job.

The guy had some skills, Steel thought appreciatively, leaning his head back and closing his eyes. He let his thoughts drift away, the only thing mattering then being the wet warmth of this guy's mouth closing around more and more of his cock.

Before the guy could get settled into a good rhythm, Steel's phone rang—Winston's ringtone. He immediately pulled his cock free of the guy's mouth and bent down to dig the noisy device from his pocket.

"Dude, just let it go to voicemail," the guy urged, flicking his tongue against the ridge of Steel's tip.

Steel ignored him, answering the phone. "Yo, what's up?"

"You at home?" Steel could hear the tension in Winston's voice in just those few words and knew something was up.

"I can be real quick."

"Good. I'm on my way there."

Steel hung up the phone and immediately tugged his pants back up and tucking his deflating cock into his pants.

"What the hell, man?" protested the guy, but Steel ignored him, heading out of the alley while he was still buckling his belt.

Winston needed him.

Eight

WINSTON SAW STEEL jogging toward his apartment as he approached the building himself. He briefly wondered where Steel had been but decided he'd rather not ask, in case he didn't like the answer. It was strange how possessive he felt over his best friend, he knew that, and yet that was how it was. He was certain Steel felt the same way.

"Everything okay?" Steel asked Winston as soon as they met in front of the apartment building.

Winston just shrugged tersely.

Steel slipped an arm around Winston, and Winston relaxed. It was as if the simple act of contact was enough to ease the tension that had built inside him since his conversation with his mother. They walked like that up to his apartment door, and by the time they reached it, most of the anger had seeped out of him.

Winston leaned against the wall next to the door while Steel unlocked it and followed him inside. A sense of belonging draped Winston as he took in the mess of the apartment. Clothes were all over the place, empty takeout boxes on the table, glasses and cups covering pretty much every surface. The couch was top of the line, though, as was the fifty-inch television. Other than that, everything was sparse; a coffee table and a lamp.

"Okay," said Steel, pressing a cold beer into Winston's hand and nudging him with his leg so he could sit on the right side of the couch, which he preferred. "I left a damn good blow job for this. What gives?"

The idea of someone giving Steel a blow job stuck in Winston's mind, spiking his jealousy. No matter how much he didn't want to, all he could think about was some stranger's lips wrapped around Steel's meaty cock and he wished it had been him.

"Winston?" Steel repeated.

"Sorry. Just thinking." Winston shook his head, clearing away the sexual thoughts. He was achingly hard right then, harder than he'd been when he woke up that morning. "I had a fight with mom." Winston explained the confrontation with Constance while they drank their beers.

"She's never understood me on this," he finished.

"It's her brother," Steel said with a shrug. "People can be blind when it comes to things like family."

"I'm not blind," Winston countered. "He's my uncle." Steel was quiet for a moment, clearly thinking about something.

"Well, you got the Dragons to keep your head on straight," Steel pointed out, patting his thigh. His hand lingered there afterward. If he said something more, Winston wasn't really listening; his eyes were focused on the hand. He could feel the warmth from it through the material of his khaki shorts, building to a fire that went right to his cock. Winston was surprised it hadn't busted through his zipper.

"You know what you need?" Steel asked him, still not lifting his hand from Winston's thigh.

"More beer?" Winston suggested.

"Nope. To get off."

Winston turned to face Steel so quickly he was surprised his neck didn't snap. He could never tell when Steel was being serious or when he was joking—though even for Steel it was often a thin line; something he was joking about could become something he decided to go through with.

"Are you serious, man?"

Steel shrugged, nonchalant, as if he were suggesting they do something as normal as watch television. "Yeah, why not? *Da fei gei*— let's shoot some airplanes, yeah?" Steel made a jerking off motion. "I'm serious," he insisted when Winston just kept staring at him. "It's not like we haven't done it before."

Winston's pulse raced, thundering in his ears as it pumped blood to lower regions of his body. He remembered each and every time he and Steel had messed around together—most of them between the ages of fifteen and eighteen—a rough time for him with his father, and dealing with his sexuality. Experimentation wasn't unusual among teenagers, right?

Now they were definitely not teenagers caught in the clutches of surging hormones and sexual discovery, though Winston felt like it at the moment. He'd never been so turned on in his life. Even though the rational part of his mind screamed that it was a bad idea, though, his body cried *Yes, yes, do it!*

"You in or what?" Steel pressed. His left hand remained on Winston's thigh, but the right hand's fingers were already reaching for his zipper. He wasn't joking, it seemed. "I've got porn in the DVD player."

Winston snorted. "Of course you do—when do you not?"

Steel must have taken that for a yes, because he reached for the remote, turning on the television and the DVD player and hitting play on the menu screen right away.

The movie that came up had a guy blindfolded and tied to the posts of a bed while another guy took care of him. After taking in that detail, Winston stopped focusing on the movie, because Steel's pants were undone and his dick was out, big and hard like Winston remembered it.

Winston hurried pulled his own free, tucking the waistband of his underwear behind his balls and shifting into a more comfortable position as he began to stroke. He tried to keep his eyes on the movie but wasn't having much luck; his gaze kept wandering back to Steel's thick length and his hand pumping over it steadily. The sight stirred Winston's blood way more than the video did.

Winston felt Steel's gaze and glanced up, their eyes meeting. There was something stirring behind Steel's eyes, something Winston couldn't name and wasn't sure he wanted to. But it was there, and his body responded to it, his arousal surging.

Steel's hand slid down to grip the base of his cock, squeezing it and causing the veins that lined the shaft to bulge even more, all the while still holding Winston's gaze. "You want to touch it, don't you?"

Winston knew there was no point in lying about this, especially since he could barely turn his eyes away from his friend's cock, so he just nodded.

"It's cool," Steel said, giving his dick a shake. "Go ahead."

Winston, suddenly trembling, reached out with his left hand and wrapped it around Steel's cock tightly. The length pulsed, the heat of it feeling like it would sear his palm. He pumped his fist slowly over it, savoring the sensation and enjoying the sighs of pleasure coming from Steel. He wanted to let his fingers explore every inch of the length, spend all day with this cock in his hand, wash away any memory of whatever random person had their mouth around it before.

"Faster," Steel commanded, and Winston obeyed, working Steel's length quickly. His right hand remained wrapped around his own cock but was still, all of his energy now focused on Steel. He alternated his grip, squeezing tightly at the top and loosening as he reached the base, twisting his hand to palm the head.

It didn't take long before Steel's body tensed, and he grunted out something unintelligible and shot his load onto his stomach, pushing his shirt up to avoid a mess.

Winston was reluctant to release Steel's cock but let it go and turned his attention back to his own cock, following Steel's example and pushing his shirt up under his chin. He pumped himself rapidly, wanting to reach orgasm now that Steel was finished. He was surprised when Steel's hand came and began to lightly brush against his balls, the soft touch unraveled him quickly, and he emptied himself onto his own stomach.

Steel held a box of tissue out to him, and he pulled a handful free, muttering a thanks before cleaning himself up. He deposited the sticky tissue in the garbage can Steel offered him.

Winston felt awkward for a moment—it had been so long since they'd done that together, and he didn't know how to feel, especially given the way he had come to feel about Steel.

Steel, though, was content to act like everything was perfectly normal. He flopped back down on the couch next to Winston, cutting the DVD off and switching to satellite television. "You want to order pizza or something?"

"Uh, sure," Winston said awkwardly, studying Steel out the corner of his eye. Yes, his friend looked the same as always. Maybe Winston was the one making it awkward. "I'll get the menus." Steel had a massive pile of takeout menus stacked up on the small two-seater table in the kitchen area. They came in handy, because Steel couldn't cook to save his own life and would definitely starve if it weren't for Constance and takeout.

As Winston made his way back to the couch, shuffling through the menus to find the pizza ones, a weird chirping sound filled the room. Both Steel and Winston looked around, confused for a moment until Winston realized what it was.

"The phone!" He patted his pockets and found it missing. He checked the couch, and there the burner phone was, shoved in the cushions. He flipped it open and examined the message he'd received.

"What does it say?" Steel asked, craning his neck to see the message.

"It's just a date and time. Nine-nineteen, oh-two-hundred." Winston looked up at Steel. "The next race is in two days."

Nine

"WHY DO I need to tell him all this?" Winston demanded of Wei obstinately. He was pacing the room above Coffee by Constance in a small circle.

"Would you just stand still?" Steel took hold of Winston's arm until he stopped moving.

"Look," said Wei, crossing his arms across his chest, "I don't like telling Hong any more than you do, but the nature of this investigation requires it. If it weren't for Hong we wouldn't even know about this."

"What happens when Hong's dirty boss finds out about it?" Winston inquired.

Conroy came up behind Winston and pat his cheek playfully. "Don't worry about Dang, little Winston. We can handle him."

"Last time I checked, Dang nearly got Noah killed," Winston pointed out.

Wei growled. "Don't remind me."

"Look, to be honest, part of what we need is for Dang to try to dip his nose back into our shit," Conroy said. "That's the only way we'll catch his sorry ass doing something dirty so we can finally fucking prove it."

"He knows I said something to Hong about him." Winston didn't know how Wei could sound so confident about that fact, but he'd learned to trust the man's instincts. "He's going to play by the rules—at least for now. He won't be a concern. This Dark Streets race, though, is a big fucking concern, especially if it's coming through my territory."

A knock at the door paused their conversation, and Conroy crossed the room and opened it, letting in Allen Hong. The inspector's body was tense, and it looked to Winston like he didn't want to be there any more than he was wanted.

He probably looks around and sees everything he could have had if he hadn't been a fucking traitor, Winston thought.

"Show me the phone," Hong said when he walked in. No greeting, no acknowledgment of Wei's grace in allowing him to be there, just right to business. Just as well, though; at least they didn't have to put up with him trying to make small talk.

Winston hesitated, glancing at Wei, who nodded. Sighing, Winston tossed the phone to Hong, not wanting to get any closer than he needed to. He watched Hong read the message, his face impassive.

"We'll have you a car by tomorrow night." That was his only statement about the matter.

"What? No way." Winston shook his head, turning to the boss. "Wei. I'm not driving a fucking police car."

"It won't be a police car," Hong corrected patiently. "It's a car we happen to own."

"I'm not driving a car the police happen to own, then," Winston spat, glaring daggers at Hong. "I'm driving my own car. I won't win in a police car."

"This isn't about you winning. This is about finding out who's running the races and who committed these murders."

Winston had never heard someone say something so stupid. "How do you think I can do that if I don't win? No one's going to take any interest in me unless I actually win. Who notices the losers? They don't get to the winner's circle."

"Drawing their attention is going to mean putting yourself in danger, isn't it?" Steel asked, his voice full of concern. "We don't know if the killer—or killers—are the people organizing this race. Maybe they're killing people for winning, or for doing shitty, or because they drive a shit car for all we know!"

Winston was touched by Steel's protective nature, but he was a Dragon—or going to be. "I signed up for this, Steel. It wouldn't be the first time a Dragon has done something dangerous."

"You're not a Dragon," Conroy reminded him, but then added, with a certain amount of pride in his voice, "yet."

Winston turned back to Hong. "I'm driving my own car."

The inspector pursed his lips but must have decided it wasn't worth fighting over, because he said, "Fine. But before the race, we're putting a tracker in your car. We will know where you are at all times. If it gets deactivated, or you take it out, I will put out an arrest warrant for you."

His face made it clear to Winston that he was not kidding and nothing they said would change his mind. Winston didn't expect anything less from the police. He knew that the police couldn't stand the way that the people in the district looked to Wei and the Dragons for their protection, not the police. It was only natural for them to try to assert their dominance in whatever little ways they could. Hong probably got an even bigger kick out of showing his control over Wei.

Smug bastard.

Winston again looked to Wei, who answered. "If you say so. But no plain clothes, no tail, nothing like that. If these racers catch even a hint of the police, they'll disband and we'll have lost our biggest chance of finding out what happened."

Hong nodded.

"There is one little thing I'd like to point out," Conroy said from where he stood next to Steel. "We still don't know where the race is."

"He won't get that message until the day of the race, about midnight, according to what little information we've been able to gather." Hong glanced at the expensive watch on his wrist. "If that's all, I'm going to go say good-bye to Constance and head out."

Wei just nodded, already turning his back on the inspector.

Winston saw what almost looked like hurt, or anger, flash behind Hong's eyes before he went out the door.

Winston followed. He didn't know why, or what he expected to accomplish, but he did.

"Wait," he said once the door was closed behind him. Hong, already halfway down the steps, stopped and turned toward Winston, face neutral but body language wary, like he was anticipating an attack of some sort. "You're not doing her any good coming here."

Hong snorted and started back down the stairs. "I mean it," Winston called after him. "You're only hurting her, you know that, right?"

"She's my sister," Hong said. To Winston's surprise, his voice shook. "You think I'm just going to turn my back on her?"

"You mean like you did my father's memory?" Winston challenged. Just bringing his father up caused an ache in his chest, stirring feelings he'd never quite put to bed. How did a fifteen-year-old come to terms with the death of a man he worshipped? Idolized? Even at twenty, Winston didn't know how to begin to do it.

At the mention of Winston's father, Hong flinched as if he'd been struck. Part of Winston was happy about that, glad to have the chance to inflict pain on this man who represented the very thing that robbed him of a father—a man that was supposed to be his family. Another part of him felt sick for using his father's memory as a weapon. He deserved better.

"You made your choice," Winston said, voice sounding thick to his own ears.

Hong glanced back at Winston over his shoulders, the quickly descending evening casting a shadow over his face so Winston couldn't quite make out his features, and then he walked to the door of the shop's kitchen and slipped inside.

Winston was surprised to realize that tears streaked his cheeks. When had he started crying? And why? He grabbed the rail of the stairs on either side, shoulders slumping forward as he stared down at the stairs through blurry eyes.

He heard the door open and then close quietly behind him. He didn't have to see who it was to know it was Steel. Somehow he recognized his friend's presence. He was not surprised when Steel's hands fell on his shoulders, squeezing them comfortingly.

"You okay, bro?"

Winston took several deep breaths, using the moment to enjoy the contact with Steel before straightening, discreetly wiping the tears clear, and leaving no trace of his weakness. "I'm fine. Come on, let's get planning."

Ten

"Stop fucking pacing," Steel snapped as Winston's feet traced the same figure eight pattern in his living room. "You're making me nervous, man. Just sit down and relax."

It was nearly midnight, and Winston had been amped the entire day. Steel did his best to keep him distracted—took him out to play a few games of basketball, get food—but every time he got Winston close to relaxed, something would happen to wind him back up. They'd spent a good portion of the evening standing over the shoulders of a police tech as they installed a new GPS console in the car, a console that would also be the police's way of keeping track of Winston's location.

Steel didn't think they needed to be there for that, but Winston had insisted, saying no one was touching his car without him being there to monitor. He wanted to make sure they didn't fuck up something.

They'd passed most of the evening playing *Call of Duty* on the Xbox One, but as the hours ticked down to eleven, Winston lost his ability to focus and his kill-to-death ratio became appalling, so Steel cut the game off, no longer seeing the fun in sniping his best friend if he wasn't going to at least make it difficult.

"You think I can relax?" Winston quipped. "I'm about to enter an illegal street race in a car that took me a long time to restore; I don't even know where I'm going to be racing or if there's going to be a killer watching me while I do it. So no, I'm pretty sure sitting down and relaxing isn't an option at the moment."

"Come on, man, you know you have nothing to worry about," Steel said, stretching his feet out and placing them on the coffee table. "I'm going to be right there."

Winston gave him an exasperated look. "I don't think they'll allow you to ride shotgun during an illegal street race, Steel."

"No, but I'll be at the finish line waiting for you."

"How are you going to get there?" Winston asked, though he sounded relieved to hear it.

"Wei already said I can borrow his bike. So once you head out to start the race, I'll be going to the finish line so I can keep an eye on you."

Winston smiled a little bit. "You that worried about me?" His voice was light, but it was not a question that Steel could reply to lightly. He stood, slipping one hand around the back of Winston's neck and giving it a gentle but firm squeeze, forcing his friend to meet his eyes.

"I owe you my life, Winston. You saved me in more ways than one. I will never let anything happen to you."

Their eyes remained locked, and Steel did not release him; in fact, he stepped in closer, minutely. Winston's breath was coming quicker, his eyes now holding a question that Steel recognized but didn't honestly know the answer to.

Winston's tongue darted out to wet his lips—Steel's gaze was drawn to it. He didn't understand why, but the simple gesture had him achingly hard. It was ridiculous—this was his best friend in the world, someone he'd known for ten years, and he'd always managed to keep whatever dirty thoughts he had at bay. Lately, though, it was becoming more and more difficult to do so.

Especially after the joint jack-off session yesterday. He didn't know what part of himself had thought that was a good idea, but it definitely wasn't the smart part. And right now, what was happening? Steel was staring at Winston's lips, now moist, slightly parted as if in anticipation of something, and all he wanted to do was use the hand he still had on Winston's neck and pull him closer and kiss him, for fuck's sake, and the longer he looked at those lips, the harder to resist the impulse became.

As if he was watching himself from the sidelines, he leaned in, set on claiming those lips and seeing—finally—what his friend tasted like. The sharp buzz of the doorbell interrupted them and the two literally sprang apart, eyes uncertain. They were both wondering what just happened.

The doorbell came again, and Steel recovered himself enough to go and open the door. "Constance," he blurted, surprised to see the woman standing on the other side, hands clutched together in front of her like she was nervous but trying not to show it.

"Mom?" Winston said in disbelief, joining Steel at the door.

"May, uh, may I come in?" Constance asked, and the two men stood aside as one, allowing her to step through the door before Steel closed it behind her.

"I'm waiting for the message with the race location," Winston said, his voice carefully neutral. Steel shot him a pointed look, trying to communicate with his eyes that he needed to talk to his mother and bring the tension between them to an end.

Winston and Constance rarely fought, and when they did, it was hard on them both. There was no one in the world whose opinion Winston cared for more—even Wei's, though Winston might not have realized that. He hated to see the two at odds, because it played hell with both of them. Considering Winston was about to walk into a dangerous situation, he knew neither of them wanted to leave things as they were.

"Uh, I'll go...into the bedroom or something," he said after a moment of awkward silence.

"Not like you won't hear us anyway," Winston muttered, appearing a bit embarrassed by the whole situation. "Mom, if you came here to—"

"I came here to tell you that I know you're going out there to risk your fool life and that I know there's nothing I can do to stop you when you get these idiotic ideas in your head—"

"Is this supposed to be an apology or a continuous string of insults?"

Constance glared at him and he fell silent again. "I love you, Winston. You have a great heart, and I know it was concern for me that caused this whole thing. I appreciate it, I do. But there is something I need you to understand right now, before you go out there. I am your mother—nothing will change that, and nothing can change that. I am the parent, which means that my life is my own, to do with as I please. Allen—" Steel caught Winston flinch at the name of his uncle; hell, he himself tensed up at it. None of the Dragons liked the fact that someone who was basically one of them could betray them, become a cop. "—is my brother, and I can't turn my back on him any more than you could turn your back on Shelby, or she could turn her back on you."

Winston opened his mouth to say something, and Steel nudged the back of his leg with his foot. Sometimes Winston just didn't know when to shut the fuck up.

Constance stepped up to Winston, reaching up and cupping his cheek. "This isn't something you can control, *jai*."

"Wei—"

Constance placed her fingertip against Winston's lips, silencing him. "I'm not a Dragon, so Wei can't give me orders. And if he tried, he'd regret it."

Steel snorted, swallowing the noise quickly when Constance glared at him around Winston. He did not for one moment doubt her words. She was a fierce woman, fighting side by side with Wei and the others during the war with the Nine Stars. Anyone who tried to impose their will on her was in for something they were not expecting.

"You're right. I'm sorry, *Mah Ma*," Winston said gently, pulling his mother into a deep hug.

A pang of jealousy went through Steel as he witnessed the sweet exchange between mother and son. He felt awful for being that way when it came to Winston and his mother, but he never had that connection, and it was something he wished for more than anything else in the world.

"Be careful out there," Constance whispered in her son's ear.

"Aren't I always?"

Constance and Steel both said "No!" at the same time.

"You drive like a deranged man," Steel added. The tension was gone, which meant things were fine between mother and son—for now, at least. Steel didn't think the Hong issue would go away quite that easily, but they deserved this moment, considering what Winston was about to undertake.

Constance met Steel's eyes around the hug. "You'll be with him?"

"I can't ride with him because of the rules of the Dark Streets race, but I'll be monitoring him the whole time. If something happens to him, I'm there."

"Wei and the others will be tracking me, too, Mom, and so will H— the police. So there's no way I'm not okay. There's absolutely nothing you need to worry about."

"What a stupid thing to say." Constance sniffed, pulling out of the hug and wiping her cheeks clear of tears. "Of course there's something I need to worry about. You're my son, and you're about to do something dangerous."

"You were my mother and you did something dangerous," Winston reminded her gently. "You could have died, like Dad, but you did it anyway."

"Because it was the right thing to do." Constance nodded. "I understand."

The burner phone they'd taken from Min's apartment let out its loud chirping noise, startling all three of them. Steel shared a look with Winston, who nodded.

"It's go time."

Eleven

WINSTON HAD NEVER felt more nervous in his life than he did right there in that moment, pulling his car up into the parking garage in Aberdeen where the night's race would be. There were seven other cars there waiting. Most of the drivers remained in their cars, content to wait out the start of the race from there. A few of the drivers, one a woman close to Winston's age, congregated in front of a beautiful fiery-red Ford Mustang.

They barely glanced his way, so Winston took the opportunity to study the drivers. Aside from the woman, who gave off a cold and distant vibe, observing the others as they interacted without actively joining in, they were all older, closer to forty than twenty, and looked like they came from the streets. The bigger man had a few scars along his face and arms—Winston guessed they were knife scars. He was probably involved with some sort of fighting ring. The smaller man looked like he'd lived his life getting punched in the face. His nose was more a mass of pulp than an actual nose by that point.

As they spoke about something, the larger man gesturing broadly, the woman turned Winston's way at last. Something sparked behind her eyes, and she raised her eyebrows. She separated herself from the group, making her way toward Winston in his car.

Winston rolled down the window, not trusting himself to get out. His heart hammered in his chest, and he hoped he would be able to play it cool. He didn't know how things worked in this situation. He'd felt somewhat confident in his ability to do this when it was an idea, something he didn't actually have to do. Now that he was in it, he felt like he was going to faint.

I'm not afraid, he told himself firmly. Wei would never be afraid. *I can do this.*

"I don't remember seeing your face around here before," the woman said, leaning on the car, tilting in to look Winston over.

"I'm new." Winston shrugged, hoping he sounded nonchalant.

Her lips, coated in a sheen of ruby-red lipstick, turned up at the corners. "I guessed that. You got a name, new guy? And not your real name. We use racer names here."

Racer names? Winston hadn't thought of one of those. Why the hell hadn't he thought up a racer name? He racked his brain, trying to think of something that sounded cool, something that would be appropriate and not give away anything about him or why he was there. He was drawing a blank. He hadn't even had his first race and he was already fucking everything up.

"Not much for words, huh?" The woman smiled wider. "Okay, then, I'll call you Noisy. I'm Mimi."

"Nice to meet you, then, Mimi," Winston said, while silently he was thinking *Noisy? My fucking racer name is Noisy now? Dear fucking God*. He hoped that his displeasure at the nickname wasn't written on his face, what with Mimi staring at him like she could see through him. "So, when, uh, is the race supposed to start?"

"We're still waiting for the escort."

"Escort?"

Mimi leaned her hip against the car, a quizzical. Expression on her face. "You know, the escort to the starting point? Have you never done this before?"

"Nope, this is my first time," Winston admitted. He didn't have to fake the sheepishness in his voice. "So this isn't where the race starts?"

Mimi snorted. "How can we start a race in a parking garage? A car will come to lead us to the site. And collect the entry fee for new drivers," she added. "You do have that, right?"

That much Winston was at least prepared for. "Yup. Ten thousand dollars, cash." He patted a duffle bag on the passenger seat next to him. If he'd been doing this independently, there would have been no way he could have mustered the entry fee. He wondered how someone like Min had managed it. "So how does this work, exactly? The money, I mean."

Mimi shook her head. "Wow, they don't explain shit to anyone anymore, do they? Basically, you pay ten thousand dollars. That gets you five races—unless you win one, then you collect a portion of the collected fee, and can use it however the fuck you want. The ten K, though, that's gone. You're not getting it back."

"What happens if I don't make any money in those five races?"

"Then you pay again or you stop racing, that simple. Oh, if you come in first, second, or third, your position in the next race is guaranteed, as well. Just 'cause you paid your fee doesn't mean you get in every race. Some races are all-arounds, but some are higher stakes, and those require wins or at least placing."

"Seems pretty straightforward."

"Good luck, Noisy." Mimi winked and walked away, and Winston let out the breath he didn't realize he'd been holding. He wanted to ask her how he would know when the escort came, but figured he'd know when the time came.

He heard the vibration of his phone in the glove compartment and surreptitiously pulled it out, looking to make sure no one was paying him any attention. A few more cars were arriving, so most of the focus was on their drivers. The light on the phone was turned all the way down to keep anyone from noticing he had it—it was his own personal cell phone, which was probably also a no-no.

The vibration came from a message from Steel.

—Everything all right?

Winston knew his friend enough to read the text in the other man's voice—probably in the exact right tone, too. He couldn't help but smile at Steel's protectiveness. It must be eating him up, not being there for something like this. Unfortunately, there were no tagalongs.

—Yeah, it's all chill. Other racers arriving. Waiting to go to the start site now.

He pushed the phone back into the glove box as a black sedan pulled into the parking garage. The other drivers scurried to their cars, all businesslike now. The black sedan drove closer to where Winston sat in his car. He squinted, trying to see the driver, but the windows were too tinted.

The car came to a stop next to Winston's, the window rolling down. The first thing Winston thought when he saw the driver was that he was exceedingly average. Nothing stood out to him about the man, and Winston doubted he would be able to remember him the next day. When the man spoke, his voice was like cement, reminding Winston of tires going down a gravel road.

"You new?"

"Yes," Winston said nervously. He grabbed at the duffel bag, holding it up for the man to see. "I have the entry fee." He passed the bag over to the man when he held his hand out expectantly. The man counted the money quickly and expertly, giving a nod when he finished, and tossing the duffel into the passenger seat of his own car.

"Welcome to the Dark Streets."

Twelve

THERE WERE FIFTEEN cars in this race. Winston, being the new guy, was in last place in the line-up at Ovolo Aberdeen Harbor. The path was laid out for them, provided on a portable GPS device given to them when they arrived. They would be going from the Harbor and back around to it, following first Aberdeen Main Street until they hit Aberdeen Reservoir Road. They'd take it until they reached Yue Kwong Road, which would eventually connect them back to the tightly interconnected streets of the Aberdeen Market District, which they would follow right back to the starting point of Ovolo Aberdeen Harbor.

As soon as he thought he could get away with it, he texted the general route they would be taking to Steel, knowing he would kill him if he didn't. Message sent, he turned the phone off. He needed to be one hundred percent focused on the race if he hoped to have any chance of not completely fucking it up.

An air horn blew once—the first warning, letting drivers know to prep themselves. The second air horn blast followed, and Winston thought he was going to pass out from nervousness. Why had he agreed to this? He sure as hell better get his tattoo after this mess!

When the third blast sounded, Winston slammed his foot onto the gas pedal, wincing as his tires squealed, spinning rapidly on the ground before the car burst into motion. It was difficult to maintain control of the car for a moment, but he managed it.

He kept his speed as even as he could at the beginning, happy just to keep the taillights of the person ahead of him in sight. He didn't have any delusions about winning, not his first race. He just wanted to prove that he could keep up with these guys.

A chance presented itself unexpectedly when the driver in front of him tried to cut off another car and got knocked up pretty roughly, thrown into a spin. Winston took the opportunity to speed past him and the car who gave it the beating.

He gained confidence as he continued on, following the road up Aberdeen Main Street, and he picked up speed, deciding he would damn well do his best. What was the point, otherwise?

By the time Winston reached Aberdeen Reservoir Road, he'd already overtaken three other cars, putting him in tenth place in the race. *I think I'm pretty good at this*, he realized with a grin. No sooner had the thought crossed his mind, though, than his body was jerked forward, his face nearly slamming into the steering wheel. Neck aching, Winston looked into the rearview mirror, squinting against the brightness of the headlights of the car behind him, a yellow Dodge Charger.

The fucker rammed his car!

Winston thought of the months of labor he'd put into repairing the car, the time spent finding parts, putting them in, making sure everything was perfect. This *puk gai* was going to fuck that all up.

No way in hell was Winston going to let that happen.

He pushed the gas pedal to the car floor as he zoomed out of the turn onto Aberdeen Reservoir Road. The lanes narrowed down beyond the turn, creating a tighter playing field. Speed alone wasn't going to work for him at this stage in the race.

An engine revved behind him and Winston barely had time to brace himself before the Charger behind him slammed into him once more. This time he distinctly heard the crunch of metal and breaking glass. One, if not both, of his taillights shattered.

"Diu lei lo mo chau hai!" he shouted at the driver, knowing Constance would have knocked him unconscious if she heard him speak like that.

I gotta get the fuck away from this lunatic. He decided to take a risky maneuver and jerked the wheel of the car to the right, slipping into the lane for oncoming traffic. As soon as the car behind him followed suit, he jerked to the left again. When his pursuer attempted the same maneuver, his tires spun a bit and he was forced to slow down. He didn't control his car well enough, though, and the car behind it clipped his front as it sped past him.

That's that, Winston thought, satisfied. He could rest a little easier and focus on the road.

The race only got trickier as they reached Yue Kwong Road. Despite the hour, there was some civilian traffic they now had to factor in. Twice Winston was nearly overtaken because he'd slowed to avoid a collision with a late-night delivery bike. He somehow managed to maintain his lead, though, and as he pulled into the civilian streets of the Aberdeen Market District, he was in ninth place, though for how long he didn't know. These streets were more dangerous than anything he'd driven before, especially at these speeds.

Glancing into the rearview mirror, he caught sight of the car that'd rammed him before. *This is a persistent* ga tsan. He was so distracted that he missed a turn. He cursed himself as he watched the other cars round the corner he should have taken.

He hit reverse and sped back, finally making the turn, though he'd dropped back to twelfth place, and he couldn't get any further past that on the narrow, winding roads. His one last chance would be the brief moment when the race reached Aberdeen Praya Road. He hoped to at least regain tenth, but he didn't have a lot of confidence that he could.

So fucking close. So fucking close, and I make a stupid mistake.

He kept his focus intently on the road, determined not to make the same mistake twice.

He took the exit onto the Aberdeen Praya Road and as soon as he left the turn, he punched down on the accelerator. At the same time another car—the fucking yellow Charger—turned after him, zooming into the left lane, intent on passing Winston. Winston slowed down for a moment, making him think he could, and then sped up. The yellow Charger swerved to avoid being hit but didn't slow down; instead, it sped up, attempting to gain two positions instead of just the one.

The Charger and the car in front of Winston, a dark-colored Nissan GT-R, traded a few side licks for a moment, until it appeared the Charger was going to get ahead. The Nissan cut hard to the left, slamming into the Charger.

Winston hit the gas hard, using the opportunity to speed through the opening provided by the Nissan, forcing it to slow and allow him into its place.

When Winston crossed the finish line, he was in eleventh place. He released a shaky breath he didn't know he'd been holding as he came to a stop. He physically could not make himself release his hold on the steering wheel in front of him for several minutes.

A tap on the driver's side window startled him and he nearly jumped out of his seat. His hand trembled so much he could barely push the button to roll down the window to greet Mimi.

"Eleventh place, huh?"

"I know, I sucked."

Mimi drummed long, manicured nails on the roof of his car. "What? No, you didn't suck. A lot of people don't advance more than one place in their first race—if they advance at all. I think you got some talent, Noisy."

"Is there any chance we could reconsider the nickname?"

"Not on your life, kid. Now, give me the GPS and you can get the hell out of here. Good job tonight. Go get some sleep. You earned it."

Thirteen

THE ONLY THING Steel hated more than waiting was feeling helpless, and at that moment, he had no choice but to do both. He leaned against the passenger side door of Conroy's car where it sat on the shoulder of the road at the predetermined meeting point. He had his arms crossed over his chest, his right foot propped up against the car behind him.

"*Puk gai*, if you don't get your foot off my fuckin' car, I'm going to rip it off your body and shove it up your ass!" Conroy pushed Steel hard enough to show that he was partly serious. "You need to just chill, man. He'll get here when he gets here."

Steel glared balefully at him. "You could have just dropped me off and gone off to fuck karaoke bar staff or whatever the hell it is you do with your free time. You don't have to wait around."

"Actually, I do." Conroy lit a cigarette and blew a plume of smoke from his nose. "Boss's orders. I don't think he trusts you by yourself here."

"Who knows, maybe he just wanted to get rid of you for a few hours, get some peace and quiet for once."

"You got a big mouth." Conroy scowled.

"So I've been told."

The two fell silent, Conroy leaning lazily against his car, Steel staring down the road, tense. What the hell was taking Winston so long? He was sure the race went fine—they would have heard the sound of emergency vehicles if it hadn't. Had he been found out? Had someone somehow figured out that Winston was there working in tandem with the police? How had that happened? He thought they'd been so careful, but whoever organized this Dark Streets tournament had to be damn smart themselves.

We were stupid to let him go in there alone, Steel thought sourly. *If anything happens to him...* Steel imagined a variety of pain-inducing things he could do to the organizers of the street races and anyone else who might have been involved in hurting Winston. The longer he thought about it, the cleverer and more inventive his imagined torture became. The ideas were nearing the point of sheer ridiculousness when Steel caught the glint of headlights off the road up ahead, followed closely by the sound of a car engine.

Conroy and Steel traded glances as they waited to see if this was their guy or another false alarm. When the car came into sight, Steel let out an audible sigh of relief. He ignored the knowing look Conroy sent his way, hurrying over to the car as the door opened and Winston got out from behind the wheel.

His face was haggard and tired, but other than that, he seemed fine, much to Steel's relief. He wouldn't have to bust any skulls tonight, at least.

"Shit, man, you look tired as hell," Conroy teased, punching Winston's arm lightly. "How did you do?"

"Eleventh place." Winston yawned.

Conroy raised an eyebrow at that. "Eleventh? Out of how many?"

Steel glared at Conroy. "It was his first race. Give him a break."

"It's not as bad as it sounds, actually," Winston said. He probably would have sounded more defensive if he weren't exhausted. "I got praise from one of the higher-ups and everything."

"The boss will be glad to hear it."

"Okay," Steel said impatiently. "He's here, so you can hop in your baby and go back home or wherever it is you're headed. I'll take it from here."

Conroy looked like he wanted to say something, but a glance at Winston stopped him. "Okay, fine. Wei wanted me to tell you he wants to see you tomorrow morning for a breakdown of what you've learned."

"I'll be there," Winston assured him.

Satisfied, Conroy climbed into his Corvette and drove off, leaving them alone on the road.

"Let's get you home," Steel said, leading Winston to the car with one hand on his back between his shoulders. He ignored the heat that seemed to radiate out of Winston and into him, seeping down his arm and right between his legs.

"Be careful with my car," Winston murmured as he slid into the passenger seat.

"You sound like Conroy," Steel muttered, taking Winston's place behind the wheel. He started the car and glanced over at Winston, a bemused expression on his face.

Winston didn't bother buckling his seat belt, just leaned his head against the door and closed his eyes. The adrenaline that kept him amped during the race was probably gone now, Steel thought, and it no doubt left a bone-deep weariness in its wake.

A strange feeling surged through Steel as he gazed at Winston, bearing an intensity and heat that he did not expect. He couldn't give a name to the emotion; it was entirely unfamiliar to him. Whatever it was, it clutched at his throat and heart with a vice grip and would not let go. Even though he knew Winston was fine after the race, the fierce worry that held him wouldn't abate.

Sure, Winston was fine this time, but what about the next time? There was nothing to guarantee that Winston wouldn't be in danger in the next race—in fact, everything implied that he would! The more he participated in the Dark Streets races, the more likely he was to draw the ire of the person responsible for the killing, making himself a target.

The idea of Winston being in danger made Steel's blood boil. That was only reasonable, though, wasn't it, after everything Winston had done for him? Everyone must feel the same way about the friends in their lives. He knew Wei felt that way about Noah.

But Wei and Noah aren't just friends; a small voice reminded him. That probably wasn't the best example for him to use. But it felt right, anyway, and he hated that. Why did things have to be so *complicated*? His life was so much better when it was simple—no confusion, no worries, no stress. Aside from the issues facing the Dragons, of course, but he didn't count those. Hell, he lived for that stuff.

It was connection, emotion, and all the trappings that came with it that he had no need for. He didn't see how anybody did. But did that apply to Winston?

Steel rolled down the window, allowing the rush of night air to chase away the thoughts. Winston didn't even stir.

Steel surprised himself somewhat when he brought Winston's car to a stop in the parking lot near his apartment. He hadn't realized he'd decided to bring Winston to his place until that moment. His original intention had been to drive him to Constance's so she could stop worrying. Now that they were there, though, Steel didn't want to have Winston anywhere else.

He didn't want to disturb Winston once parked, but didn't think he'd manage to get him up the stairs and to his apartment alone, at least not without attracting some looks. He didn't seem to mind that when he was drunk and it was Winston doing his best to help him, but that was another issue all together.

Steel got out of the car and walked around to the passenger side, opening the door slowly so Winston didn't fall out. "Yo, Winston. Wake up, man." He shook his best friend gently awake. "We're here. I need you to walk, at least until we get inside."

Winston made a grumbling noise, but stirred, unsteadily exiting the car. Locking it up tightly behind them, Steel guided Winston toward the apartment. It took a bit of effort to navigate the stairs, but eventually they made it into the apartment.

Winston's autopilot seemed to kick in, and he made his way immediately to the bedroom where he collapsed on the bed.

Steel opened and downed a bottle of Tsingtao in two deep gulps before he entered his bedroom. Hands on his hips, he surveyed his best friend, collapsed on the bed, shoes still on.

The things I do for this guy. Steel methodically removed Winston's shoes and helped him get under the cover. That done, he flicked the lights off and got in bed on the other side, body relaxing the moment his head touched the pillow. He lay there for five minutes or so, listening to Winston's breathing, before he fell asleep.

Fourteen

HE WATCHED THE car taillights fade into the night from his concealed position, a satisfied smirk on his face. Everything was going exactly how he anticipated. There was no better feeling than when a carefully laid plan fell into place. It was a wonderful vindication all its own.

Confident they would not be coming back, he pulled his cell phone out of his pocket and dialed the one number saved in it. As he expected, it rang once before it was answered. His employer was no doubt waiting anxiously by the phone.

"Yes, what is it?"

"Everything is going exactly as I said it would."

"The Dragons?" His employer was near breathless with excitement. "They've entered the Dark Streets?"

"Just like I said they would. I don't mind pointing out that everything is following my plan to the letter."

His employer snorted dismissively. "Don't get cocky."

It wasn't cockiness; it was confidence, but he didn't think there would be much use in explaining the difference to the likes of his employer, so he simply stayed quiet and listened.

"That's still only the next big step in the plan. We have to make sure everything else follows along, as well. Don't get sloppy on me now."

He scowled. Just who did his boss think he was? "I don't get sloppy. I know my role here; you've been very kind, and I always provide the service I've been asked for. Don't worry; it will get taken care of in the manner we discussed."

"It has to be done perfectly," his employer warned. "We can't risk any mistakes."

"Yes," he drawled, bored with the conversation and implications that he didn't know how to do his job. "That's why you're paying me."

"A lot of money," his employer huffed.

"I'm worth every bit of it. I'll be in contact with you once I'm ready to proceed to the next stage." He hung up without waiting for a reply. He didn't suffer fools lightly, and his employer fell into that category. Oh, hiring him was a stroke of genius, but one smart action didn't make him any less of a fool. Even if he weren't a fool, micromanagers made the worst employers in his field. He couldn't understand why they didn't see they hired a professional because they could not do the job themselves, so what was the point of attempting to offer instruction on how to do it?

He'd been doing this too long to let fools and idiots tell him what to do. They might provide the money, but that was it. He liked to make it quite clear they had no say otherwise in just how the deed was done. After all, in the end, the job was always finished, and that was all they cared about, wasn't it?

Phone call finished, he made his way to his discreetly parked car and climbed behind the wheel. The ball had been nudged, and now he just had to make sure it rolled off the cliff.

Fifteen

"WIN, WHAT ARE you doing? Hurry up," the voice called out to Winston. It was a deep, melodious baritone, the laughter clear within it. Only one person in the world ever called him Win, and that was his father. Winston was fourteen again, sitting in his room doing something or other. The moment his dad called, though, Winston shot up from his bed and hurried out the door so quickly he nearly tripped over a pile of dirty clothes.

"Dad," he called. "Where are you?"

He found himself walking through a strange hall he didn't recognize. This wasn't his home. A dark, splotchy wallpaper covered the walls, peeling in places. The wooden floor was creaking, scratched and scuffed, the entire place devoid of any warmth.

"Win?" His dad's voice echoed off the walls, the acoustics making it sound like it was coming from everywhere all at once. Was he down the hall behind Winston or in front of him?

Winston decided to go forward. The hall stretched on forever, like one of those looped backgrounds. When he looked back, he couldn't see where he'd been. There was no sign of the door to his room, just the continuous expanse of the unending corridor.

"Winston?" Real fear colored his father's voice now. "Winston, where are you?"

Heart pounding in his chest, Winston began running. The hall had to end somewhere, and when it did, he'd find his father. Somehow, impossibly, the hallway began to slant uphill, the going becoming more and more difficult. Winston was quickly out of breath, his lungs burning and his legs aching, but he pushed on. This was his father.

"Winston! Please! Help me!"

The sheer emotion in that voice, in the way he cried out to his son, wrenched at Winston's heart. He needed to get to him, needed to save him, like he couldn't before.

Where is he? Where is he, damn it? He could barely force himself to keep moving. He'd almost entirely given up when he saw the end of the hallway ahead.

Finally.

Adrenaline surged through his body, and he rushed forward, leaving the hallway, only to find himself in a jail cell, everything surrounding him gray concrete and cold, metal bars. Harsh, palpable dread bubbled inside him, threatening to burst through his chest.

No. No, no, no. He closed his eyes to ward off the sight of the cell, but it persisted, the image burned into his mind in a way that no amount of time would erase.

"Winston…"

This time the voice was soft, weak, almost inaudible. Winston hesitated, knowing what he'd see when he opened his eyes. It wouldn't be the first time, nor did he think it would be the last. Keeping his eyes closed only delayed the inevitable, though. Like a Band-Aid, it was better to get it over with quickly.

When he opened his eyes, he was greeted with the sight of his father lying on the floor of the cell. It was no longer a monotonous gray. Long lines of crimson streaked the ground, pooling around his father's beaten and broken form.

"Winston…" His father reached out a bloodied hand toward him. "Winston… help me."

"*Aa de,*" Winston whimpered, reaching for his father's hand. Before he could grasp it, though, two men in police uniforms—faceless, they were always faceless—grabbed him under his arms and dragged him away, through the cell door. No matter how much he struggled, he was not strong enough to resist them. He could only reach helplessly toward his father as he was dragged off until he was no longer visible.

The men carrying him threw him down hard on the concrete floor, their blurred visages looming over him like monstrous, faceless shadows. One of them raised their foot, bringing it crashing down toward Winston's face—

—Winston jolted awake, sitting up and wrestling with the covers he was under for a moment before he fully processed where he was. It was still dark, though gray light was slowly making its way into the room through the window, telling Winston that morning couldn't be too far off.

"S'thamatter?" Steel asked groggily beside him, still mostly asleep.

"Nothing," Winston lied quickly, feeling guilty for waking Steel. "Go back to sleep."

"Liar," Steel muttered. He reached over and patted Winston's arm gently.

The brief moment of contact made Winston shiver. He broke away, using the motion of drawing his knees up to his chest as cover. "I had the dream again." He didn't need to explain *what* dream for Steel to understand, and that was part of what made their friendship so perfect for them both. They understood each other—were in perfect sync.

Steel sat up, shaking his head as if attempting to shake some of the sleep away. "You all right?"

The lie sprang to his lips before he reconsidered. There was never any use lying to Steel. "I will be soon."

"You know there's nothing you could have done, right? You were just a kid."

"I know that," he said wearily. He'd heard it a million times, from the moment he first told someone—Steel, as a matter of fact—about the dreams. He wasn't lying; he did know that, academically. Telling that to his unconscious was another thing entirely. "It's not like I really think I'm responsible—just like I didn't actually see him there in that cell. But in my dream, it's like I did. I can only imagine what he looked like afterward, and whatever my imagination comes up with is so much worse than the reality must have been, for all I know."

"You let these dreams torture you too much," Steel told him. "I know you can't stop yourself from having them, but you have to teach yourself to shake them off. You can't let them linger. It's only going to drive you crazy."

"I know," Winston replied quietly. It seemed to be the only thing he could say.

"Come here." Steel pulled Winston close to him. Winston was still dressed, though Steel seemed to be wearing only boxers; the warmth of his body passed through Winston's clothing, setting a fire in his veins that helped to chase away the dream's lingering chill. He said nothing about it, of course, and pulled away from Steel as soon as he could without it being odd.

"Thanks, Steel. You go on and get some sleep, though. No use both of us being kept up all night because of my dreams, you know."

Steel yawned theatrically. "I guess you're right. I've got an alarm set for ten, by the way. Wei wants you at the shop at eleven to give a report."

"Thanks. Go to sleep."

Steel grunted and settled back onto the bed, rolling onto his side with his back to Winston.

Winston lay back down as well, mostly so Steel wouldn't get too suspicious. He stared up at the same ceiling he'd awoken to with a hangover a few days ago—a few days, was that it? It felt longer; he'd been given his first true task for Wei and the Dragons that day.

He'd woken up with no clothes on next to Steel that day.

The memory brought a stirring in his cock, and he shifted uncomfortably. It turned his mind toward the feeling that shot through him when Steel touched him, and the way he'd felt jerking off with Steel—which only made him think about Steel's cock.

What the hell is wrong with me? No way in hell I should be thinking about this right now. If Steel woke up and found him lying there with a boner he'd never live it down. He mirrored Steel's action, rolling onto his side with his back to Steel's, allowing himself a small bit of privacy.

He doubted sleep would come to him again that night, considering it rarely did after the dreams about his father. He lay there, watching the room slowly brighten as morning made its arrival, listening to the sound of the city streets outside the window and Steel's steady, rhythmic breathing, content to stay that way until the alarm clock went off.

Sixteen

STEEL DROVE WINSTON to his mother's coffee shop the next morning, not trusting his friend's alertness. He knew Winston hadn't gone back to sleep after his dream; he almost never did. As he drove, Steel kept glancing at Winston out of the corner of his eye. Winston couldn't even argue, since the police had swooped in to take his car in for repairs after the race and the damage it took. Steel's blood still boiled when he thought about it. He still couldn't believe he hadn't paid any attention to it the night before.

"I'm fine," Winston said irritably, noticing the looks. "Really, I am. You don't have to worry."

"Me? Worry? You know I never worry." He did his best to keep his glances more concealed after that.

They walked into the coffee shop to be greeted by Noah behind the counter with his apron on. He'd taken a job at Coffee by Constance in part to get a work visa and in part to maintain some independence, living with Wei in a foreign country. The nature of Wei's position meant that Noah had more limited freedom, so he grabbed freedom where he could—even if that freedom did involve working in the coffee shop that also played host to the Dragons' gathering place.

"Damn it," Noah cursed when they walked in. "I owe Conroy twenty bucks."

Steel frowned. "What the hell did you bet on?"

"I bet Conroy that you two would be late today. He disagreed. He said you'd be here between ten fifty-five and eleven." Noah checked his watch. "Yeah, it's ten fifty-three. I owe him. Although"—he went on slowly, a devious smile coming to his face—"if you were to just stay down here until after eleven, he'd never know."

Steel smirked. "Screwing Conroy out of money? I'm in."

"I already know you're here," Conroy said, emerging from the kitchen, hand held out in a "gimme" gesture. "Pay up, *gweilo*."

"You're insufferable sometimes, you know that?" Noah placed the lost money in Conroy's hand, sighing overdramatically.

"The boss wants you upstairs," Conroy said to Winston and jerking his head back the way he'd come. "I'd go if I were you. He's a little grumpy this morning. My guess is *this one—*" He elbowed Noah so it was clear everyone knew who he was talking about. "—didn't put out last night."

"*Sau seng,*" Noah muttered. Steel grinned and Conroy gaped, surprised, before he turned accusatory eyes on Steel.

"You taught him that, didn't you?"

"No. Did you?" he asked Winston.

"Nope."

"I learned it watching a drama," Noah said. "Don't look at me like that," he added defensively. "I've got to learn somewhere, don't I?"

Conroy rolled his eyes and turned to Winston. "You, let's go. Not you," he added when Steel started to follow. "Boss said just Winston."

Steel scowled but didn't argue; Conroy was speaking for Wei—he was being an ass about it, but he was speaking for the leader. Steel wasn't about to get all pissy about it. Besides, if it meant getting out of a boring meeting, he wasn't exactly complaining. He could pass his time down here annoying Noah and eating some of Constance's baked goods. He didn't know how he never grew fat with the way he ate with Winston's family when he was young. Constance had no problem making sure someone was full—she always offered Steel more food, especially when he had been a young child fresh off the streets, nothing more than skin and bone. He hated to think just how much money Constance spent keeping him fed, along with her own children.

Once Winston disappeared upstairs, Steel turned to Noah and ordered a large coffee and a banana muffin.

"Long night?" Noah quipped, getting the coffee ready.

"Baby, with me every night is a long night," Steel replied with an overly lascivious wink.

Noah groaned. "I think I'm going to throw up."

"Don't worry, *gweilo*, you're not my type."

Noah placed the coffee and the big muffin on a tray. "Thank god for small favors. Please tell me you're going to eat this somewhere that's not at the counter?"

"You don't deserve my presence anyway," Steel drawled. He wandered over to one of the far tables near the window, sitting in the sun to enjoy his coffee and muffin.

He'd been there for nearly half an hour, his muffin gone, his coffee all but finished, when several customers entered the shop—a group of pretty girls, no doubt from one of the nearby universities. Big tits, friendly smiles, nice curves, soft bodies.

Not like Winston.

It was such a strange thought—coming from nowhere and catching Steel off guard. Once it came, though, he found he couldn't shake himself free of it. No, there wasn't anything soft about Winston, despite what someone's first impression might make them think. He was hard, firm. He had his own curves—the swell of his ass, for instance—but there was nothing feminine about him.

For fuck's sake, stop it, he chastised himself firmly. *Winston is my best friend—that's it. The last thing I need to do is complicate anyone's life by getting any other thoughts in my head.*

What better way to chase away the strange thoughts—at least temporarily, since they always seemed to come back lately—than to go and chat up some pretty girls? Who knew, he might even get lucky in the deal.

Steel strolled over to the table the girls were sitting at, near the front counter. They talked amongst themselves about something or another they'd done together recently, though their conversation came to an end when Steel approached; they fell silent and examined him. One looked a bit apprehensive, but the other two showed signs of vague curiosity or interest.

"Good morning, ladies," he said with his most dashing smile in place.

"Do we know you?" asked one of them, eyes narrowed suspiciously. Given the rash of girls going missing not too long ago, Steel couldn't say he blamed them for their caution.

"No, probably not—which I would say is unfortunate, considering how beautiful you all are. I wish I could have met you all before." A loud snort came from the counter. Steel glanced toward Noah to see him miming vomiting.

Well, what the fuck does he know about talking to girls? The girls giggled a little—they were still uncertain about him, he could tell, but they were warming up, even the suspicious one. "My friends call me Steel—it's nice to meet you."

The suspicious one hid a laugh in her coffee cup. One of the other girls had no problem asking, "Steel? Why?"

"You don't want to know," Noah muttered from the counter, loud enough for them to plainly hear. When Steel glared at him, he just kept his eyes fixed on the counter in front of him, like he hadn't said anything at all.

If he wasn't Wei's boy toy... Steel brushed the angry thought aside, pointing to the empty chair at the girls' table. "Mind if I sit down—I'm here alone, and that can be kind of a bummer, right?"

The girls traded looks, a conversation taking place between them without any words. Finally, the suspicious one nodded, gesturing toward the chair. Steel slid his long body into the chair, tapping his index fingers on his coffee cup and smiling at the girls. "You ladies on your way to class or something?"

They giggled again—this time Steel couldn't begin to fathom the reason—before they answered. "No, we're skipping class today. Just boring economics lectures anyway."

This really might be my lucky day. Steel leaned forward a bit. "Oh? Did you have something better in mind to do today?"

Behind the counter, Noah scoffed. "Certainly not you."

The girls gave Noah sidelong glance, brows furrowing.

"Oh, I'm out of coffee," he said quickly, flashing his empty coffee cup to the girls. "I'll be right back."

He left the table at a leisurely walk, not wanting to give the impression that anything was wrong. When he reached the counter, it was all he could do not to lunge over it and grab Noah by the throat.

"What the fuck are you doing?" he hissed, voice low.

"What am *I* doing? What the fuck are *you* doing? You're flirting—badly, I might add—with those girls!"

"If you know what I'm doing, what the hell are you asking me for, then?"

"*What about Winston?*"

The question struck Steel hard, catching him off guard. What about Winston? What did that even mean? Why was his best friend being shoved in his face in an effort to shame him for trying to pick up a girl or two? "What does that mean? What about him?"

Noah looked at him as if he'd asked a ridiculous question. "How would he feel about you going off with these girls?"

"I don't know—proud his friend is getting some action?" Steel shrugged. "How should I know? More importantly, why should it matter?"

Noah's eyebrows came together, and he shifted from foot to foot uncomfortably behind the counter. Part of Steel enjoyed seeing him squirm, but the other part, the part that suspected what he was going to say, just felt uneasy.

"Aren't you two...?"

"What? No!" Steel exploded. He looked over his shoulder, saw the shock on the girls' faces, and lowered his voice before continuing. "What the fuck, man? Did we say we were—that we were—"

"Together?" Noah supplied helpfully. "No, I mean you didn't, but I just...the way you are together..."

"He's my best friend. That's it. I love him—because he's my best friend. I would never do anything to—I wouldn't want to mess it up."

Noah made a face like he wanted to say something else but then shook his head. "Okay, whatever you say."

"Damn right whatever I say," Steel huffed. He placed his empty coffee cup on the counter and spun on his heel, heading back to the table of girls.

"So," he said as he sat down, "where were we?" The girls chattered on about potential plans for the day, but Steel didn't pay attention. Noah's question kept echoing loudly in every corner of his mind.

What about Winston?

Seventeen

SITTING IN HIS meeting with Wei, Winston struggled—he did his best not to show it, but he was really tired. As he'd thought, he hadn't gone back to sleep after the dream, so now it was barely after noon and he was fighting off exhaustion, that familiar feeling of strain behind his eyes that made him just want to run home to his bed.

"Conroy said you made contact with one of the higher-ups in the race," Wei remarked, sitting in one of the chairs dragged over from the poker table while Winston, Tony, and Conroy sat on the couch. It was plain from the way he said it that Wei meant it more as a question than a statement.

"Yeah. Some girl. Told me her name was Mimi," Winston explained. "Not her real name, though, I don't think; everyone there seemed to go by nicknames."

Conroy snickered. "What was your nickname? Baby Face?"

Winston's face burned. "Is that important right now?" He looked to the father figure of the group for help. "Tony, tell him that's not important right now."

Tony shrugged, mouth tight as he struggled to suppress a smile. "I don't know, Winston, it might be. Especially if you don't want Conroy to go around calling you Baby Face from now on."

"For fuck's sake." Winston sighed heavily. "Fine. Noisy. My nickname is Noisy."

Conroy laughed so hard for a moment that Winston thought—hopefully—that he might choke. "I gave a guy that nickname once, too. Doubt it's for the same reasons, though."

"Can we focus, please?" Wei said, though he, too, was smiling lightly. "She tell you anything interesting?"

Winston thought about his encounter with her for a moment and then shrugged. "Not really. She broke down the race structure for me— the ten thousand bought me in to five races. Top placers are guaranteed spots in the big races. Right now that's all I know."

"It's a good start for the first run," Wei said, reaching over and patting him on the leg. "I didn't even think you'd make contact at all. No reason for them to talk to the new guy. You must have been pretty impressive."

"Persistent, more like it." He remembered the plain, nondescript guy he'd received his GPS from and paid money to. "There was a guy there for the organizers, though. He gave me the GPS that had the race route. I couldn't tell you much about him, though; he was pretty average. I probably couldn't even pick him out on the street if I saw him."

"You gonna need to work on that, man." Conroy punched Winston's arm playfully. "Keep your eyes open. Take in every detail. You never know what's gonna be important. Thought you would have learned that after what went down at K."

Winston flushed at the unsubtle reminder of his failure at the nightclub where the Twisted Vipers had been running their kidnapping and underground porn ring. He'd looked away for one moment, dropped his guard for the smallest amount of time, and Noah had nearly gotten knifed.

"He learned his lesson, Conroy," Wei said, coming to Winston's defense with a bit of a reprimand in his voice.

He says that now, sure, Winston thought, remembering how pissed Wei had been at the time. Winston couldn't remember ever seeing Wei that mad before, and he definitely didn't like being on the receiving end of the anger. He must have been angry after his old man was killed, but that was during the war with the Nine Stars, and Winston's mother had kept him away from all that.

Winston thought about his dream, the death of his father in the prison cell, taken down by Nine Star bastards after being set up by the Hong Kong Police Department. *Did he get like this when my dad was murdered?* That was dangerous territory, though, and he didn't really want to go down that road, not so soon after that fucking dream.

"Any idea when the next race will be?" Tony asked, helping Wei steer the conversation back to business.

"No idea. I won't know until they send me a message on that phone."

Wei grunted. "Then keep that phone on you at all times. Carry extra batteries or something for it if you need to—buy one and I'll make sure the police reimburse you."

"Speaking of the police...when will I have to brief them about all of this?"

"You leave that to me," Wei said firmly. "I've already made it clear to Hong that the only one the police will be talking to about this is me. I know you don't need that right now."

The gratitude that rushed through Winston at that moment was overwhelming. He wanted to hug Wei, but figured he'd get punched if he tried. He'd settle for an appreciative nod—it was much more manly.

Wei stood up, signaling the meeting's end. "You've done a great job, Winston. Just like I knew you would. Keep up the good work. Hopefully we can find whoever's behind this before any more bodies turn up."

The comment sent a chill down Winston's spine, a grim reminder of what he was doing there. He felt a little guilty, focusing only on what he got out of this situation—primarily showing Wei, once and for all, that he belonged in the Dragons—and forgetting that there were people whose lives had been lost. He thought of that poor little boy who'd lost his brother, arguably the only parental figure he had, and his resolve deepened. He would do this—and not just for himself but for Yao and the others who'd lost loved ones.

Winston followed Wei down the stairs back toward the shop, Conroy and Tony coming in behind him.

"Let us know when you get the next call," Wei said, looking over his shoulder toward him.

"Of course."

They entered the coffee shop through the kitchen and then went out into the main area. Wei immediately crossed to Noah, pulling him into his arms and giving him a deep kiss. When they separated, Winston noticed the deep red spread across Noah's face.

"I've got to go meet Hong," Wei told his lover, kissing him quickly one last time. "After that, I've got some business to take care of. See you at home later."

"Don't kill a police official," Noah called after Wei, who smirked.

"No promises."

"Noah, when is my mom coming..." Winston happened to glance toward a table of girls and trailed off. Steel was seated at the table with the girls, talking and laughing. He leaned pretty close to one of them, a girl with hair dyed blonde like a Westerner. He had that look on his face that he got when he was flirting with someone—the same one he'd had the other night at the bar with that flamboyant twink, the one that had made Winston drink an unremembered number of tequila shots and gotten him ungodly drunk.

"What—? Oh." Noah patted Winston's shoulder, but Winston barely noticed.

As if he could feel Winston's gaze on him, Steel glanced up, catching Winston's eye. He said something to the girls and rose, heading Winston's way. Winston watched the way he walked, the smooth swagger he had so naturally. He doubted Steel even knew just how he actually appeared to others.

Winston cleared his throat. "Hey."

"Hey. How was the meeting?"

Winston shrugged, trying to match the effortless way Steel moved and feeling ridiculous. "It was fine. Just telling them what happened."

"Cool, cool. Hey, look, these chicks over here know this cool new place that opened up in Aberdeen, and we were going to go check it out and then hit up a few places, have a little fun. You in?"

Winston didn't have to think hard about it. Did he want to sit around all day, watching Steel flirt with some college girls he picked up? Definitely not. "Sorry, bro, but I told Mom I'd spend some time with her. Haven't done much of that recently."

"Okay... You have your car here, so you don't mind if I...?" Steel gestured over his should with his thumb.

"No, no," Winston said, throat feeling tight as something coiled in his stomach. "Go. Have fun." He couldn't believe he'd even gotten those words out, because the thing coiling in his stomach screamed at him to say *No, no, you can't go with these* tsau hai.

Something flashed across Steel's face, too fast for Winston to read it, and then he smiled. "Great. I'll catch you later."

Winston waved, a smile that he just knew everyone could tell was false plastered on his face.

"Are you a complete idiot?" Noah demanded from behind him.

"Hey," Winston said defensively. "What the hell are you talking about?"

"You just let him walk out the door with those girls." Noah gestured emphatically toward the door. "So, I repeat my question—are you a complete idiot?"

Winston knew what Noah was asking—Noah was damn perceptive and had caught on a long time ago, no doubt. But there was a reason that old white guy called it the love that dare not speak its name. Steel was his best friend, and he would be damned before he let something like feelings getting out of his control ruin an eleven-year friendship.

"I think you've got me confused with his mother," he quipped. "Speaking of mothers, do you know when mine will be back?"

Noah made a face at him, like he'd really like to continue the conversation, but glanced at the clock on the wall. "She said by one thirty. Listen, Winston—no, it's not about that," he added quickly, seeing Winston's face. "It's just that you don't seem to have any plans tonight, and we haven't had a chance to hang out since I got back—"

Winston sneered good-naturedly. "Too busy getting the D to make time for friends, huh?"

"—so I was hoping you'd come over tonight for dinner," Noah finished, glaring at him. "Of course, if you want to be an asshole about it, feel free to go fuck yourself."

Winston considered the option. He'd not spent a whole lot of time at Wei's apartment, aside from when he was on guard duty, protecting Noah. But his options seemed few at the moment: either sit at home and mope about, feeling jealous about Steel, wondering what he was doing with those girls, or else do the same thing but with company, so that he could distract himself better.

"You know what? Sure. What are you cooking?"

"Actually, it's Wei's night to cook."

Winston's smile faltered. "Oh. Then, uh, maybe not."

Eighteen

WINSTON SPENT THE majority of the day regretting accepting Noah's invitation. The more he thought about it, the worse it sounded. There he was, about to be the third wheel. He didn't know how he'd thought that being around a couple as plainly in love as Wei and Noah would help distract him.

The only thing that had managed that recently was the Dark Streets race. He'd been entirely focused on the road, the maneuvers necessary just to stay alive. For once, there were no thoughts about Steel—no worries about what might happen with the Twisted Vipers.

God, he wished he could be in a race right that moment.

When the elevator dinged at Wei's floor, Winston considered going right back downstairs. If Noah had just been some friend of his, he would have, but Noah happened to be Wei's lover, and upsetting him was likely to upset Wei himself. Winston had done enough of that to last a lifetime.

A smile slapped on his face—one he hoped was more believable than the one he'd given Steel earlier in the coffee shop—Winston rang the doorbell. A delicious scent wafted out from the apartment when Noah opened the door, hinting of spice and something more. It was a familiar odor, and Winston's stomach growled to life in response.

"Winston!" Noah greeted him, beaming. "You're right on time. Come on in. Wei's making *fo wo*."

"*Fo wo*, huh?" Winston was impressed. Most Westerners just called it hot pot and were done with it. "We're going to turn you into a true Hong Konger yet."

Winston slid off his shoes and followed Noah into the apartment. It hadn't changed much since he'd last been there—the same wallpaper, the same furniture, the same stained-glass half-wall dividing the front of the apartment from the bedroom area.

One thing that was different was Wei. He'd never seen the leader of the Dragons look so utterly at peace. He stood at the counter, cutting various vegetables in a pair of simple gray sweatpants and a white wifebeater that showed off his several tattoos, including the beginning of his own Dragon, which Winston knew came to an end right over his heart.

Damn it, when am I going to get one? He longed for a tattoo, longed to be marked, to show that he was part of the extended family that was the Dragons, that he belonged—and he did, he knew he did.

"Go on and have a seat anywhere," Noah said, bustling back and forth between the counter—taking things Wei was finished preparing—and the small four-seater dining room table. A pot sat over a portable burner, the red broth of its contents bubbling merrily. It was the source of the spicy smell. Several plates of various vegetables sat there already—chopped mushrooms, bean sprouts, some carrots, a block of tofu cut into four big wedges. There were also three tall cans of Tsingtao beer and a plate laden down with raw, thinly cut beef.

Winston settled himself in one of the chairs, watching the way Noah and Wei moved together in the kitchen. Noah reached for a big wooden spoon under Wei's arm, which he lifted for him without Noah needing to say a word. He moved his arm aside for Wei to slide the knife and chopping board he'd been using into the sink before ducking back behind him and crossing to the table with the spoon in hand.

It was like choreography. Is that what happened when you became a couple? They'd not even known each other six months and yet it was like they shared a mind. Winston and Steel had known each other for nearly eleven years, and it was more like they were on different wavelengths entirely.

Was that just another sign that he and Steel weren't a match for each other?

"I think we're good," Wei said, approaching the table with three sets of chopsticks in his hand. He passed them around and sat down, leaning over the pot to give it and inhaling deeply.

"Smells great," Noah enthused, rubbing his hands together in anticipation.

"It really does," Winston offered, feeling a bit out of place. He was intruding on this moment between the two of them, and he'd never felt more plainly that he didn't belong. "Thanks a lot for having me over."

"Don't mention it," Wei said with a shrug of his shoulder. "Now let's eat." He unceremoniously dumped the vegetables and tofu into the pot, using the wooden spoon Noah'd brought to stir them around a bit.

They each had small bowls, but hot pot wasn't like soup. These bowls were used for the meats and other ingredients they fished out of the pot. They also had traditional ladle-like soupspoons to scoop up the broth if they so wished.

Knowing how Wei ate, Winston wasted no time taking a long, thin slice of beef with his chopsticks and dipping it into the simmering pot. It didn't take long to get the meat perfect, and thirty seconds later, he held his spoon under it to catch the dripping as he guided it to his mouth.

It was all he could do not to cough when the spicy broth struck his tongue. He hadn't expected the intensity level. That was a mistake, considering he was well aware that Wei loved spicy food. He'd just assumed Wei would tone down the spice for the white guy eating with them.

Noah, to Winston's surprise, showed not even the slightest hesitation about the heat level. He ate the meat, fished out a carrot, and promptly ladled some of the broth out to sip down without missing a beat. *Damn,* he thought, impressed, *we might really make Noah into a Hong Konger yet.*

"Too spicy?" Noah asked Winston innocently, catching on to the expression on Winston's face.

No way I'm letting an American outdo me. Winston doubled down and began eating in earnest. Now that he knew what he was getting into, the *fo lo* was just right and, somehow, familiar.

"This reminds me of the *fo lo* my dad used to make," he said when he realized what it was.

"That's because it's your dad's recipe," Wei explained. "He taught me how to make it. He didn't like it as spicy as I do, so I had to pump it up a couple notches, but at its heart, it's still his."

Winston smiled wistfully. "He used to love to cook. I remember always being happy when I came home from school and saw he was cooking."

"From the way he told it, that's the only way he got your mom. He couldn't cook worth shit until he met Constance and learned to impress her."

"Wow," said Noah. "That's some dedication."

"Seems like it," Wei reasoned. "But I don't know. There isn't much of anything someone won't do for someone they love."

The look the lovers shared made Winston feel once again like he was an interloper.

"What was my dad like with you?" Winston asked, eager to change the subject and also very curious about the dichotomous nature of his father—a man who both helped him make his lunches for school and also waged a war against a violent and destructive street gang. "I don't know anything about his involvement with the Dragons or what he was really like."

Wei sat his chopsticks down and leaned over the table toward him. "Listen, Winston. The man you remember, that's who your father really was. You have this crazy idea the man you knew was a mask he was wearing, but you're wrong. The things he did in our fight with the Nine Stars, that was out of necessity—it wasn't who he was. I doubt he would have done any of it if it weren't to keep you, your sister, Constance, and Allen safe."

Hearing Wei say Hong's first name, and without malice, in the same sentence as his father, set a hot stab of anger through Winston's chest. He hated the reminder that a man he worshipped like his father had anything to do with a bastard like Hong. It only made it worse to know that Hong was the best man at his parents' wedding. Clearly the friendship didn't mean that much, though, because Hong had the audacity to turn his back on the Dragons—on Winston's father's memory—and join the *police.*

"Too bad the *puk gai* didn't return the favor," Winston said through gritted teeth. He caught the moment that Noah and Wei shared. "What? You think I'm being too hard on him?"

"Winston, this is me you're talking to," Wei said firmly. "You know my history with your uncle. But to blame him for your father's death—that's just wrong. He suffered, too."

"Did he?" Winston couldn't hold back the sneer. "Did he suffer? I don't see how, when he turned around and joined the bastards who caused my father's death."

"Let's talk about something else," Noah said quickly in an attempt to head off the rapidly building anger.

"I'm not much in the mood for talking anymore," Winston said stiffly. He placed his chopsticks down on the table as calmly as he could manage. "I'm going to go on and get home. Thanks for the food."

"Come on, Winston, just stay and finish dinner," Noah pleaded, but Wei placed a hand on Noah's arm, silencing him.

"You know what, Winston? You say you're ready to be a Dragon, and then you constantly turn around and prove just how you're *not*. You want to act like a child and storm out when you don't like a conversation? Do it. Prove you're still a boy, not a man."

Winston forced himself to meet Wei's gaze, despite how much he wanted to look away. He had steel in his spine, and he was going to prove it, one way or another.

"If that's what you think I'm doing, I can't do anything about that," he said simply. Despite how much his feet pleaded with him to race out of there and to the safety of the solitude of his car, he walked calmly, slid into his shoes, and closed the door quietly behind him.

He even managed to make it to his car before he let out a throat-ache-inducing sound, somewhere between a howl and a shout.

Nineteen

STEEL COULDN'T HAVE felt more miserable if he tried. It wasn't that he even wanted to spend the day with the girls—come on, what guy did?—but he'd been willing with even the possibility of getting laid. It had been a while, and he was in real need. There was only so long a guy could be satisfied shooting airplanes every night.

Shopping with a bunch of college girls was a nightmare for him, but it was endurable. He just plastered an interested look on his face, commented on their conversations sometimes, and gave his opinion on outfits they tried on. He thought that part would be fun, but it was actually like a form of torture. He didn't give a fuck about clothes, and why should he? They were just going to end up on his floor later.

To make the whole day worse, Winston's expression kept popping up in Steel's mind, along with Noah's stupid question. *What about Winston?* Steel wasn't an idiot; he could see that Winston hated the idea of him going out with these girls, even though he said it was fine.

If he didn't want me to go, he should have said so. But why would he, Steel, expect him to? Like he'd told Noah, they were best friends. Winston *should* have been right there encouraging him, cheering him on as he scored—metaphorically, of course. Then again, considering their mutual jerk-off the other night...

Don't go there, he had to tell himself. The last thing he needed was to get a hard-on while sitting close to a women's changing room. He could just imagine the uproar that would cause.

Things got progressively worse as the day went on. They stopped for lunch, and the girls spent the entirety of the time talking about people Steel didn't know and couldn't give two shits about. He wanted to tell them how petty their problems seemed in comparison to the bigger picture, but that would not really serve any purpose other than to piss them off, so he held his tongue.

He got a grace period of several hours before they met again at the bar. He almost didn't go to meet them, but he convinced himself he needed the night out and he needed the score. If he could get just one of them, he could give her other things to talk about, like how great his dick was.

He had hopes that once they got out and about in an adult environment their behaviors would shift, but they didn't. They dressed the part, but they still spent the majority of their time there drinking cocktails and complaining about the same people from lunch.

The longer it went on, the more sour Steel's mood became. He didn't know how long a man could sit around while people talked about other people he didn't know, didn't want to know, and didn't care one tiny ounce about. He kept pounding back whiskey, hoping it would alleviate some of the stress, but unfortunately it didn't. What it did was make him impatient.

"I kept telling everyone she was like that," the suspicious girl was saying. "She always had something nice to say about people to their face. She always called Aily her best friend, but I heard her saying some terrible things about Aily to other girls."

Dear god in heaven, whatever sin I committed to earn this, I'm sorry.

"God, she's such a bitch," one of the other two said, putting her half-full drink down on the table.

"I'm going to get another," Steel muttered, holding up his empty whiskey glass.

The suspicious girl snorted. "That's like your fourth already. What, are you an alcoholic?"

"I wasn't before spending the day with you," Steel muttered. He regretted it the moment he heard the gasps of indignation from the table. The whiskey made his tongue more slippery than he would have liked.

"What's that supposed to mean?"

"Nothing, it didn't mean anything," Steel said dismissively.

"I'm sorry," said the one girl that Steel was most interested in, crossing her arms over her chest, her eyes flashing dangerously. "Are we boring you? No one forced you to come. *You* came waltzing over to *our* table and sat down, not the other way around."

"You're not boring me," Steel said quickly. His whiskey-soaked brain was trying to navigate a path through the dangerous waters he'd steered himself into, but he didn't see that happening. "It's just that I thought—"

"Thought *what*?" she demanded hotly. "Thought that today would be some massive orgy, or you'd have us fighting over you?

"What? No—"

"He probably thought we'd be easy lays," the suspicious one said scathingly. "In and out by lunch time, is that right? Sorry we disappointed you there!"

"You know what? I don't need this. Sure, I was hoping to get laid— who the fuck isn't? Isn't that why you agreed to bring me along, with the potential of one of you getting laid? Or maybe *you* were the ones who were hoping for a group fuck? I don't even care—I've spent this entire day listening to you girls ramble on and on and on. It's driving me crazy. I could understand putting up with this shit if we were dating, but at this point, we're not even fucking, so forget this shit."

His voice had grown progressively louder, until he'd shouted the last words. Though he didn't realize until he'd finished his tirade.

The four girls watched him with expressions ranging from disgusted to almost pitying. "You know," said the suspicious one. "Maybe you should go back to your sad little life and drink alone. You're used to it, right? You were alone at the coffee shop, too. Now we see why."

The three girls rose as one and walked off. Before she disappeared, the third girl, who'd been quiet up until that point issued a parting shot: "You know, this sucks for you. A little booze in us, and at least one of us was a sure thing." She looked him over from head to toe once more before walking off, shaking her head in disappointment.

Great, he thought. *Just fucking great. I pissed Winston off for this?*

Damn it, why was Winston the only thing he could think of today?

He made his way to the bar. If he was going to be alone and guilty— was he guilty for the way he'd just talked to those girls, or because of Winston? If because of Winston, *why*?—he damn well was going to be drunk, too.

"Another whiskey." He slid his empty glass to the bartender. "Actually, make it a double this time."

"I have to admit," said a voice from the stool next to him, "that was entertaining for me. Probably more than it should have been."

Steel glanced over with a scowl at Allen Hong. The inspector was propped up on his elbows, nursing a beer and smiling at Steel from the corner of his eye.

"I didn't know they let asshole cops in here."

"They let you in, so clearly they let assholes in—and not everyone is as ridiculously prejudiced against the cops as you and the rest of the Dragons." He casually took a drink of his beer. Not many people would openly say something like that about the Dragons while in Dragon territory. Then again, not many people would turn down a spot in the Dragons, either. Hong had done both of those things.

"Are you just here to kick me when I'm down, *put gai*?" Steel grumbled. He nodded his thanks to the bartender as he received his drink.

"No, that's just a bonus. I thought tonight would just be me drinking alone and bored—lucky me, you were here making an ass of yourself."

"So glad I could be of assistance," Steel snarled, flipping Hong his middle finger. "Now, if you'll excuse me, I've got better things to do than talk to you—like get completely shit-faced alone."

He started to go, but Hong grabbed his arm. It took every ounce of self-control Steel had not to clock him instantly, but Wei didn't like it when they caused a scene and got arrested—and punching a cop would definitely see him arrested.

"I want to ask you something," Hong said, and Steel stiffened. Nothing good could come of anything that Hong wanted to ask him. "It's about Winston."

That didn't make Steel feel any better. "What about him?"

"I just want to know how he's doing. He won't talk to me, of course, and Constance and I don't talk about him much, either, when we talk. I've tried asking Wei, and he just freezes me out—not unexpected, again, but I can't learn anything that way."

"What, nothing to report to your boss?" Steel asked coldly.

Hong reeled liked he'd been slapped. "You think I'm Dang's spy?"

"What reason do I have not to?"

"I'll ignore the fact that I've known you since you were ten years old and instead say how about the fact that Wei doesn't think so?"

"I don't have to agree with everything Wei thinks," Steel fired back, even though he knew Wei wouldn't have made that decision lightly.

"Wow, a Dragon with an original thought." Hong's words dripped with sarcasm.

"So why did you pick me to ask questions you wouldn't ask your sister or Wei? You think I bend over easier, is that it?"

"What? No. I'm asking you because who knows him better than you? You two have always been close, and lately..." Hong trailed off with a shrug.

"And lately what?" Steel snapped.

"I don't know—it just seems like you two are even closer than you used to be, that's all."

Steel wanted to ask him what he meant, but decided he didn't want to know. Something in Hong's expression put a tiny crack in the mortar of Steel's disdain, and he felt himself empathizing with the man somewhat. "Why wouldn't Winston be okay?"

"Everything going on with the Dark Streets now," Hong said as if it were obvious. "That's got to be stressing him out. He's undercover in a criminal outfit when he's never in any way been trained or prepared for it. I hate that he's been put in this situation."

"I don't think he sees it that way. He's thrilled to have this chance, man."

"I'm sure he does feel that way now," Hong allowed. "But it's not going to be easy. I'd feel better knowing he had someone to turn to, someone who...who had his best interests at heart."

"He has—" *He has me* Steel wanted to say, but couldn't get the words out. It was true, Winston did have him, and he definitely had Winston's best interests at heart—or tried to, anyway. Instead of saying that, though, he finished with "—he has the Dragons. We look after our own, Hong, in case you forgot."

Hong's face clouded for a moment. "No, I didn't forget."

"I have a question of my own. Why do you care so much?"

Hong blinked, genuinely caught off guard by the question. "Why do I care about Winston so much?"

Steel nodded.

Hong's brow furrowed, like he was searching for the words, or for a reason. Maybe he didn't know. "Because," he said at last, "he's family."

Twenty

WINSTON'S ANGER HADN'T entirely dissipated by the time he arrived home from Wei and Noah's apartment. Part of him knew the anger was irrational, but that didn't matter; he couldn't simply reason away his emotions, no matter how ridiculous they might be.

He didn't think they were ridiculous, either. Maybe he'd overreacted, but he couldn't stand hearing Wei of all people defend *Hong* to him. He'd never thought that day would come; Wei had as much reason—or almost as much—to hate Hong as Winston.

Calm down, he told himself as he entered the home he shared with Shelby and Constance. The last thing he wanted was for Constance to ask questions about why he was upset.

"That you, Winston?" Constance called from the kitchen. A moment later she poked her head through the doorway, expression surprised. "I didn't think you'd be back so soon. Your sister and I are in here."

Winston followed her back into the kitchen-slash-dining room, where Shelby sat at a table, making dumplings.

"Well, Noah and Wei wanted a little...alone time," he lied, grinning as Shelby made a face. Constance rolled her eyes and sat back down at the table, joining Shelby in making the dumplings—doing a much better job of it than her daughter, too.

"You want to sit down and join us?" Constance asked. "You're stuffing them too much, Shelby. You can't get them sealed tightly if you stuff them like that. They'll burst in the pot."

Winston started to say no, but thought about it for a moment and realized there was nothing he'd rather do more at that moment than sit down and spend some time with his mother and sister. It wasn't a desire he found himself with a lot, but today it felt like just the thing he needed.

"Okay," he said, sliding a third chair out and lowering himself into it.

"Okay?" Constance blinked. "I mean, great. Shelby, pass your brother some of those wrappers and the gloves."

Shelby complied wordlessly. Winston slipped them on and reached for the bowl containing the stuffing mix with one hand, sliding one of the wrappers free with the other. The stuffing was a mixture of minced meat, spring onion, and various seasonings—a recipe Constance said their mother passed down to her.

"This is nice," Constance said, watching Winston and Shelby prepare their dumplings with an indulgent smile on her face. Winston couldn't recall the last time he'd seen her so happy. "My kids and I making dumplings together."

"Don't cry about it, Mom," Shelby scoffed, but gently so Constance would know it's good-natured ribbing.

"This just makes me think of when I was a young girl," Constance said, eyes growing wistful, like she was looking out onto some scene that neither of her children could see unfolding before her. "As a family, we'd sit at the table and make dumplings just like this. It was nice."

"You don't talk much about when you were younger, Mom," Shelby commented. "I've always wanted to hear stories from when you were my age."

"I don't know how much there is to tell, really. We were a normal family at that point. Your grandfather was already gone—he died when I was eleven, from cancer. It was just your grandmother, me, and your uncle."

The mention of Hong made Winston's stomach clench, but he stayed quiet, listening. He didn't say it, but he wanted to hear Constance's stories as much as Shelby did.

"Allen wanted to quit school, get a job as a fisherman or something, but your grandmother wouldn't have it. She told him in no uncertain terms that he wasn't meant for that sort of life, and she'd be damned if he'd condemn himself to it for her sake. She took on the responsibilities—got several jobs, actually. Allen got part-time jobs while he stayed in school. When he was sixteen, he ended up in the hospital because he'd worn himself out studying for entrance exams and working his jobs. It was a miracle he didn't do worse than just drive himself to exhaustion. But he's always been that way—the protective brother, even though he's younger."

Winston bit back a dirty comment, not wanting to ruin the moment.

Shelby, though, leaned in, eyes alight with interest and seemingly forgetting the dumplings. "Really?"

Constance nodded fervently. "Oh yes. Allen and your dad became good friends when your uncle was in high school. They met at one of Allen's part-time jobs cleaning up and answering the phones for a kung fu teacher—your father. The age difference never mattered much to them. They bonded over their love of various hobbies—mostly martial arts. Despite the fact that your father was older and clearly worlds better in martial arts, the day Allen learned we were dating, he pulled him aside and told him, 'If you ever hurt my sister, I'll kill you.'"

Winston couldn't help but scoff. "As if he could."

"He probably couldn't, but I know, as your father did, that he would have genuinely tried. He would have done anything to protect me. He still would."

Winston had a hard time believing that. He didn't think that his mom was lying in her story, but he couldn't reconcile the image Constance had of Hong with the one that he had. How could the protective big brother, who became best friends with a man older than him, be the same man who joined the very organization that led to his best friend's death?

Could they possibly be the same person?

"Protecting others has always been something your uncle did," Constance added, her voice gentle, as if she understood the conflict of thoughts in Winston's mind. "He shielded people from bullies at school—usually against people much bigger than him. If there's one thing Allen didn't lack, it was courage. He has it in spades."

"Had, maybe," Winston muttered under his breath, not loud enough for anyone to hear. Hong didn't have courage now—if he did, he'd be standing up to his corrupt slug of a boss. He'd rather have his job than stand up for the people of the Eastern District. What was courageous about that?

"He joined the fight against the Nine Stars before even your father did," Constance went on. "In fact, Allen convinced your father to become involved. Even with Wei and everything going on, your father wanted to stay out of it."

That caught Winston's attention. He hadn't known that. "Why didn't Dad want to fight?"

"The same reason I didn't, at first. We had you. It didn't make sense to endanger ourselves when we had two kids to think about. Allen—and Wei, of course, but mostly Allen—convinced us that having you was exactly why we needed to fight. If it weren't for him, I don't know when, or even if, your father and I would have joined Wei and the others."

"Maybe it would be better if you hadn't," Winston blurted before he thought better of it. "Then Dad would still be alive."

"Maybe," Constance said slowly. "Or maybe we'd all be dead. Who knows what would've happened with the Nine Stars. People were dying all the time—people not involved. Innocent people. That's what made Wei fight; that's what made us fight."

"Do you regret it?" Shelby asked, voice soft. She was the most emotionally fragile of the family, and even then, the death of their father struck her quite painfully when they talked about it.

"No, sweetie," Constance said without hesitation. She reached across the table, taking Shelby's hand in her own. "Not even for one moment. We made the right choice—I know that even now. Your father sacrificed everything for you two, to keep you safe, and I'm sure if he'd known the outcome, he would have done it anyway. Everyone made choices that we have no option but to live with."

"That's right." Winston scowled. "Everyone did—including Hong. Dad chose to die protecting his family. *Uncle Allen—*" He said the words with as much venom as he could. "—chose to join the people who killed his brother-in-law."

"That's not what happened, Winston, and you know it," Constance said, exasperated. "He joined so he could—"

"Mom, there's nothing you could say that would make it okay!" Winston cried, rising to his feet. He was raring for a fight, and he certainly couldn't sate that urge with Wei or Noah. Here, though, he could. It helped immensely that his mother was always defending Hong, even though her husband was dead and he'd thrown his lot in with the people who killed him.

"No, I guess not, since you don't want to hear anything but the sound of your own voice anyway!"

Winston opened his mouth to fire a rebuttal back, but before he could, a knock came at the door, followed by the doorbell repeatedly buzzing. "Who the fuck...?"

"Watch your mouth," Constance called after him as he made his way to the door.

"What the fuck is your problem?" Winston demanded, pulling the door open. To his great surprise, he was greeted by a very noticeably drunk Steel.

"My problem?" Steel slurred. "My problem? I'll tell you my problem! I want to talk to that *puk gai* Winston!"

Twenty-One

STEEL'S ENTIRE WORLD was whiskey-filtered. He felt like the apartment complex where Winston lived was somehow slanted now; he couldn't manage to stand up straight for some reason and resorted to supporting himself against the doorframe of Winston's apartment door.

He knocked and no one answered, so he couldn't be certain if he'd knocked at all. Maybe they couldn't hear his knock. Had he knocked softly or hard? He couldn't remember, so to be safe, he began furiously ringing the doorbell.

Steel heard a male voice saying, "What the fuck is your problem?" as they pulled the door open.

An irrational, whiskey-fueled anger welled up in him. "My problem? My problem? I'll tell you my problem! I want to talk to that *puk gai* Winston!" It was Winston's fault that Steel's night had been shit—Winston and his guilt and his stupid face constantly popping up in Steel's head and Hong—but mostly Winston, and the way he'd been making Steel feel lately.

"Steel...?"

Suddenly, the male voice was familiar, and Steel blinked through the alcohol. Winston stood there at the door, an uncertain expression on his face.

"Winston!" Steel threw his arms open and stumbled into the apartment, pulling Winston into his arms. "Just the *puk gai* I was looking for!"

"For fuck's sake, Steel, you smell like you took a bath in booze." Winston tried to push him back at arm's length.

"Yeah, you do," Constance said from behind Winston. The sound of her voice sent guilt reeling through Steel. In his drunken state, he hadn't even taken into consideration that Constance would be there, as well. And Shelby? Yup—he saw her, a bleary figure standing behind her mother. "You also sound like you *drank* a bathtub full of booze. Maybe you should get a shower and sober up a little, Steel."

Steel stood there blinking a few times, processing Constance's words. Okay, yeah, maybe taking a shower would be a good idea. He was immune to the smell of the liquor at that point, having been exposed to it in great concentrations for a long time. The last thing he wanted to do was offend or piss off Constance. "Maybe. Maybe you're right," he managed.

"No maybe about it," Winston said, nose wrinkled. "Come on. I'll help you so you don't fall over."

Winston slipped an arm about Steel's waist, guiding Steel's own over his shoulders and walked with him back toward the bedroom and bathroom. "Your night not go so well, huh?"

Steel thought he heard a bit of satisfaction in those words, but it might have just been the whiskey whispering in his ear, so he ignored it for the time being. "Those girls were annoying," he muttered instead.

"That sucks."

"Yeah, man. All they wanted to do was sit around and...and..." Steel struggled to find the right words. "And say things. It was too fucking boring, man."

Winston helped Steel into the bathroom, finally releasing him so he could stand unsteadily in the middle of it. "You've still got some clothes here in my room, right? I'll grab those for you. You go on and get in the shower."

Steel stood there for a moment, wobbling and unable to make himself focus on anything. Thoughts just flitted in and out of his mind, not lingering long enough to leave an impression.

What am I supposed to be doing? He stared at himself in the bathroom mirror, trying his best to concentrate. He watched as his brow furrowed, lines forming on his forehead. It was strangely surreal, watching that happen on his own face right before his eyes.

Clothes. Shower. Right. He shook his head, the gesture making his stomach churn a bit. He needed to take a shower. Hands fumbling, he managed to remove his shirt and get his pants down to his ankles, though from there he couldn't quite master what to do. Every time he bent forward to push his pants off his feet, he felt like he was going to tip over, and he didn't have the balance necessary to force the pants off with his feet.

It was in this conundrum that Winston returned to. Steel gave him a sheepish smile. "I'm having a lil trouble with my pants."

Winston gave him a put-upon smile. "I see that. Here, let me help you."

Winston crouched down, helping Steel slip the bunched up jeans off his feet. Steel peered down at Winston, on his knees in front of him, and his dick stirred to life. In a matter of seconds, he was rock hard. His dick took over for his alcohol-impaired brain, and began conjuring all sorts of images of things Winston could be doing on his knees that were more fun than just helping his drunk ass out of his pants.

Steel's whisky-soaked mind didn't even pause to think about what Winston's reaction might be when he looked up and noticed his current state—and he'd definitely notice; a family of four could sleep under the tent Steel was pitching.

"Jesus, man," Winston said, looking up and promptly looking away. Steel noticed how the back of his neck reddened a bit.

"Sorry. It's got a mind of its own tonight."

Winston stood up, keeping careful distance between them. "You can handle the rest from here, yeah? 'Cause if you think I'm taking your boxers off for you, you're fucking crazier than you look."

Steel chuckled. "Yeah, I think I got it from here."

Winston left him to it. He was ashamed of just how long it took him to get his boxers off, but he finally managed it and padded into the shower. He stayed upright long enough to turn the water on as hot as he could stand before he plopped down right there on the shower floor, head on his knees, letting the hot water beat against his back and head and breathing in the steam that slowly filled the shower stall.

He jarred awake, no idea how much later, and felt sober—well, more sober than before, anyway. The world spun a bit around him, but he had his bearings, and when he stood up, he found his balance mostly steady.

He turned the water off and stepped out of the shower, noticing a towel sitting on the edge of the sink, along with some of his clothes he kept at Winston's for just such an occasion. Winston must have brought it in while he was showering, and he hadn't even noticed.

Fuck, how long did I pass out for?

Steel dried himself and dressed. When he emerged from the bathroom, he was pleased to see there were still lights in the kitchen, and he could hear Shelby and Constance talking, their conversation occasional broken up by the deeper timbre of Winston's voice.

Steel didn't feel up to facing them—he was sober enough to feel embarrassed about the state he'd shown up in, especially in front of Shelby. Instead, he made for Winston's bedroom, flopping down on the bed. He intended to stay awake long enough for Winston to return to talk to him—he couldn't remember what his drunker self wanted to say to Winston, but he figured he'd remember it eventually—but the moment his head hit the pillow, he was asleep.

Twenty-Two

SITTING AT THE table with Constance and Shelby, Winston heard Steel stumble out of the bathroom nearly an hour after going in and make his way into his bedroom. He was in no rush to follow, though. He didn't want to talk to him at the moment; Steel had seemed pretty pissed at him when he'd gotten there, and he had no idea why. Drunk Steel could get angry at someone for saying thank you if he set his mind to it.

He continued making dumplings with his mother and sister, though he could only partially listen to their conversation; half of his mind kept straying to his friend in his room, no doubt asleep by then. Constance and Shelby took pity on him and didn't direct any questions his way, just letting him sit there and be lost in his own thoughts.

He put it off for as long as he thought he could get away with, but eventually he knew he needed to go to his room and confront whatever it was Steel wanted to present him with. "Okay, I'm going to go check on the drunk idiot," he announced, pushing his chair back from the table and rising.

"Good idea," Constance said, her mouth stretching into a tight line. "Let him know I'd appreciate it if he refrained from coming to my home smelling like an entire distillery, if he can manage it."

"Why should I? Won't you just tell him the same thing in the morning?"

"I will, but I imagine you'll be quite a bit nicer about it than I'm going to be."

Winston started to challenge her on that and then thought about it. "You're probably right. He should be warned. *Joutau.*"

"Good night."

Winston peed, brushed his teeth, and went into his bedroom. As he'd expected, Steel had passed out on his bed, dead center, making it impossible for Winston to get in bed without disturbing him.

Asshole, Winston thought, slapping Steel's bare foot. "Steel. Oi, Steel! Wake up."

Steel stirred, tossing his head back and forth and bending his foot away from Winston's reach. He mumbled something under his breath, but Winston didn't catch it. He figured it was something inappropriate, though, knowing Steel.

"Steel, I can't get in bed with you laying like this."

"Sorry," Steel muttered and shifted his body minutely.

"You're gonna have to move more than that," Winston said, giving his leg a shove.

He shifted more, until there was room for Winston to lay down, too. "Better?"

"It's fine," Winston said with a sigh, lowering his body to the bed. He lay on his stomach, head resting on his arms, facing away from Steel. Winston was grateful Steel seemed to forget the reason for his abrupt arrival at his place, but he also had an irritating desire to know what brought him there.

"Steel," he muttered after a moment, repeating once more when a reply didn't come. The second time did it, and he got a sleepy sound of inquiry from his friend. "Why are you here?"

"'M drunk," Steel muttered.

"No, I mean why are you at my place?"

"'Cause you're here," he answered.

"So you were looking for me?"

"Uh-huh."

"Why?" Winston waited in silence in the dark, suddenly aware of just how rapidly his heart was beating. After several agonizing moments, no answer came. "Steel?"

Another beat before an answer came. "Huh?"

"Why were you looking for me?"

"'M always looking for you," came the slurred response.

"You are?" The words escaped Winston's throat in a choked whisper; it was all he could manage.

"'Course. I love you."

Winston rolled over and sat up, certain his ears had deceived him. "You...you do?"

Steel reached blindly over, patting Winston's right arm. "You're m'best friend."

Winston's heart fell. "Oh. I mean, I know."

Steel rolled over, facing him, watching him through heavily lidded eyes. "Really, you are. You're the only one who knows m' real name's Jian. You've been here for me through everything. Worst time in my life, and you were there."

"So why were you mad at me tonight?" Winston cautiously asked.

"N'mad at you," he muttered. "Mad at me. I abandoned you for some stupid girls. I don't know why I did that. The thing I value most is you. Your friendship, I mean."

"Me, too," Winston said, feeling a little light-headed. They might not have been the exact words he'd wanted to hear, but they still meant a lot to him. "Listen, Steel—"

The scent of alcohol flooded over Winston as Steel's lips pressed against his own, cutting his words short. The kiss lasted only a moment before Steel broke away, rolling onto his back, eyes closed. "My best friend," he repeated almost too softly for Winston to hear.

Winston lay there, listening to Steel's breathing as it deepened again. Looked like another night he wouldn't be able to sleep. How could he when his body was on fire, his lips still tingling, still able to feel Steel's pressed against them?

Twenty-Three

WINSTON WOKE WITH an uneasy feeling the next morning. He'd managed to get a little sleep, though it was fitful and he didn't feel rested afterward. He didn't want to think about how awkward things would be with Steel when they were both awake. What would he be thinking after last night?

Even in the light of day, Winston couldn't stop thinking about the feel of Steel's lips. It was such a sudden gesture, but it meant something, didn't it?

Don't be stupid, he told himself firmly, laying still in bed, eyes squeezed tight so he could pretend he was still asleep in case Steel was in the room. *He was drunk, that's all.*

But didn't people say a drunk tongue speaks a sober mind? Did that apply to kisses, as well? He thought about the line of different people he'd kissed while drunk over the course of his life. Sure, he'd been into a lot of them, at the time. But some of them were women, and unlike Steel, he just wasn't bisexual. Those kisses definitely weren't about being sexually attracted to someone.

Great. He was second-guessing every thought that had hounded him the night before. It was impossible to figure out what might or might not have been running through Steel's head. The only person who would know that was Steel himself—and he wasn't so sure Steel did, either, as drunk as he'd been when he'd gotten there.

Winston tensed when he felt the bed move next to him as Steel sat up.

He couldn't put it off forever, so he decided to man up and face him. He sat up, rubbing the sleep out of his eyes.

"Good morning," Steel said, sounding much more cheerful than he should.

"Aren't you hungover?"

Steel stood up and stretched, shaking his head. "Nope. I feel great."

Lucky bastard, Winston thought, then: *Does he not remember the kiss?* Acting casual, he said, "You might not after Mom gets through with you."

Steel cringed. "I didn't even think about Constance. She pissed?"

Winston nodded.

"Fuck me. Okay, maybe I should at least *act* like I'm hungover so she'll cut me some slack."

Winston walked to his dresser and started digging out clothes. "I don't think Mom has ever cut anyone slack in her entire life."

"Think I'm screwed?"

"You're screwed."

"Damn it. Well, better face the firing squad."

"You sticking around today?" Winston asked, pulling a shirt over his head and stepping into his pair of khakis. He tried to keep the question casual, not wanting to sound hopeful or needy about it.

"With a bitchy Constance running around?" Steel snorted. "Not likely. Besides, there's something important I need to take care of today."

Winston was crestfallen, but hid it well. "Oh, okay."

"I'll try to catch you later tonight, though," Steel said quickly, like he sensed Winston's disappointment. "This shouldn't take all day."

"Okay, sounds good." Winston smiled.

Together they made their way out into the front of the apartment. It was dead quiet, though, not a sound or sight of either Constance or Shelby.

"Looks like you're in luck," Winston said, elbowing Steel. "Mom and Shelby must already be at the coffee shop. You can stop shaking, now."

"Who's shaking?" Steel protested indignantly.

"You are! The thought of my mom being pissed off has you trembling like a little kid again."

Steel flipped Winston off and made for the door. "All right, I'm gonna get going. I'll message you when I'm done or something." He stood there in the door for a moment, and in that was the first sign of awkwardness, the first tell that Winston could see that indicated Steel might remember the night before, or at least enough of it. Something flickered behind his eyes, words unspoken, and then vanished, like the blinds had been lowered on the windows of a house. "Catch you later."

"Later," Winston called behind him, feeling miserable. He sat down on the couch and then buried his head in his hands. Why was it that Steel acting normal made him feel *worse* than if he'd just said the previous night was because he was drunk and didn't mean anything. At least he'd have acknowledged that it was *something*. This—pretending it never happened when he knew damn well it did—it hurt way more.

Maybe I am just being an idiot, Winston thought forlornly. *Reading meaning into something that was nothing more than a drunk blip—not even worth mentioning.* Was he really that desperate? Maybe Steel was just trying to spare him the embarrassment of shooting down the ridiculous hopes and fantasies he harbored of them ever being more than just friends.

He sunk into a deep melancholy that persisted for most of the morning. He couldn't bring himself to get off the couch; he sat there in a droll fog, staring without really following at the television where one of the cheesy daytime dramas his sister loved was playing.

He sat there in the same spot until just after noon when his stomach growling for food stirred him from his stupor. He was halfway to the kitchen when the doorbell rang.

"Steel should know it's unlocked." He reversed course. He opened the door, ready to tease Steel, and the words froze in his throat.

It wasn't steel standing there, but Allen Hong.

"What—what the hell are you doing here?" Winston spat. "You know what? I don't give a fuck. Fuck off, *jin jang*."

He started to shut the door, but Allen held it open with his hand.

"I need to talk to you," he said grimly. "It's about the Dark Streets."

Winston stopped trying to close the door, but he studied Hong suspiciously. "Did Wei tell you you could come and talk to me?"

"I don't need Wei fucking Tseng's permission to do my damn job," Hong snapped, and Winston felt a surge of what felt like victory. It looked like he'd touched a nerve for the seemingly unflappable inspector. He'd have to file that one away for future use. "He's not in charge of this; I am. End of story. This can't wait for him to decide to take my calls or call me back."

Winston reluctantly stepped back and allowed Hong into the apartment. "Make it quick."

"When the next race rolls around, you've got to work faster. We need something *now*. This isn't some long-term sting we've set up. It's great that you established some connection last time. We need to see some results from that the next race."

"You make it sound so simple, but it's not! These guys barely know me; it's been *one* race."

"Just tell me if you're not up to it," Hong snapped. "I'll put one of my officers on it instead."

Winston sneered. "Because you cops have been so successful before now? Why did you need me in the first place? I'll do it—but I'll do it on my own time."

"This isn't a game, Winston," Hong nearly shouted. "People are dying, and things are about to get much uglier!"

Hong's outburst took Winston aback. "What's happened? There's something that you're not telling me."

Hong sighed, as if he was debating what he should and shouldn't say. "There's been another death, and we're pretty sure it's connected to the races. This one could make things way worse than they already are, though—that's all I'm going to say on the matter," he added, seeing Winston about to ask a question. "You've got to get something, and soon, Winston."

"I'm doing what I can, but I can't just force them to talk to me. These things take time. I'll have a much easier time of it if you and your cop friends stay the hell out of it." He opened the door, making it clear that he was done talking to Hong.

Hong sighed and walked out of the apartment.

"Oh," Winston added to his back, "one more thing. The next time you want to talk about the Dark Streets, call Wei." He closed the door at that, taking a moment to feel a little self-satisfied with his last words. The moment was brief, though, and he hurried to find his cell phone.

He needed to talk to Wei.

Twenty-Four

STEEL SAT ON Wei's motorcycle outside of the rundown apartment building for a long while, staring up at the windows, lost in his own memories. So much about the place reminded him of where he was born, the place he ran away from. It was nicer than his old place, though, so there was that. Fewer windows were boarded up, too.

The place he'd stayed with his worthless mother didn't even have electricity; they were squatters. Looking back on it as an adult, he recognized it as a drug den, but as a child, he just thought it was normal. The place itself wasn't why he'd left—neither was the hunger, really, though that was something he could still remember wrestling with every day, even now, when he hadn't known true hunger in ten years.

He didn't like to think about that time of his life, the time before he'd become Steel—when he was just Jian, a weak and helpless kid. No one liked to be reminded of the darkest time of their lives.

Eager to shake off the shadow that seemed to have fallen over him, Steel glanced at his watch. Almost four, so it was as good a time as any to go in. He dismounted the motorcycle and crossed the street to the apartment building. It smelled as bad as the last time he and Winston were there. Hopefully the same wouldn't be true for the particular unit he was visiting.

He knocked on the door, and a moment later it opened, little Yao's wide, wary eyes peering up at him through the crack. He visibly relaxed, like he was relieved to see a familiar face, and opened the door wider.

"Hey, little man," Steel greeted, looking into the apartment as the door opened. It was somewhat cleaner than it had been before, he'd give the old addict that. "You shouldn't open the door if you don't know who it is."

"I can't know who it is if I don't open the door," Yao said in that plainspoken way that children had.

He's got me there, Steel thought with a wry grin. He swiped playfully at the kid's head, pulling him in close. The boy laughed, squirming to get out of his arms. *I wonder if this is the first time he's laughed since his brother was killed?* It was a grim thought and a reminder of why he was there.

"Hey, Yao, listen. Where's your mom?"

Yao shrugged. "She said she had to go to work."

Steel's upper lip drew up at the thought of what his mother was doing for "work"—if that's even what she was doing. He thought it more likely she was getting high somewhere. Even if she was working an actual job, it was probably just so she could buy more drugs.

"Does she ever bring work here?" Steel asked Yao carefully. He didn't want to lead the kid on, but he wanted to know.

Yao shook his head. "Sometimes she brings Mr. Yang over, and they go in her room and it smells funny, but that's all."

Steel nodded. "Okay, that's good. I've got something for you." Steel dug into his pocket and pulled out a cheap little flip phone. "This is for you. My number is saved in there under Steel. If you ever need anything—and I mean *anything*, you call me. If you're hungry, call me. If your mom brings back not nice people and you're scared, call me. Anytime, okay?"

Yao nodded, his face showing he didn't really understand what was happening. "Why are you giving me this? Because you were Min's friend?"

"Kind of." Steel struggled with how to explain it to a kid. He decided the best approach would be not treating him like a child, but like a person. A kid who went through what Yao must have gone through wasn't really a kid on the inside. "Listen, little man, I'm going to tell you something I've only told a few people, okay? You've got to keep this between you and me, our little secret. Agreed?"

"Okay."

"There was this boy named Jian. He was a lot like you, I bet. He had a ma and a pa, but they didn't care about him. They spent all of their time getting drunk and high, and Jian spent all of his time pretending he wasn't there. He lived in a terrible place—no lights, no TV, no water, and usually no food. He was all alone."

The telling was harder than he thought it would be, and for a moment, the words just wouldn't come, but he soldiered on. "You had your brother—and now you have me—but Jian had no one. When he was nine years old, his life became worse. His father left and his mother started bringing her work home with her. All these different men. Some of them ignored him, but some of them liked to hurt him. All Jian wanted to do was hide somewhere no one could find him. But the ones that wanted to hurt him, they always found him."

Even so many years later, the memories had a powerful hold on him. The feelings of helplessness washed over him, and he was once again the lonely, frightened little boy trying to find dark places to hide, places where he'd be untouched by the world around him.

"What happened?" Yao prompted, and Steel fought back the feelings and forced himself to return to the present, to where he was no longer powerless.

"Jian made it through that year, but when he was ten years old, something else happened. One night, his mother called him to her room. He didn't want to go, but she sounded like she needed help—sometimes the men she brought home hurt her, too—so he went. One of those men was there, was still there. His mother called him over to them, so he went, and the man looked him over.

"For some reason his mother started crying. She told this man that she changed her mind. He told her to think about the money, how she'd be able to live for such a little thing—and she'd have more of the money, too, because she wouldn't have a kid to feed. Still, his mother protested, so the man hit her. He grabbed Jian's arm, threw some money on the bed, and started dragging Jian from his home."

Yao's eyes were wide with fear. "Why was the man taking Jian?"

"He said he owned Jian now, and he knew people that would pay a lot of money for Jian in sweatshops. There are some very bad people out there, Yao."

"Did the man give Jian to other people?"

"No. It was raining that night, a huge storm. Jian managed to escape the man, and he ran and ran for hours. When he was too tired, he snuck through an unlocked window into an apartment. He found a family there, and they helped him. They fed him, took care of him. He grew up to be someone strong, someone who could protect people who couldn't protect themselves. Are you ready for the part that's a secret, the part you can't tell anyone else?"

Yao nodded eagerly.

Steel leaned close, looking the little boy right in the eyes. "Jian is me. That's my real name. I know how you must feel—but like I found a family to help me, you've found a family to help you. I'm that family. I know your brother is gone, and I can't replace him, but I will be here for you." He nodded toward the phone Yao clutched in his little hands. "All you have to do is give me a call."

Twenty-Five

As SOON AS Hong left, Winston called Wei and then hopped in his car and made his way to the coffee shop. Wei sounded pretty pissed, and he felt bad for stirring up trouble, but it would have been even worse if he hadn't said anything at all. At least Wei was pissed at Hong and not him.

Winston stayed downstairs in the shop while Wei made a phone call to Hong himself upstairs. Every now and then he thought he heard shouting, but it might have been his imagination.

Nothing better to do with his time, he helped Noah at the front of the shop while Shelby helped their mother in the back. When he first began, they were far too busy for idle conversation, which Winston was okay with. It kept his mind from focusing on Steel every moment, which was good, because every time he thought about the kiss he wanted to curl into a ball and hide from the world. He was an idiot for letting his imagination run wild and assign meaning to the kiss.

He liked to think that kisses meant something, though. It wasn't a drunken make-out session in some noisy bar. It was a quick kiss on the mouth in bed.

But still drunk, he reasoned with himself. No, he would not let his mind get the better of him here. He wasn't about to walk into that heartache. Where had eleven years of a crush gotten him? Nowhere. He didn't need to waste any more time.

"Listen, Winston," Noah said to him once things slowed down a bit. "About last night, I'm really sorry. We didn't want to upset you."

Winston shrugged off the apology. "It's nothing; I shouldn't have gotten so worked up about everything. That was on me."

"So everything's cool?" Noah asked hopefully. Winston wasn't surprised; Noah had a small circle of friends, so he likely wanted to keep the ones he had.

"Everything's cool," Winston affirmed. They fist bumped and Noah looked relieved. To be honest, Winston was too. The last thing he needed was for Wei to be pissed at him. He knew he'd have to go and apologize to the big guy himself in person, and he absolutely dreaded it. He would do it, though, because if there was one lesson his father taught him that stuck with him more than any other—besides family takes care of family—was that a man owned up to his mistakes when he made them.

Maybe, just maybe, apologizing would help show Wei, and himself, that he *was* a man and he could act like it.

Something started vibrating in his pocket, startling him. He grabbed his phone, but it wasn't ringing. It took him a full minute to realize it was the burner phone he had for the race. He'd received a text message:

—*Nine, twenty-nine, oh-two-hundred.*

The next race.

"There you are," Steel said as he came into the coffee shop. "I went looking for you at your place, but you weren't there."

"Did you put Wei's bike around back?" Noah called to Steel. "You know he's going to get pissed if you don't."

"It's been done," Steel assured Noah, his eyes not leaving Winston's face. "What's up?"

Winston showed him the message.

"Okay. We need to tell Wei."

"Tell me what?" Wei asked, coming out of the kitchen. He paused long enough to slide a hand down Noah's back, a gesture that looked almost unconscious, like it was the most natural thing in the world.

If it wasn't for the message, he'd have felt a stab of envy. As it was, he just passed the phone to Wei.

"Goddamn it," Wei huffed. "I *just* got off the phone with Hong. Last thing I want to do is call him *again.*"

"Tell me about it," Winston huffed.

"Did I miss something?" Steel asked.

Winston started to explain, but Conroy hurried into the coffee shop. "Wei, we've got a problem."

Wei pressed a hand against his head. "Of course we do. What is it?"

"Johnny Hwang just called. He wants a meeting."

The tension in the room seemed to multiply at the mention of the leader of the Twisted Vipers.

"Noah," Wei called, sounding tired, "call the red poles, get them here. Meeting in twenty minutes."

"Use the phone in the back," Constance told him quietly.

Steel grabbed Winston's arm and led him to the corner of the shop. "Do you know what this is about?"

Winston shrugged. "No idea. Maybe it has something to do with Hong coming to see me earlier, but I'm not sure."

"Wait, Hong went to see you?" Steel bristled. "Wei said you weren't going to have any contact with that sonofabitch." Steel started past Winston toward Wei, but Winston grabbed his arm, stopping him.

"Wei didn't know, but he handled it," he assured Steel.

The last hold-out voice in the back of his mind became emboldened. Steel was concerned about him, protective. Did the kiss really mean nothing? Then again, Steel was a Dragon; he'd protect anyone in that building without a second thought.

But would he kiss them?

Winston didn't have a ready answer for that.

"What the hell did he want?" Steel asked, fists clenched. "I told him—"

Winston cocked his head to the side. "You told him?"

"I meant we, as in the Dragons. Wei told him to leave you alone. What did he want?"

"He came to talk about the Dark Streets. He said someone else was dead, and it would cause problems. Maybe this is what he meant." Winston couldn't think of any other reason Hwang would want to see Wei. It certainly wouldn't be good; tension between the groups was at an all-time high. Constance seemed to think it was only a matter of time before violence broke out, and Winston couldn't say he disagreed.

"Great," Steel muttered, hands on his hips. "The last thing we need is more bullshit fromthe fucking Twisted Vipers."

Winston said nothing, eyes trained on Wei. Their leader stood next to Conroy, who was on the phone, presumably with the Twisted Vipers. Wei's face was a mask, though the tension in his body gave away his thoughts. He was worried about whatever this was. Then again, since the incident with the kidnapped and murdered girls and Noah himself being targeted by a supposed rogue Viper, Wei hadn't exactly been the picture of serenity, not that Winston could blame him. He didn't envy Wei the position.

"You all right?" Steel asked, drawing Winston's attention from Wei and Conroy.

"I'm fine. Where were you today?"

"I went to see Yao."

Winston's eyebrows rose; that wasn't the answer he'd been expecting. "Min's little brother? Why?"

Steel shrugged. "Someone needs to keep an eye on him. With his brother gone, he's all alone in the world."

Winston couldn't help but smile. "You're looking out for him? That's awesome." Steel ducked his head, but not before Winston caught sight of the blush creeping into his cheeks. "Look, I totally get it. He reminds you of yourself when you were his age. You want to spare him the pain and hardship you went through. I think it's incredible." He put a hand on Steel's shoulder and squeezed, trying not to note the intense heat of his body radiating through his clothes.

The two locked eyes for a moment, Winston's searching, though for what he didn't know yet. There was something there, dancing behind Steel's eyes, something that might have been anticipation or fear or something else entirely. Magnetic tension sparked between them, a pull that drew them toward one another, though neither of them noticed it at first.

"Steel," Wei called, the sound of his voice severing whatever invisible force acted between them. For a wild moment, Winston felt a surge of anger at Wei, but it faded quickly as reality set back in. "Get over here. You, Smile, Jesse, and Chris are going with me to meet Hwang."

Winston's heart leapt into his throat at Wei's words. "You're actually going to meet with him? But—but what if it's a trap?" A thousand different scenarios played through his head, all of them ending with Steel—and the others—injured or dead.

"That's why he's taking us along," Steel reminded Winston, patting his shoulder. "Don't worry, we'll be fine."

"I know you will," Winston said because it was the right thing to say, not because he actually believed it. "Just be careful."

"I'm always careful," Steel answered before following Wei out the front door as Chris Ma's car pulled in front of the coffee shop.

Like hell you are, Winston thought darkly. *But you sure as hell better be this time.*

Twenty-Six

STEEL HATED RIDING in the backseat of cars. He felt like he never had enough legroom, especially with someone like Chris, who insisted on sliding his seat back to accommodate his own lanky, long legs. He ended up scrunched up in the back next to Jesse, a cheerful, short guy, who somehow felt the need to manspread and take up a full half of the backseat.

God, he hoped that the meeting place was close.

"So, Wei," Chris said, drumming his long fingers on the steering wheel. "Did Hwang say what this meeting is about?"

"No, but I've got my theories, and they're not good."

Steel frowned. That made it sound like Winston's theory was right, unfortunately. If the meeting *was* related to another death, it would mean an escalation of tension, and things were already pretty damn tense. He didn't know how much higher it could go before everything exploded and a whole shitstorm came their way.

"Let's hope it's not a trap." He sighed.

Jesse looked at him like he was crazy. "What are you talking about? I'm jonesing for a fight. I didn't get to have any fun last time."

"This shit isn't fun," Wei growled. "This isn't some shoot-'em-up game with no consequences. I don't need you going in there half-cocked, do you hear me?"

"Don't worry, Wei, I'm all cock," Jesse assured him, to the groans of everyone else in the car. Steel elbowed him hard in the side. "I deserved that," Jesse winced.

The meeting place Hwang selected was inside Twisted Viper territory, but not so deeply as to make Steel nervous. That was how it tended to work; the one who called the meeting called the place. Steel knew Wei would have picked a place in his own territory, too. It looked like it was one of those family-style restaurants that served a variety of dishes.

"Could they be any more fucking stereotypical?" Steel asked, rolling his eyes.

"I think it's got style," Jesse said, craning his neck down to peer at the restaurant.

Steel slapped him on the back of the head.

"Ow! What's that for?"

"For acting like the youngest guy in the car when that's me. Keep your head on straight."

Jesse made a face but said nothing more.

"Listen, I meant what I said about going in there half-cocked." Wei turned in the front seat to study Steel, Jesse, and Smile in the backseat. "Smile, you're head muscle. I'm counting on you to make sure these idiots don't get in any trouble."

"You got it, boss." Smile nodded grimly. He'd been so quiet on the car ride over that Steel had basically forgotten he was there. His name was meant to be off-putting; Steel couldn't recall ever seeing the man smile. He was menacing and brooding, and Steel understood immediately why he was there.

"Yo, Wei, it's go time," Chris said, jerking his head toward the restaurant. The doors had opened and four guys in expensive-looking business suits came out, making their way toward the car.

Steel tensed. The men might have been dressed civilly, but there was no mistaking the violence that lurked beneath them, like a coiled snake, waiting to strike. These were murderers, not businessmen.

"Be cool," Wei instructed. "You know what to do."

Smile nodded and climbed out of the car first. Steel, Chris, and Jesse followed suit, eyeing their Twisted Viper counterparts, sizing them up to see how they'd come out in a fight.

At the thought of violence breaking out, Winston's face flashed before Steel's eyes. Winston would be so pissed at him if he got hurt. It wasn't like he was charging around, looking for a fight, though. Besides, he couldn't be thinking about Winston at a time like that. Wei needed him to have his head in the game. The part he played in the Dragons was dangerous, but he'd accepted that when he'd joined up—and Winston understood the risks involved, too, and he was just as willing to deal with them as Steel was.

The Viper Steel selected was an ugly brute of a man, looking like a frying pan had been smashed into his face a couple of times. He was muscle-bound, though, looking as out of place in his suit as Steel would look at an all-girls school. Smash Mouth met Steel's gaze, his own beady eyes narrowing. Looks like he was down for a fight, too. That was just fine with Steel.

Smile opened the door for Wei, and Steel and the others fell into place. Smile was in front of Wei, Chris and Steel to his left and right, with Jesse bringing up the rear.

As they passed, Smash Mouth muttered to his companion, loud enough for Steel to hear, "These *sei gei lou* don't look so tough."

Normally that sort of comment would have just slid right off Steel's back, but considering how tense he was it sent him careening over the edge. He turned to the *puk gai*, walking up on him until they were standing almost toe-to-toe. "You wanna see just how tough we are, *puk gai?*"

Smash Mouth grinned, showing a collection of broken teeth. "Bring it, *ong lan gau.*"

"Steel," Smile barked. It took every ounce of willpower that Steel had not to ignore Smile and slam his fist into Smash Mouth's face in an effort to break more of his teeth. He pulled himself back, the action as taxing as if he was climbing back up onto a rock ledge after falling over it. He took a step back from Smash Mouth; lip curled up in a sneer.

"Looks like Mommy's calling you," Smash Mouth taunted. "Maybe she'll let you out to play next time."

"There's definitely going to be a next time," Steel growled. "You can fucking count on it."

He held Smash Mouth's gaze for a moment, long enough to make sure he understood just how serious Steel was, before he fell back into place. He shrugged sheepishly at the look Wei sent his way.

He was definitely in for some words later, and he deserved it, too. Seeing Smash Mouth's smug look, though, he didn't care if he'd get verbally reamed later. It was worth it. Somebody had to show these Viper *ga tsan* that the Dragons weren't to be fucked with. Wei had to be all political and shit, but Steel didn't. He'd gladly take the chewing out if he could accomplish that goal.

The interior of the restaurant was precisely what Steel expected: gaudy, over the top Chinese-themed decorations, from lion dog statues to big paintings of the zodiac signs on the walls. Every table was round, like in most dim sum places. The place was empty, aside from one table in the very center of the restaurant.

Johnny Hwang occupied that table, sitting to where he was looking at the door so he could observe them when they came in. Two men stood behind him to either side, and the men from outside followed Steel and the others in.

Steel couldn't help but tense. They were outnumbered in Viper territory. If ever was a good time for a trap to be sprung, it was now.

"Wei," Hwang called across the restaurant as they came in. "I trust you had no problems finding your way here?"

Wei gave Hwang a cold but polite smile. "No, it was very easy to find."

"Unlike the places you always pick." Hwang leaned forward, sharp, intelligent eyes studying Wei and the others to see if his barb landed home. He'd have to try a lot harder than that to shake Wei, though. "Was there a problem outside?"

"No," Wei said coolly.

Hwang's face was full of insincere relief. "Oh, that's good to hear. It sounded for a moment like you couldn't control one of your people."

Steel's hands tightened into fists, but he kept himself reined in. He might have no problem showing dominance in front of some lowly red pole or grunt, but doing something stupid here would likely get them killed—and even if it didn't, Wei would kill *him* afterward anyway.

Smile shot him an unnecessary warning glance. He nodded ever so slightly to say he was cool.

Wei didn't wait for an invitation. He sat down at the table directly across from Hwang, Smile and Steel taking places at his sides, while and Chris and Jesse stood closer to the men at the back. It would work well, since people often underestimated Jesse because of his size, but he was one hell of a fighter, and it would work to their advantage.

"I'll just get right to it, since I'm sure neither of us has the time or patience to dick around right now," Hwang said, casual attitude he'd had when they first walked in melting away, revealing the hard persona of the Twisted Viper Dragonhead. "It's come to my attention that one of my men is dead—murdered, to be precise, in *your* territory last night. What I want to know is simple—which of your men is responsible?"

So, Steel thought grimly, *Winston was right. The death Hong mentioned is connected. This isn't good.*

"I appreciate the bluntness, Johnny. And I know what it looks like," Wei said slowly. "But none of my people had anything to do with this."

One of Hwang's muscle snorted derisively. "Bullshit."

Who the fuck did this guy think he was? Steel started around the table, intent on teaching that piece of shit a lesson about respect. Smile grabbed his arm, jerking his head toward Wei to indicate that they should follow his lead on this, and he didn't seemed the slightest bit perturbed by the comment—he didn't even look as if he'd heard it. All of his attention was on Johnny Hwang.

Hwang, for his part, studied Wei incredulously. "You expect me to believe a Twisted Viper ended up murdered in Dragon territory, but it wasn't at the hand of a Dragon?"

"I see how it could seem that way," Wei conceded. "But it's true. What was your Viper doing in my territory?"

Hwang's mouth narrowed into a sharp line. "Nothing untoward, I am sure."

"They were part of the Dark Streets, weren't they?"

Hwang's face didn't give away more than a flicker, but it told Steel they were right. "You punish all outsiders who enter the races, do you?"

Wei sighed. "No. Just a few days ago, one of my own was killed— gunned down. He was involved with the race, too. I don't think that's a coincidence, do you?"

Hwang thought for a moment. "I think you'd say anything to cover for your people. I don't think you ordered it done—if I did, this meeting would not have been called. What I think is that one of your people saw an opportunity to draw blood and took it. Given the current climate, I think I've been more than accommodating to your people, especially after the amount of *our* blood that was spilled not too long ago—"

"Leo Tong is the one responsible for that," Wei interrupted brusquely. "You know as well as I do that we weren't the aggressors in that."

"Which is why I've been accommodating," Hwang said tersely. "But I cannot sit back quietly while even more of my own blood is spilt. What kind of leader would I be, in that case? My people won't tolerate it anymore, and neither will I. That's why I called you here, Wei. This is a friendly warning: if there is any more Twisted Viper blood shed at the hands of the Dragons, there will be war."

Steel felt like cold water had been dashed over him; his chest constricted and he couldn't draw in a breath, and goose bumps rose all along his body. Of course they'd been living with that potential for weeks, but to hear it given voice, to hear the promise made, it made the reality of it that much clearer. He could see it plainly then: there would be violence, there would be bloodshed, and there would be lives lost. It was inevitable; their set course since before Noah got there. His arrival—or more precisely, his sister's—was the catalyst. But it didn't set the course. The vision terrified him in a way it wouldn't have a few weeks before, and when he tried to figure out why, Winston was the only thing that came to mind.

He had to live for Winston, and he needed Winston to live for him.

"You should think very carefully about your words, Johnny," Wei said. Steel couldn't see his face and couldn't tell what he was thinking based on his voice, but the men who were looking at Wei began to shift their weight, looking like men who were only just now realizing the stray dog on the street had teeth.

"Trust me, Wei, I've thought about this for a long time. We're done here. Show our guests out, boys."

The men who'd greeted them outside straightened, waiting for Wei and company to get up. Wei sat still at the table for a moment, eyes locked on Hwang. Steel was desperate to know what was going through his head. He figured Wei would say something, try the diplomatic path, but when he moved, it was simply to rise and leave the restaurant.

This time Steel was the last one out the door, and before he got outside, he heard Johnny Hwang say, "I'm hungry. Find the *bat po* who runs this place and get some damn food."

Wei remained silent for a long portion of the drive, so when he spoke, it startled all of them in the car. His words mirrored Steel's earlier thoughts.

"It's only a matter of time."

Twenty-Seven

WINSTON HATED NOT knowing what was going on. Waiting drove him crazy, so to keep himself occupied, he went out to his car in the alley and went to work on it. The car was one of the few things that could actually distract him. He'd spend hours working on it, tuning it up, getting its engine purring just right, and making sure the outside shone with the beauty a car like it deserved.

Every now and then, thoughts of what might be going on at the meeting Wei had dragged Steel off to rose up, but he drove them down by diving into a new task. He had a race in two days and needed the car to be ready for it. Sure, the police had done a quick job repairing it, but that didn't mean there was nothing for him to do. Shelby had come out once to get his help with something, and he'd told her just that. She'd made the mistake of asking, "What does waxing the car have to do with getting it ready?"

"Image is just as important in this as the car's functioning," Winston had told her impatiently. "You should see these guys, Shelby. Their cars look like they've just been driven off the lot. Someone who's willing to pay ten thousand dollars to enter the race is going to take pride in how their car looks driving in it. I can't show up with a dirty car and expect these guys to take me seriously."

Shelby didn't have much to say to that, just turned around and went back inside.

The afternoon wore on into evening, and still no word came their way from Wei and the others. Wei didn't say where the meeting was taking place, so who knew how long it would take to get there. The lateness was just a matter of travel time, that was all. He wouldn't allow his mind to drive toward more sinister explanations, because it was hard to rein it back in once it did. Once the images of Wei and Steel and the others lying around, splattered in blood, gaping holes in their chests or heads, dead at the hands of the Twisted Vipers—

Damn it, man, stop!

Winston forced his focus back to the car, circling it, hawk-like, searching for any blemishes or smudges in the coat of wax he'd just applied. It was tedious work, seeking out and removing even the tiniest of smudges, but it was exactly what he needed to keep his mind in safe territory, his imagination effectively bridled.

The sun had sunk low enough that the narrow alleyway behind the coffee shop was cast in shadow when the sound of car doors in front of the shop and familiar voices chatting away drifted back to him. Winston's first instinct was to rush into the shop and see Steel, to make sure he was okay, but he resisted. He didn't want to look like an idiot, and besides, Steel probably still had Dragon business to tend to. He didn't know if Steel even wanted to see him.

Did he care?

Though he didn't run inside to see him, he couldn't stop staring at the door, waiting. When Steel emerged, their eyes met; Steel had been searching for him as he came out.

Winston didn't have the vocabulary to adequately express his relief at seeing Steel alive and unharmed, especially after going into the den of the enemy. For a moment, it was as if his emotions were about to pour out, his joy so overwhelming he might burst. With their eyes locked, Winston felt like he could see right into Steel's heart; they were connected for that moment, suspended in time.

Just as suddenly as the connection formed, it broke, and Steel went upstairs after the others. Winston was left feeling hollowed out, like something was suddenly missing, the echo of that connection.

You're being stupid, he thought, giving his head a violent shake, as if he could physically dislodge the feeling.

He threw himself back into the car, forcing himself not to look up at the door to the Dragons' meeting place. It was harder than he thought, so he turned his attention to cleaning the interior of the car.

He was halfway through the task, bent over the backseat on the rear passenger side and replacing the floor mats he'd just cleaned, when a strong hand grabbed his shoulder and jerked him to a standing position. The protest died on his lips when he whirled around and saw that it was Steel.

"You scared the shit out of me," he scolded shakily. His heart was beating faster than "Flight of the Bumblebee."

Steel smiled apologetically. "Sorry. Seemed like a good idea when I did it."

"What are you doing out here, anyway?" Winston asked. His heartbeat was racing still, though this time for an entirely different reason. Since the kiss, Winston found being in close proximity to Steel almost painful. It was like his body went on high alert, entering a state of hyperawareness. Steel's scent reached him, manly and sharp, stirring his blood to arousal. "Shouldn't you be in a meeting or something?" He hadn't heard Wei and the others come down yet.

"It's almost done," Steel said with a shrug. "They don't really ask my opinion in decisions, so they won't miss me. Besides, I come bearing gifts." He held up a bottle of *shaojiu,* and Winston had to fight to suppress a groan at the sight of it. "Get in the car."

Winston balked at that. "We're not drinking this in the car," he said firmly. "I don't want the whole thing smelling like *shaojiu*—the fumes will get me drunk during the race, and that won't help me win."

Steel snickered. "I forget how weak you are sometimes."

Winston punched Steel in the shoulder. "I'm not weak. I just can't drink as much as you without getting alcohol poisoning."

"Right, weak. That's what I said. If we're not drinking in the car, where are we going to drink?"

Winston thought for a moment. The shop was still open, and the Dragons were meeting upstairs. An idea came to him. "I guess we could do it on the roof. We'd be out of the way."

"Sounds like a great idea," Steel said cheerfully, slapping Winston on the back. "Let's get going." He jogged off for the ladder on the side of the building that led up to the roof. Its original purpose was to provide access to the HVAC unit on the roof in case there was a problem, but Winston had used it quite often in his teenage years to hide from his mother. He'd actually had his first taste of alcohol up there, as well as his first—and last—cigarette.

Steel managed to scale the ladder with no problem, even with the *shaojiu* in hand. Winston stood at the bottom of the ladder as Steel went up, staring up at his ass as he did.

"You comin' or what?" Steel called, spurring Winston into motion. He was glad Steel couldn't see how red he felt his face become.

Steel already had the *shaojiu* open and was taking his first swig when Winston reached the top of the ladder. Steel held the bottle out, waiting for Winston to take it. Winston did so reluctantly. He hated the smell and taste of *shaojiu*, pungent and burning like rubbing alcohol, but Steel was offering, so he was drinking.

Steel at least attempted to hide his amusement at Winston's sour face as the alcohol burned its way down his throat, for which Winston was grateful.

They drank and shot the shit about random things, letting the alcohol seep into their bones. Once he was good and tipsy, Winston worked up the nerve to ask Steel about what'd happened at the meeting with Hwang. The more Winston heard, the more worried he became.

He knew things were getting bad between the two rival gangs, but he always assumed Wei would find some way to keep the peace. It might have been foolishly idealistic of him, but he wanted to hold on to that hope. Now, though, Winston could see the end to the fragile peace quickly approaching, and he felt truly afraid in a way he hadn't since his father had been killed. He knew his family might not be spared death and despair, pain and lies.

"I was worried about you," Winston admitted quietly, staring down at the patch of roof between his feet, not wanting to look at Steel. "While you were gone, it was all I thought about. I kept...I kept seeing all these different, terrible things that could have happened to you—to all of you."

"I'm fine." Steel touched Winston's arm and squeezed it firmly. "Nothing bad happened to us, Winston."

"But it might." Winston was unable to hide the tremble in his words. Now that he was voicing his fears, he couldn't stop. They flowed from him, coming faster and faster. "If it's like you say, there's going to be a war—it's just a matter of when. No one is guaranteed safety, you know. Last time I lost my Dad; who knows who this time? Shelby? Mom? You?"

"You're not going to lose me," Steel said before taking a deep pull of the alcohol.

"You don't know that," Winston argued. "You're not invincible, Steel. None of us are."

Steel turned his body to look into Winston's eyes. "You're really worried about this, huh?"

"Yes! I don't see how you aren't!"

"I learned a long time ago that there's nothing you can do about the future, so there's no use worrying about it."

"I wish it was that easy," Winston muttered.

"You need to relax. I think I know exactly how to make that happen, too." Steel set the all but empty bottle of *shaojiu* aside before he shifted position, kneeling on the ground between Winston's legs and using his elbows to nudge them open wider.

"Uh, Steel, what are you doing?" Winston's pulse fluttered rapidly.

"You're my best friend, man. I hate seeing you so stressed out, so I'm helping you relax. Nothing wrong with that, right?"

Winston didn't know what to say. If Steel was going to help him relax the way it looked like he was, Winston sure as hell didn't want to argue. Even if a niggling voice in the back of his mind whispered that there was something really wrong with this.

His suspicion was verified as Steel grabbed his belt and began undoing it with surprisingly nimble fingers.

Oh my fucking god, this isn't happening. Winston was unable to take his eyes away from the sight of Steel's fingers working to free him from his clothes. *Am I really about to let my best friend do this? Do I have the willpower to stop it?*

The answer to that was no, he decided.

The button and zipper of his fly followed the belt, and soon Steel's hands were parting the fabric, exposing the front of Winston's boxer briefs. The moment Steel had gotten to his knees before him, Winston's cock had stood ramrod straight. Steel's eyes flicked toward Winston, an amused smirk on his lips. He reached for the waistband of Winston's underwear.

That was where Winston's nerve failed him. "Uh, Steel, maybe this isn't a good idea," he said, throat dry, while a voice in his head screamed at him *What the hell are you saying?*

"Why?" Steel asked, eyes once again meeting Winston's, but this time holding them. Winston could see the need in them, hot and primal.

"Uh, we're on the roof," he said quickly. "Someone might see."

"It's dark," Steel countered, fingertips slipping beneath the waistband. "You know you want it," Steel purred.

Winston squeezed his eyes shut, unable to come up with a sensible, logical argument. It was like his brain was shutting down, diverting power elsewhere. Steel was right, wasn't he? Winston wanted this *badly*, more than he could possibly express. So why was he fighting it?

Steel must have seen the surrender in Winston's face, because he pulled the front of the boxer briefs down and exposed Winston's cock to the warm night air. "Oh man, I'm going to enjoy this."

Twenty-Eight

WINSTON'S COCK STOOD proudly in front of Steel, just waiting to be touched the way it deserved. Steel slowly closed his fingers around it, feeling its warmth, the throb of Winston's heartbeat through it as it pulsed at his touch. Winston let out a low moan as Steel's hand made contact. The sound spurred him on more, and he tightened his grip, giving it a few testing strokes.

Arousal coursed through Steel's veins, emboldened by the copious amount of *shaojiu* he'd consumed. It would be so easy to blame everything on the alcohol or hormones, but deep down, Steel knew that would be a lie. The alcohol might have made him act on the desire, but it didn't put it there. He'd been wrestling with it for far too long.

The *shaojiu* had provided him an opening tonight, and he was going to take it, that was for damn sure.

He looked up into Winston's face and saw that his eyes were squeezed shut, as if he was afraid opening them would bring it to an end—or maybe afraid it would make it real. But Steel wanted to look into Winston's eyes, wanted Winston to see it and know it was happening.

"Open your eyes, Win," he breathed, voice sounding deep and husky to his own ears. "Open your eyes and look at me."

Steel waited until Winston complied before he moved further, pulling the foreskin back off Winston's blood-engorged glans and slowly taking it into his mouth. He and Winston moaned together, Winston from the sensation of Steel's wet mouth closing around his cock, Steel from the way Winston's flavor exploded on his tongue, filling his senses with his essence.

Now that he'd started, Steel knew he wouldn't be able to stop until they were done, even if he'd wanted to—which he didn't; every second-guessing thought he'd had was driven out by the taste of Winston on his tongue.

He took Winston's cock further in, making sure his lips rounded out to provide good suction. While he'd been with plenty of men—he got his jollies from sex, no matter the gender of the person it was with—he'd rarely felt the need to perform that he felt then. This wasn't just some guy; it was *Winston*. That meant something to him. He would make sure this was the best damn blow job he ever gave, anything to make Winston feel better than anyone else had.

Steel took Winston in as far as he could manage, stopping when his cock struck the back of his throat. He was out of practice; recently most of his encounters with guys had involved *them* on their knees, not him. He was doing a fine job, though, he supposed, because Winston let out a hiss of pleasure, throwing his head back and muttering something under his breath that Steel didn't catch.

Encouraged, Steel gripped the base tightly, making a ring with his thumb and index finger while the rest of his hand pressed against Winston's abdomen, feeling his muscles contract as he set a deliberately slow pace. He made sure to swirl his tongue around the sensitive head on every upstroke, something he personally liked when he was on the receiving end. Based on Winston's moans every time he did it, they had that in common.

"Don't stop, don't stop," Winston breathed when Steel let his length fall from his lips. Steel ignored him, though, trailing kisses to the crook of his thigh before moving lower to lap at his balls and draw a whimper from him.

"You like having your balls licked, huh?" He lapped at them harder, savoring the way Winston writhed from his ministrations. "Stand up," he ordered. Winston complied instantly, and Steel tugged his shorts and boxer briefs down to his ankles and went back to sucking him.

It took a few minutes of practice, but he soon was able to deep throat Winston with no problem. After the first time he managed to swallow around Winston's cock, Winston had to sit down quickly, his knees trembling.

"I'm close," Winston warned, breath hitching.

Steel showed no acknowledgment of the warning except to speed up his bobbing, adding his fist to the mix and dragging it over Winston's spit-slicked cock. Steel had seen the telltale signs of Winston's orgasm before, during their joint jerk-off sessions, and he recognized them now: the way his legs tensed, his back arching a bit, his hips thrusting upward.

Winston tried to push Steel's mouth away, but he didn't budge. He was expecting the sudden explosion in his mouth, but he hadn't anticipated its volume. He persisted, swallowing as quickly as he could, barely noticing the salty taste as it went down.

Steel kept it up until Winston's limp cock slid from between his lips. "Feel more relaxed?" he asked, clearing his throat. He fumbled around for the bottle of *shaojiu* to wash away the final remnants of Winston's release.

"I think so," Winston replied breathlessly, leaning back and staring up at the stars beginning to appear in the evening sky.

Steel wanted to lean over Winston and claim his lips in a kiss. That frightened him way more than whatever sexual desires he harbored for Winston. Sex was sex—messy, fun, and ultimately uncomplicated. He had no problems with the concept of a jizz and split—in fact, he preferred them. He didn't want strings and emotion; he'd much rather find a random person in a bar or use Unzipped or other dating apps, meet, have fun, and never see each other again.

He couldn't not see Winston again. Aside from the logistics of being a Dragon and Winston's eventual entry into their ranks, Steel couldn't imagine not having Winston in his life.

The drunken kiss, the blow job—if he could make them mean nothing, pass them off and pretend nothing had changed, he could preserve their friendship. The thought of losing Winston's friendship was like a knife burning in his gut.

They were fine, until emotions were brought to the light.

"Good," he said, pushing himself to his feet and cramming any emotion he might be feeling deep down. "You should get your pants up before someone looks for us and catches you rocking out with your cock out."

Winston blushed and pulled his shorts and pants back up, looking confused. Steel did his best to ignore the pang of guilt that stabbed at his chest. "Listen, Steel, I need to—"

"What we need to do is get back inside and see what crazy plans they've concocted while the voice of reason was up here helping you relax."

Winston snorted. "If you're the voice of reason, the Dragons are in trouble."

Steel flipped him off and made his way to the ladder, grateful that, at least for the moment, Winston was going along with it and acting like everything was normal. Who could say if things would be the same tomorrow.

But Steel would think about tomorrow when it came.

Twenty-Nine

THE DAY OF the race came faster than Winston expected. It had been quiet around Dragon headquarters since the meeting with the Twisted Vipers. Wei had set in place some contingency plans, but Winston wasn't in on anything. If he asked, everyone just told him not to worry about it or that it was being taken care of.

That left him nothing to distract him from the nervousness leading up to the race, except perhaps Steel, and that was just as bad, or perhaps worse. Since the...events on the roof, he'd seen Steel for all of maybe ten minutes total. Every time he did, Steel acted normal, but Winston could see the invisible wall that now stood between them. Steel assured him he was just busy doing things for the Dragons, but Winston wondered if it was Wei's instructions or if Steel was volunteering for them in order to keep his distance from Winston.

After the roof, Steel went right back to acting like his normal self. He joked around and laughed with Winston, no indication that things were strained between them, and nothing but the completely satisfied feeling Winston had in the wake of his orgasm to prove to Winston that it really happened and he hadn't dreamt the whole thing.

Now that the day of the race had come, Winston had the impending evening to worry about instead of his relationship—or lack thereof—with Steel. It actually made things worse. He spent most of the day at home, doing his best to keep his mind off everything. No matter what he tried, it just didn't work. Porn, television, movies, video games, none of it distracted him like he'd hoped it would.

As evening approached, he was a bundle of nerves, incapable of sitting still for five minutes. He really wished Steel were there to see him, like he had been before the first race. That would help him tremendously. If he was honest with himself, he just wanted to see Steel, to have a little time in his presence. It didn't need to involve anything serious; simply being in the same space for a bit would make him feel worlds better.

When nine o'clock rolled around and Steel still had not showed, Winston gave up hoping for him. He was probably caught up in Dragon business or whatever—it didn't mean anything. No matter how many times he repeated that to himself, though, he couldn't make it true.

It did matter to him.

He'd never imagined that Steel, his best friend in the world, the one person he'd come to count on more than anyone else in his life, the one he'd come to love, would abandon him on such an important night. Steel knew what these races meant, not just for him but for the Dragons. He knew Winston well enough to know he'd need support before it, and yet he hadn't bothered to show up.

He sat at the dinner table, an uneaten bowl of his mother's vegetable soup in front of him. He clutched his phone in his hand, the screen displaying Steel's contact information. His finger hovered above the Call button, but he couldn't quite bring himself to push it, no matter how much he really wanted to. He didn't know what he could expect to come of it, except perhaps for Steel to ignore his call.

Winston didn't have the courage to find that out, didn't think he'd be able to withstand a flat-out rejection from Steel, which left him in a torturous limbo where he could not have what he wanted, but it remained dangled in front of him, taunting him.

He thought about Wei and Noah, how happy they were and how frequently he had to see it, and it made him feel even worse. In the back of his mind, somewhere he rarely, if ever, acknowledged, he'd thought that maybe he and Steel could have that. Now, though, it was looking like anything involving Steel would just bring him pain and misery.

By the time Constance came home from the coffee shop, just before ten, Winston had worked himself into a good and proper funk. He was at the table, head on his arms as he stared blankly at the refrigerator.

"Well, this isn't exactly what I expected to come home to tonight," Constance said lightly, pausing in the doorway. "Tonight *is* the race, right?"

"Yes." Winston didn't look away from the refrigerator.

"Well then, shouldn't you be getting pumped up or something?"

Constance crossed to the stove, picking up one of the bowls she'd set down beside the simmering pot of soup that morning before she left. "If this is you pumped up and excited, I'd really hate to see how you act around something you have no interest in."

Winston forced his head up from the table with great effort. "I'm ready for the race." He couldn't even get himself to believe it, so he doubted his mother was fooled.

Constance walked her soup to the table and sat down opposite her son. "Usually when you're home all day, the sink is full of dishes. I can't help but notice it's empty, and I doubt you took it upon yourself to finally wash your own dishes. Have you eaten anything today?"

"I haven't been very hungry." Winston used his spoon to stir the now cold soup in his bowl.

"I know you're worried about the race," Constance began.

"It's not the race," Winston interrupted. "It's—" He stopped, realizing how close he was to opening up and pouring out everything to his mother. "I just have a lot on my mind," he finished weakly.

"You have for a while," Constance remarked, carefully eating her soup. Something in her tone told Winston she knew more than she was letting on. "Listen, Winston, you're about to go into a situation where you need your wits about you. You can't afford to be distracted by anything. Even love."

The last two words struck Winston as if he'd been slapped. He gaped at Constance. Was he that transparent? He thought he did a better job of hiding his feelings. He'd worked so hard constructing a mask of indifference to hide behind, and he couldn't figure out how Constance had seen through it.

"I'm your mother," Constance said, as if she were answering his silent question. "You might put on a good show for others, but I've studied your face your entire life. I know you. I know it's none of my business..."

Winston wanted to snap at her, wanted to tell her *Damn right it's none of your business!* but he stopped himself. He wasn't angry at her, and the last thing he truly wanted was to pick a fight right before the Dark Streets.

"It's just hard to explain," he said instead.

"I don't know if it's all that hard," Constance said with a small smile. "A matter of feelings and not knowing if they're returned, right?"

"Well, when you say it that way, it doesn't seem so hard," Winston mumbled. "You're not entirely right, though. It's not that I don't know if they're returned—that I'm sure of. It's more about whether or not he wants to return them."

Once he started, Winston couldn't stop. He told Constance about how things had become between him and Steel, leaving out a few details like the mutual masturbation and the great blow job he'd gotten. He kept in the kiss, because that was an important element relating to his state of mind.

There might be something to say for getting it off your chest, he thought when he was done. He felt no lighter, but he did feel better, somehow. Putting all of his fears and doubts into words had a calming effect on him, like it had stripped them of their power.

Constance seemed to listen carefully to everything he said, reserving any comment she might have for when he finished. He knew she'd have some things to say about it; in fact, he was counting on it.

"You know," she said after a full minute of silence. "Those dramas your sister loves—"

"What does this have to do with my situation?" Winston asked, exasperated.

"Just listen, now. Do you want my advice or not?"

"I don't know, do I? Okay, okay." He threw his hands up in surrender. "Go on."

"Those dramas your sister loves usually have stories that revolve around the idea that you can't help who you fall in love with. And while that's true enough, to an extent, you *can* help how you act on those feelings."

Winston thought for a moment, with no luck. "I don't think I'm following you."

"What I'm saying is you're putting all of the power in this on Steel, like you don't have a choice to make. Why?"

Winston furrowed his brow. He'd never thought of it that way. He considered carefully before he answered. "I guess because he's the one who can't seem to decide, not me."

"But you *do* have something to decide," Constance chided him in that way mothers had—gentle, but firm. "You need to decide what you're worth and what you'll live with. If you'll settle for what you've been offered, or if you decide that no, you need more."

"But how do I—?"

"That's something only you can do." Constance reached across the table to squeeze his hand. "I can tell you what to do, but only you can decide *how* to do it." She rose, carrying her now empty bowl to the sink. As she walked back out past Winston, she paused long enough to squeeze his shoulders gently and kiss the top of his head.

"Make sure you eat something," she said, and then she was gone, leaving him alone in the kitchen with his thoughts.

Thirty

STEEL SPENT MOST of the day before the race in the poorer neighborhoods that separated the Eastern District from Twisted Viper territory. Wei thought of it as an extra precaution, something that needed to be done just to be safe. He didn't think that Hwang or his Vipers would lash out, not right after issuing the kind of warning they did.

Steel thought otherwise. Wei was an honorable guy, and as such, he thought other people would operate on the same honor system he did. Steel had plenty of experience with men like Hwang, men who could not possibly be called honorable. He didn't doubt for one second that the Twisted Viper *ga tsan* would strike, given he was sure he could get away with it.

"You've been looking at your phone a lot," Jesse commented from the passenger seat. His arm hung lazily out the window as they drove at a low speed through the neighborhood. "You expecting a sext or something?"

"You're supposed to be watching for trouble." Steel scowled. "Keep focused."

"You gonna sit here with a straight face and tell me to stay focused?" Jesse scoffed. "You're so distracted you almost ran over the same old lady twice!"

Steel shrugged. "Old bat shouldn't be in the road. How was she standing in the *same* place when we circled back around? Doesn't make any sense."

"Maybe she was waiting for us to come back by. She did flip you off."

Steel chuckled. She had, at that, and it had been damn funny. If his mind weren't so occupied he would have found it downright hilarious. However, all he could think about was the impending Dark Streets race Winston would be involved in later that night.

What was Winston doing at that moment? Steel hoped he was relaxing so he would be refreshed when it was go time.

Steel thought he felt his phone vibrate and glanced down at it where it rested between his legs on the seat. Nothing. God damn it, why did that keep happening? Actually, he knew why, he just didn't want to admit it. He was waiting for Winston's text. It was nearly four in the afternoon, and he'd been expecting it since this morning. Nothing had come, no *Where are you?* or *What are you doing?* Not a single message all day.

"You're starting to drive me nuts with that shit, man," Jesse groaned, catching Steel's glance at his phone. "Just text whatever score you're waiting for already and get it over with. You're making *me* anxious."

Steel wanted to punch Jesse right in the mouth. The only thing that stopped him from doing exactly that was the fact that Jesse didn't know it was Winston he was talking about.

"So who is she? Or he?" Jesse went on, drumming his fingers against the side of the car in as irritating a way as one possibly could.

God he acts like a high schooler sometimes, Steel thought, ignoring his question. Hopefully he'd catch a hint and shut up about it already.

"You know," Jesse went on, shattering any hope Steel had that he'd drop it, "I never figured you for the kind of guy who'd hang around waiting to get hit up. More the man of action type, I thought. Whoever it is, they must be pretty damn good in bed—"

"Do you ever shut up?" Steel snapped, losing control. "I don't think you've been silent for more than twenty seconds since we got out here! Give a man a break, for fuck's sake!" He regretted the outburst as soon as it happened. The last thing he wanted to do was alienate any of the Dragons, and Jesse was just being Jesse, but he was so tightly wound he felt like he would come apart at the seams at the slightest prodding.

"Sorry," Jesse muttered, seemingly hurt and turning to stare out the passenger side window.

Steel heaved a sigh, pulling the car to a halt at a stop sign and then resting his head momentarily on the steering wheel. What he really wanted to do was bash his head against it, maybe knock some sense into himself, but then that would leave Jesse to drive, and he was even worse than Winston behind the wheel.

"I didn't mean to snap," Steel apologized gruffly. "Everything going on right now has me on edge, that's all. Sorry for being a dick."

"There's always something to have us on edge," Jesse said in a whiny tone, but he looked back at Steel, appearing to have forgiven him.

"Seems like since Wei's lover boy came things have been pretty shitty here."

Steel understood Jesse's sentiment. "I know it looks that way, but this shit was building long before Noah got here."

"Don't get me wrong, I'm not blaming Noah," Jesse said quickly. "I'm just saying that things haven't settled down once since he got here."

"Would you be happy with a boring life?"

Jesse thought about it for a moment and grinned. "Nah, I don't think I would."

"Me either." Steel didn't even know what a boring life would be like. His entire life had been a struggle, from his upbringing to the war with the Nine Stars, and now this. All he knew how to do was fight. Could he do anything else?

Sometimes he liked to imagine what it would be like to be normal, to have a quiet life, settle down with someone—with Winston—but he couldn't see it, not really. It was a fantasy, a dream that couldn't come true. Steel wasn't meant for that sort of happiness, and he sure as hell had no intention of binding Winston to a life like that. He deserved better.

When Jesse and Steel were finally relieved, it was nearly eight o'clock. Part of Steel wanted nothing more than to go to Winston, to see him before the race, to comfort him, tell him things would be all right, and he'd be there for him after the race. He held off, though, because seeing Winston would only make the feelings worse.

It was harder and harder to pretend everything was normal when he was around Winston. Even the brief encounters they'd had since that time on the roof had been almost like torture for Steel. Every fiber of his being demanded he touch Winston, claim him, taste more of him, show Winston pleasures that only he could. The primal beast inside of him, the element of ancient pathos that had survived in mankind through millennia of evolution, demanded he make Winston know he belonged to Steel and Steel alone. That urge was dangerous, but it was getting harder and harder to resist. So he kept his distance. It was for both their sakes, or so he kept telling himself.

He went to a pool hall Jesse recommended, hoping it would distract him from his worries and from Winston, but it didn't work as intended. The later it got, the more the guilt began to eat at Steel, driving his already sour mood further south.

After Steel had snapped six or seven times at him, Jesse tossed his pool stick onto the table. "Dude, seriously? I thought you were pissy earlier, now it's just plain ridiculous. You need to go and see whoever the hell this is so you maybe stop being such a *fucking ass!*"

The outburst caught Steel off guard. Jesse was normally a very laid-back and easygoing person, and the fact that it was him of all people reached Steel more than the actual words he used. Steel took off at that moment, making right for Winston's apartment. He didn't even look at the clock on the dash until he pulled up and saw Winston making his way to his car. *Fuck*, he thought. *It's midnight!*

"Hey, Winston!" Steel called, jogging to meet him. He didn't know what he expected, but it wasn't the almost-angry look in Winston's gaze when his eyes fell on him. "Listen, I'm sorry I'm late, I was just doing rounds for Wei and—"

"And then had time to go to a bar, by the smell of it," Winston added coldly.

Shit. I didn't think about the beers. "Yeah, I went with Jesse for a bit but—"

"Listen, Steel, I don't really have time for this. I've got to get going to my race. It's tonight in case you forgot."

"No, I didn't forget. I'm sorry I didn't—"

Winston sidestepped Steel and made his way to the driver's side door. He opened it and climbed in. All Steel could do was stand there, mouth agape. A flicker of hope kindled in his chest when the car door opened once more and Winston climbed back out. The look on Winston's face extinguished the hope as fast as it had formed.

When Winston spoke, his voice was full of some sort of kinetic energy and excitement, like something drove him to speak—a feeling Steel could understand. "I'm done being confused, Steel. I'm done not knowing where I stand—where *we* stand. Especially with all the uncertainty around us already. I'm done. I need to know, Steel. How do you feel? How do you feel about me—about...about us?"

How do I feel? How do I feel? A thousand and one answers flitted through Steel's mind in a matter of seconds, but it wasn't so easy to give them voice. How did he feel about Winston? He felt aroused, he felt understood, he felt connected, felt a love that went deeper than anything he'd known before. But, louder than all those, he felt *fear*, fear of what all of that meant.

Tell him, you idiot, tell him! something in him urged. Everything that he fantasized about in the darkest moments of the night was standing right there in front of him and wanting him, too. All he needed to do was open his mouth and say it, open his mouth and tell him he was wildly, madly in love with him, had been for just about as long as he could remember. It was as simple as that.

And yet, he couldn't do it. The only words he could choke out through the lump that had formed in his throat then was "Good luck."

He thought there might have been tears in Winston's eyes, but he'd turned around and climbed back into the car before Steel could get a good look. Before he'd even realized it, tears had welled up in his own eyes, turning Winston's taillights into glistening blurs.

Thirty-One

GOOD LUCK.

Steel's parting words echoed painfully in Winston's head on a continuous loop, tormenting him with their implications. Two simple words, but to Winston they had so much dire meaning. He'd tried to prepare himself for that eventuality, but hadn't done such a good job of that, apparently.

This wasn't supposed to be how it went. Every romance movie or novel or comic told him that if he was brave, if he faced his fears and owned up to his feelings, he'd get the guy in the end, not have it made clear that the guy didn't want to pursue anything more meaningful than they had.

The fairy tales were full of shit, and he was an idiot for believing in them. Sure, Noah and Wei seemed to have gotten their fairytale ending, but Wei didn't lead a charmed life, and he never had. Maybe he didn't *deserve* a happy ever after.

"You don't look like your head's in the game tonight," Mimi commented, leaning into Winston's open window and surprising him. "What's wrong, Noisy, having girl problems?"

"Something like that," Winston muttered. He was parked in another parking garage, this one in Central, not far from Causeway Bay, which meant they weren't far from Twisted Viper territory. Given everything, Winston was a little on edge about that. He prayed the day's course would take them in the opposite direction, clear of Viper land all together.

"Aren't we all?" Mimi blew a tuft of hair out of her face. "All I can tell you is that you should concentrate on winning. If being a champ doesn't have her throwing herself at your feet, the amount of money you'll get sure as hell will."

Winston found himself actually chuckling. Mimi's coarse joking managed to crack the shell of gloom he'd raised up about himself. "Is that why you do it?"

"You bet your ass it is," she replied with a cheeky wink. "No girl can resist the sexy illegal street racer vibe. Combine it with this body, and you've got a recipe for instant sex." She studied Winston for a minute. "You, though, I can see how you might have a few problems in that department. But nothing winning and money can't fix. And maybe a makeover."

"You definitely know how to fix a guy's bad mood," Winston said with a dry smile.

"What can I say? I'm a people person."

"Yo, Mimi," a rough voice called behind her. A dark shadow fell over her face, and Winston wondered who it was to have such an effect on her. She turned, and Winston caught sight of a guy in tattered jeans and one of those sleeveless vests, no shirt under it. His entire arm was covered in an intricate sleeve, but Winston couldn't make out the design details. His hair was dyed an acid green color, shaved into a mohawk. "If I win, you gonna finally let me give you this dick?"

"*Yan you*," Mimi spat at him. He just answered her insult with a broken-toothed grin.

"He's a charming guy," Winston observed.

"A real prince among men," Mimi said, a look of utter contempt on her face.

If I had to deal with that sort of shit on a daily basis, I'd probably have that look too.

"Everyone calls him Rundown. He runs with the Twisted Vipers," Mimi said suddenly, eyes hard, still focused on the guy. "He's not a member as far as I know, and if he is, he's low down the totem pole, not even worth thinking about, but he acts like he runs the place. Just a low-ranking slimeball with delusions of grandeur."

A Twisted Viper? Winston frowned, studying the guy closer and seeing him in a new light. He wasn't just a prick; he was a dangerous prick. Mimi thought him being a lowly grunt made him less dangerous, but Winston knew it made him *more*. Moving up the ranks of an organization like the Twisted Vipers wouldn't be a simple thing; it wasn't like he'd have work evaluations or be earning merit badges to reach the next level. He'd have to prove himself, and he'd be out to do it any way possible. With the Dragons being Twisted Viper public enemy number one, the quickest route to the upper ranks would be striking a blow against them.

Hopefully, this Rundown didn't know Winston was connected, even tangentially, to Wei and the Dragons.

Any further conversation between Winston and Mimi was brought to an end when a long black sedan pulled into the parking garage behind them, just as it had before. The arrival of the car flipped some invisible switch. All of the talking, joking, and grandstanding that had been going on ceased in seconds, and every driver made their way to their car. The air was suddenly full of tension, and Winston had no doubt that each and every one of them was wondering the same thing: where would they be racing next, and how dangerous would it be?

They followed the car—Winston breathed a sigh of relief when it led them away from Causeway Bay.

As they drove, he reached for his cell phone to send a message to Steel that they were on their way to the starting point. He'd typed half the message before he stopped himself. What was the point go sending the message to Steel? He wasn't settling for whatever relationship they'd had before. It no longer worked for him. He deserved to be happy, and he wanted that happiness to involve Steel, but not on uncertain terms. He'd made that clear, and Steel had made it clear he couldn't—or wouldn't give him certainty.

Winston copied the text he'd typed and pasted it in a new message, this one to Tony.

A minute or so later he got a confused reply:

—*Uh...Okay. I'll tell Steel.*

Just seeing Steel's name typed on the screen fanned the ache in his chest from small embers to a roaring fire and his throat constricted, a familiar burning sensation growing in his eyes. He pushed it away by sheer strength of will, though for a moment it felt like it would consume him. He couldn't race if he couldn't see the road, and the farther they drove the more certain Winston became of their destination—it loomed ahead of them, growing larger with every meter they drove.

Victoria Peak.

He couldn't believe they were going to have a race there; it would be crawling with the authorities. It was home to several high-ranking members of the Special Administration Region government—including the Chief Secretary of the Administration. The organizers of the Dark Streets were out of their minds. There were no lights on in most of the buildings and residences in the area that locals referred to as the Peak, due to the time, but there would still be security, and it would without a doubt be risky as hell.

Steel would flip his shit, Winston thought, staring up at the mountain. But why did he give a fuck what Steel would think? If Steel actually cared, he would have had more to say than *good luck* when they'd met. He would have been in the apartment with Winston, passing the time, making sure he was mentally and emotionally prepared for the race to come, not out carousing with Jesse and whomever else he was with.

Fuck him, he thought, redirecting his pain into anger, an emotion he could use in the race.

They drove farther and farther along Victoria Peak, and Winston had to wonder who the organizers were and how much power they had, because they encounter no security, and the gates that barred civilians from the radio tower that topped the mountain were open. They drove in, turning around awaiting further instructions.

The driver of the black sedan—the same nondescript man who'd handed Winston his GPS system last time—went from car to car, though he carried nothing. He didn't spend more than thirty seconds at each car. As the man approached, Winston rolled his window down.

"The race is simple," the man said, leaning down, gray eyes—the first distinguishable feature Winston could note—boring into Winston's. "The goal is the base of the mountain."

"That's it?" Winston said incredulously. He hadn't imagined it would be so simple.

"Yes," the man said with the barest hint of a smile. "That's it."

Thirty-Two

ONCE ALL THE drivers were informed of the details of the race, they were instructed to circle the radio tower, getting into a line in the order they'd been told on the message they'd received before. Winston was in eleventh place, which meant he was starting about halfway around the tower, while the higher ranks were much closer to the road down. In such a straightforward race, he'd have to work really hard to gain any ranks.

He typed a message—again to Tony—informing him of the basic route of the race, and letting him know he'd meet them at the meeting place as soon as the race was over and he could get away. He returned the phone to its place in the glove compartment and turned his attention to the car ahead of him. In front of him and behind, cars were starting to rev their engines. He wondered if they were all as anxious as he was.

Some of them had done this race who knew how many times, so they probably weren't. He imagined Mimi was sitting in her car, cool and composed, as if she was just about to drive to the supermarket, not compete in a dangerous illegal race *downhill* in an area where there was a high chance of them getting arrested.

He wished he had some of that same ice water in his veins. In reality, though, the fact that this race was going to be particularly risky weighed heavily on him—especially the part where he might end up in jail. Bad things tended to happen to the men in his family when they went to jail, if his father was any indication. He would *not* go there. He didn't care if he had to drive off a cliff, he wasn't letting himself fall into the hands of the people who killed his father.

A loud air horn sounded, snapping Winston free of the dismal thoughts, He didn't have time to dwell in the shadows of the past when he had a race to win. He had to place higher up, had to get Mimi to talk to him so he could put an end to the whole situation and hopefully prevent a war with the Twisted Vipers while he was at it.

No pressure, he thought as he pushed his foot down on the accelerator, car launching smoothly into motion, and the race was off. He had a stroke of luck right at the beginning, seeing an opening between the driver just ahead of him and the exit down onto the road, and he took it, tires squealing as he wedged into the space, just barely missing clipping the car in tenth place—well, now eleventh place.

Not bad, Winston. Moving up the ranks in the first minute of the race. He could imagine the half-terrified, half-impressed look on Steel's face if he'd seen that little maneuver. Steel's face swam before his vision, and he felt like he couldn't breathe and could no longer see the road.

The car behind him nearly passed him, and he realized he'd let his foot off the gas. He snarled, pushing his foot down harder, closing the gap.

Steel had already ripped his heart out that night; he wasn't going to let him take the race from him, too. No, he was going to do his damndest to win this race. He tightened his hands on the wheel, looking out as the first turn on the mountain path came before him.

It was a sharp one, but he knew what he was doing. He made the turn at as sharp an angle as he could, using the momentum to speed past the ninth-place car, the driver having made too wide a turn.

Ninth place. He was now in ninth place. He'd advanced two places already! Maybe he was getting the hang of this racing thing. Maybe it was something he could take pride in, after all.

Tension grew as he descended further down the mountain. They'd soon be in the dangerous areas where the important people lived—the places risk of arrest would be greatest—and then they'd be in potential traffic.

Winston found that he was sweating way more than he had in the first race. Maybe it was the conditions—speeding down a mountain going more than eighty kilometers an hour—or maybe it was that there was so much at stake, with Wei counting on him and god only knew how many people might die if a war broke out between the Dragons and the Twisted Vipers.

It was more than all of that, though. Of course, all of those elements were factors, but he knew it went deeper than that. He wanted to win, wanted to prove himself worthy. Maybe, just maybe, if he showed Steel he could do something, be of service to the Dragons, Steel would see him differently.

Halfway down Victoria Peak, Winston had made it into seventh place and was trying his best to claim sixth. The car in sixth place was a big Dodge Magnum, its longer front giving it a slight edge over Winston's car.

The driver, Winston saw with a little apprehension, was that prick Rundown.

I'm beating him. Remembering the disgusting way he'd talked to Mimi, nothing would give him more pleasure at that moment. He'd managed to convert a lot of his feelings toward Steel into rage, and with Steel not there to bear its brunt, it needed to be redirected. Rundown was a deserving surrogate.

He gained ground as they sped toward another curve, determined to get the lead there. Rundown noticed him coming up on his left and glanced over at him. The two made eye contact for a split second, and in that small window of time, Winston saw a surprising amount of hatred directed his way.

He knows, he realized grimly. *He knows I'm connected to the Dragons.*

Winston didn't anticipate the way Rundown jerked the wheel suddenly, bringing his car into rough contact with Winston's own. The night was filled with the sound of plastic scraping and cracking at the force of the contact. The wheel in Winston's hand shook, and a hot spike of fear shot through him. *I'm going to lose control of the car.*

Miraculously, though, he maintained control, slowing down enough to take the turn, letting Rundown gain a little distance on him. The lead didn't last long, though, but not because Winston sped up; Rundown slammed on his breaks.

Winston swerved, barely avoiding a collision.

This left an opening for Winston to get ahead, but he was suspicious of it. He had no choice but to take it, however; the cars behind him wouldn't be so hesitant, and he needed to win, needed to get a step closer to the top and finding out what was going on. If he made no progress, then the cops would have no problem calling off the mission, and he'd never prove himself.

He had to risk it.

His instincts were right; it was a trap. No sooner had he sped up and passed Rundown's Magnum than the Twisted Viper wannabe sped up, clipping the back left of Winston's car. The impact jolted Winston forward and then back, but he'd been expecting it, so he didn't need to struggle for control this time.

"I can do this," Winston said, urging the car forward. He wasn't going to let some guy who wasn't even good enough to really be part of the Twisted Vipers get the best of him. No way, no how.

Rundown was likely thinking something along the same lines, because he too sped up. His car had superior horsepower, and Winston couldn't accelerate fast enough to avoid the impact. The direct-on blow was worse than everything before that; it jarred Winston right to his teeth, and he was certain it caused a lot of damage. The blow propelled his car forward just as another turn was coming up, this one overlooking a fairly steep drop. He spun the wheel and hit the brakes, managing to right the car before he could go over, but Rundown moved past him.

Sonofabitch. There is no fucking way I'm going to let this guy get the best of me. He floored it, which Rundown probably didn't expect, given the tight confines of the road. He slipped into the lane for oncoming traffic, ready to retake sixth place. If he didn't move any further than that, he'd be happy. The race was now personal; his only goal at that moment was to put that *puk gai* in his rearview mirror.

The round beams of car headlights coming toward him set Winston's heart racing. What the hell was someone doing driving here at this time of night? He thought about getting over back behind Rundown—he'd rather be alive and able to beat Rundown next time than dead because of the race—but the car behind him had moved forward, and there was no room for him that way—nor did it look like he'd have any luck falling behind for safety either. He had no choice.

I'm going to make it, he told himself, though he couldn't really speed up any more than he had. He didn't let himself get caught up in thinking out his steps—there was no time for thought and consideration. Instead, he let instinct take over. He jerked his wheel to the left, the left side of his car colliding hard with Rundown's. As Winston hoped, the force of the impact forced Rundown even farther left, his wheels veering onto the median. The impact forced him to slow down, and Winston just barely managed to slip in front of him before the car going his way—which had been laying on its horn, though he hadn't noticed the sound until just then—sped past him.

He was alive. His crazy-ass stunt had been successful. He was alive, and he was in sixth place. He remained in sixth place when he passed the designated finish line at the base of Victoria Peak. He didn't realize until he parked the car that his entire body was trembling. He didn't think he'd be able to stand if he tried, so he just relaxed back against his seat, feeling exhausted and sticky and actually content.

He almost dozed off when Mimi rapped her knuckles against the glass of the passenger side door. Surprised, Winston unlocked the door and she slid inside and pulled the door closed behind her.

"From what I hear, you did a damn good job out there," she said with a flash of the barest smile. "Sixth place is quite a jump. I knew you had potential the moment you rolled up, and you proved me right."

"How did you do?" Winston asked.

"Third. Went down one, but the race was dumb. I'll get first next time."

"Maybe not. I might beat you to it," Winston joked.

Mimi studied him, face serious. "You actually might. That was the single most impressive thing I've seen in a while. I'm sure the big guys will be impressed when they hear about it, too. If I were you, I'd be on the lookout for invitations to some of the special races. Glad to know I put my money down on a winning horse."

Mimi exited the car without saying anything else, pushing the door closed behind her.

Winston wanted to let out a whoop of joy. *I did it!*

Thirty-Three

"I CAN'T BELIEVE they have them racing down a goddamn mountain," Steel muttered darkly. Just the thought of Winston—who worried him with his driving on a straight road—driving down Victoria Peak at high speeds set him on edge. Steel sat in the passenger seat of Tony's car, Tony himself behind the wheel.

The older Dragon gave him a bemused look. "Conroy said you were annoying to wait with."

Steel scowled. "What does that mean?"

"It means you're bad at waiting. All you're doing when you worry about this shit is psyching yourself up. We'll know what's going on when we know, and until then there's not much you can do about it. So just calm the fuck down."

"That's easy for you to say. It's not your...your best friend out there."

"No," Tony conceded, voice gentling. "I guess it's not."

Steel couldn't stop thinking about his last encounter with Winston. The hurt on Winston's face when he couldn't bring himself to say anything after Winston poured his feelings out to him, it tormented Steel. Here he was, hurting the one person in the world he most wanted to protect, and he couldn't see a way to make it stop. He knew Winston thought he wanted to be with him, but Steel knew that wouldn't make things better. He'd only end up hurting Winston, and he couldn't live with that.

What do I have to offer him? Steel wondered bitterly. *I'm a worthless gutter rat. I might not live in the gutter anymore, but it doesn't change my past. One way or another, he's going to end up with a broken heart, and it's going to be my fault.* Since that was the case, he'd rather leave things the way they were—you couldn't miss what you never had, right?

Whatever it took to keep him sane.

Steel sank deeper into his foul mood. He could feel Tony's eyes on him, but the older man held his tongue. He no doubt knew that whatever it was he had to say would fall on deaf ears at that moment.

The gratitude that welled up in Steel's chest surprised him; he hadn't expected to be able to feel anything but bitterness and self-loathing. He appreciated Tony's ability to keep his own counsel. Conroy, Jesse, even Noah—they all saw fit to give advice he never asked for. Tony, though, was wise enough to wait.

Steel was about to buckle under the weight of his own thoughts, moments away from caving and asking Tony what he thought he should do, but the sight of headlights moving their way made him swallow the words. It was Winston; he knew it. He must have had a sixth sense, when it came to Winston, because sure enough the approaching car pulled off just in front of them.

Steel was out of the car in a flash, striding toward Winston before the engine was even cut off. The sight of Winston well and unharmed permitted Steel to let out a breath he didn't know he'd been holding. The tightness in his chest relaxed a bit, just a bit.

He forgot his dilemma, his stress, relief rushing them aside. It only lasted a moment, though; the look on Winston's face—a mixture of uncertainty and hope—brought everything crashing back, and his heart hurt more than ever. This relief he felt, all of it made him painfully aware of just how much he loved Winston and how much it hurt him that he couldn't let himself have him.

I'm no good for him, he reminded himself firmly.

"How'd the race go?" he asked, keeping his voice cool and distant. He should have asked him how he was first, but he had to keep that distance there; otherwise, the walls he'd built between them would fall to pieces, and he couldn't afford that.

Steel could see the transformation in Winston, the hope in his eyes flickering out, his back stiffening. "I got sixth place," he answered, his own voice equally cool. He tossed his keys to Steel, like he was unwilling to make physical contact. "I'm ready to go home."

"Okay, hop in, and I'll drive you to your place." Steel started for Winston's car as Winston went the other way.

"No thanks," Winston said. "I'll get Tony to drop me off at home. You just get my car to the coffee shop."

Steel tried—unsuccessfully—not to feel hurt. *You knew you couldn't have it both ways*, he told himself accusingly. *Not going to make a big deal out of this. I asked for it.* Steel nodded, unwilling to test his voice at that moment, and started for the car.

He stopped short when he noticed the rearview mirror on the passenger side looked broken, resting off-kilter. His heart surged into his throat when he saw the damage. He circled the car slowly, taking in everything. When he'd seen it all, he stormed over to Tony's car, pulling the passenger side door open, startling both men.

"What. The. Fuck. *Happened*?" He could barely squeeze the words out, such was his rage.

"I don't know what you're talking about," Winston said, staring stonily out the windshield, refusing to look at Steel.

"Don't fuck around with me on this, Winston," Steel snarled. "What happened?"

Winston was silent for a long moment—Steel thought he'd have to shake the answers out of him—but he finally spoke. "There's this other racer, Rundown," he started. Steel stood there, listening to Winston fill him in on the midrace skirmish he had with the Rundown guy.

Before Winston even finished, Steel turned on his heel and made his way for Winston's car.

"Steel, don't do anything stupid," Winston called behind him, but Steel barely noticed; he was too pissed off to think straight. He climbed behind the wheel of Winston's car and sped off. The entirety of his awareness was boiled down to the red-hot rage that coursed through his veins. He paid very little attention to the sound of a honking horn coming from a car he'd sped past at an intersection when he wasn't paying attention to the lights. The only thing he had on his mind right then was revenge.

He sped into the parking lot Winston mentioned, tires squealing, smoke rising as the tread burned as he came to a stop. The first thing he noticed was that the Dodge Magnum Winston mentioned was still in the parking lot—and there was Rundown, with his acid green hair, leaning against the front of it and laughing and talking with three guys who were no doubt his wastrel friends.

He jumped out of the car and stomped toward the guys in front of the Magnum, ignoring the small crowd of onlookers lingering after the race. Rundown didn't notice his approach until he was almost upon them.

He straightened from the car, eyeing Steel with a sneer. "What the fuck—"

Steel's fist cut him off as it slammed into his jaw, sending him sprawling back onto the hood of his car. His friends started to come to his defense, but the heat of Steel's gaze made them stop.

Rundown stood, rubbing his jaw. "You got a fucking death wish, *ong lan gau?*"

Steel grabbed him by the front of his shirt, tugging him until they were nose to nose. "You're going to be dead if you don't leave Winston the fuck alone."

Rundown jerked away from Steel. "Who the fuck is Winston? Get the fuck out of here!"

"I mean it," Steel said through gritted teeth. "The next time you want to try to run someone off the fucking road, you think about this: you'll have *me* to deal with, and I won't be nice twice."

"Yo, Rundown, I recognize this piece of shit," one of his friends said. Steel turned to study him and saw that it was one of the thugs present at the meeting with Hwang and the Twisted Vipers. *Well, Winston was right about this guy being one of them.* Some part of Steel knew that once the rage died down, he'd regret this action—it might complicate things not only for Winston but for Wei as well. "He's a fucking Dragon."

Rundown sneered, a bit of red showing from where he was bleeding somewhere in his mouth. "Should have known. Get the fuck out of here before you get dead, Dragon asshole, unless you want to end up dead."

"I'm right here," Steel hissed. "Too scared to do something about it? Going to wait until you have better odds? I can wait for a few more of your buddies to show up."

"*Diu lei lo mo chau hai,*" Rundown spat venomously.

Steel chuckled coldly. "No thanks, why don't you? You're just the type of guy she liked—*jin jing.*"

Rundown threw a punch. Steel had been expecting it and ducked past it, slamming his fist into Rundown's gut, doubling him over.

"That's enough," a woman Steel didn't recognize said, coming between Steel and Rundown. "You want to get the cops here? I don't know who you are, but you need to get the fuck out of here."

Steel glared past her at Rundown. "I'm not fucking kidding. Leave Winston alone."

Steel returned to Winston's car and drove off, ignoring the baleful glare and middle fingers thrown his way by Rundown and his companions in his rearview mirror.

Thirty-Four

AN OPEN PLACE had purposefully been chosen for the end point of the race. Some might have thought it a foolhardy decision, considering the illegality of the Dark Streets and the desire of some to see it brought to a close. That was not his concern, however. The location made it easy for him to keep an eye on the racers, to pick the perfect next target.

He took his work seriously; he would not pick just any racer. Where was the artistry, the message, in that? Oh no, he'd pick a target designed specifically to have the biggest effect on the state of things. It was a minor action, but if he played his cards well it would have *big* results—and he always played his cards well, because he always played to win. Losing simply wasn't an option.

He had a feeling when he saw the car that belonged to the mole the Dragons had sent in speed back into the parking lot after leaving that he was about to be handed a wonderful opportunity. He watched the scene that unfolded for a moment—the brutish Dragon's encounter with one of the racers, the heated exchange, the scuffle that would have turned into an all-out brawl if others hadn't intervened.

The universe provides. He pulled out the phone and dialed the single number he had stored in its memory banks. As always, it was answered on the first ring. "It's me. I've found the next target. I'll let you know when it's done."

Thirty-Five

WINSTON SLUMPED OVER on the counter, head buried in his arms, doing his best to ignore the cheerful jazz his mom had playing over the coffee shop sound system. The music's peppy, upbeat rhythm seemed a glaring, stark reminder of just how miserable he felt at that moment. Was the entire world against him that morning?

"Hey, Winston," Noah said, emerging from the kitchen with a plate full of muffins to go in the display case. "Wei just called and said your car's been towed to the shop. It'll be fine by tomorrow. The police are footing the bill for its repair."

"Yippee," Winston said, voice a dull hum.

"I thought you'd be more excited than that," Noah commented. He leaned forward on his elbows at the counter next to Winston.

"That's about all the excitement you're going to see me muster," Winston said dully.

"Uh-oh." Noah straightened, studying Winston with sharp eyes. "I know that voice. That's a heartbroken voice."

Damn gweilo *always did notice too damn much.* "Leave me alone, Noah."

Noah shook his head firmly. "Not going to happen. Since you idiot Dragons have some sort of code against talking to each other about things, I've appointed myself the listener of the Dragons. I'm not a member, so that makes it perfect. You guys can talk to me about things you can't—or don't want to—talk to the others about."

Winston tilted his head enough to look up at Noah. "You're just going to go and tell Wei whatever we talk about."

Winston couldn't remember ever seeing a more offended face. "I would never do something like that! Anything you chose to tell me in confidence would remain between us."

I can't believe I'm considering this, Winston thought to himself. Then again, he *was* at a point he couldn't really see himself moving past on his own. It couldn't hurt to open up and share with someone, and Noah was as good a person as any. "Fine." He sighed, forcing himself to sit up off the counter. "I'll tell you. But just you—this stays between us."

Noah clapped his hands in giddy excitement. "Okay, great! Hold on, let me get us some coffees!"

"I'm already having regrets," Winston muttered as Noah hurried to fix two cups of coffee—it had to be some sort of record, how quickly he got the coffee prepared and set out on the counter before them.

With the warm coffee and a little cajoling from Noah, Winston told him about his encounter with Steel, the confession he made and Steel's reaction to it. He couldn't be one hundred percent positive, but Winston was pretty sure he heard Noah mutter "Fucking idiot," when he told him about Steel's "Good luck" comment. He said nothing, though, because he didn't disagree with the sentiment. Steel *was* a fucking idiot.

"Okay, you know what?" Noah said when Winston was done.

Winston grimaced. "Please don't give me advice, Noah."

"I wasn't going to give you any—you wouldn't listen even if I did, so what's the point? All I was going to say was tonight I'm going out with a few expat friends and figured you'd like to come along."

Winston cocked his head quizzically. "You have friends outside the Dragons?"

"Yes," Noah said disdainfully. "You guys aren't the entirety of my world, you know."

"How did you meet them?" Winston demanded. He couldn't say why he found the idea of Noah having non-Dragon friends so confusing, but he did.

"Is this an interrogation about my friendships? Did Wei put you up to this? If you must know, I met one of them here—he actually comes in a lot, and we chat when he does. He invited me to this Facebook group for foreigners in Hong Kong and some of the guys are having a get-together tonight at this bar in Aberdeen."

Meeting people off Facebook sounded dubious to Winston, but he'd never really been up on the whole social media thing. Given the life of the Dragons he was exposed to every day, it didn't really seem that important. Americans were crazy about it, though, from what he could tell.

"I can't imagine Wei actually letting you go to something like that," Winston remarked.

"I'm a grown man," Noah said defensively. "Wei doesn't tell me what to do!"

Winston snorted. "You're asking me to go with you because he won't let you go if a Dragon isn't with you."

"I'm asking you to go with me because you look like you could use a boost," Noah said huffily. Winston kept a steady gaze on Noah until he sighed. "Fine, it will kill two birds with one stone, but still! My motivations are truly pure."

Winston wanted to say no. He really, really wanted to say no. Looking into Noah's pleading face, though, he found he couldn't. Why should he make someone else miserable just because he was? Sure, misery loved company, but he'd much rather take the off chance that an outing with Noah could cheer him up instead. He'd enjoy that much more than Noah being down, as well.

His answer must have been on his face before he spoke, because Noah was grinning before Winston could say "Fine."

"I'm only going so Wei will let you out of your cage," Winston told him. "I'm not going to have fun."

"Whatever it takes to get you out," Noah said giddily. "We're meeting here at nine, right after closing, and then riding together to Yau's in Aberdeen."

"I'm driving you there. Tell these friends of yours to just meet you there. You know Wei's not going to want you riding with a bunch of strangers, and I'm sure as hell not riding with them."

Noah heaved a put-upon sigh. "Fine, I will. See you here at nine o'clock?"

"I'll be here," Winston said, though he could think go nothing he'd like to do less.

Why do I let people talk me into these things?

At nine o'clock, Winston saw Noah waiting for him in front of Coffee by Constance. He quirked an eyebrow at the pale blue minivan that Winston arrived in.

"Don't judge me," Winston scowled. "This is my mom's car. Mine is in the shop, remember?"

"No judgment," Noah said as he climbed into the passenger seat. Winston caught his quiet chuckle as he looked at Winston's graduation tassel hanging from the rearview mirror. "Do you know where to go?"

"I looked it up earlier. Don't know why you and your friends want to party in Aberdeen; there's plenty to do in Dragon territory, where it's safe." Winston turned the car onto the road and headed toward Aberdeen.

Noah groaned. "God, you sound like Wei. Do you Dragons have a book you read from or something?"

Winston scowled, and Noah blinked in surprise. "What? What's with that face?"

God, he's really going to make me say it. "I'm not a Dragon, remember?"

Noah winced, but recovered. "A technicality. It'll happen soon, I'm sure."

Winston thought he caught a hint of something, Noah's voice teasing Winston, perking his interest. He didn't want to get his hopes up, but the idea that Wei might finally let him join, after all these years, was a bright light ahead of him that just might help him navigate the darkness he was in at that moment.

The two lapsed into silence for the rest of the drive until they finally arrived at the place called Yau's. It turned out to be a karaoke bar and not a dance club like Winston expected and was much more intimate than he'd thought it would be. The main floor was an open karaoke area, the sort where people signed up with the bartender or whoever was running the machine, and went up when their time was called. Upstairs, customers could enter private karaoke rooms for a fee.

Even before entering the building, Winston could hear whoever was at the microphone that moment doing an incredibly bad rendition of "Strawberry Fields" by the Beatles. *So it's going to be one of those kind of nights, huh?*

Noah's four friends were waiting for them just inside the door. Noah introduced him to each of them in turn.

"This," he said, indicating a tall and slender Korean man with delicate features and soft eyes, "is Songmin Choi."

"Nice to meet you," Songmin said with the slightest hint of accented English, shaking Winston's hand. His handshake was firm, though his skin was soft and smooth. Winston wondered what his job was.

Next he was introduced to Paulo, a man originally from Brazil, with the dark features and sensual smile Winston pictured when it came to Brazilian men. Then was Ed, a black British guy with an easy smile and flirty nature. Last was a guy named Ray from Texas in the United States. Winston had a hard time understanding him when he spoke due to a thick twang in his accent.

"We figured we'd just stay down here," Songmin informed Noah and Winston. "The fee for the private rooms is a little much."

"That's fine, right?" Noah glanced to Winston, who shrugged. He didn't have a preference; either way he couldn't see the night being enjoyable. Might as well save money if at all possible.

Noah damn near skipped to the bar to place his song request and order drinks. Winston fell behind, watching Noah with a bit of detached amusement. *At least one of us is having fun.*

"Winston, what are you having?" Noah asked over his shoulder.

"I'm the designated driver, so just a water," Winston said quickly.

With their drinks secured, they found a table halfway between the bar and the small stage where a drunk man and a girl who might be his girlfriend were doing a duet of a love song. They actually weren't half bad.

"Noah tells me that the coffee shop that your mom owns Coffee by Constance," Songmin said, leaning in close to Winston to be heard over the song. "That's pretty cool. I love that place. Your mom makes great coffee."

"Thanks. I guess it's cool. Gives me a place to work and make some money, so that's good."

"And free coffee?" Songmin chuckled.

"Something like that."

Noah's name was called for his song, and he, Ed, and Ray hopped up and hurried to the stage.

"So what do you do here in Hong Kong?" Winston inquired. At least talking would offer him a distraction from his thoughts and from the spectacle about to go down on stage.

"My father's mother is from Hong Kong," Songmin explained. "He moved here about ten years ago, opened a restaurant. I work for a Korean company called HanTech, and when they realized I could speak Cantonese, they asked if I was willing to move to Hong Kong to work in the Hong Kong office. I'd never been before, and I hadn't seen my father in many years, and never really knew this part of my grandmother's culture, so I said yes. I've been here about eighteen months."

On the stage, Noah and his Western friends started singing "You Give Love a Bad Name."

"They're...really into the song," Songmin observed, a strange expression on his face. Winston couldn't argue with him there; they were not lacking enthusiasm. Noah didn't sound half bad, but the other two were completely tone deaf, it seemed, and drowned out Noah's okay voice.

Winston wasn't sure when exactly it happened, but as the night progressed, he found he was actually enjoying himself. The thought of Steel still occasionally swam into his mind, but Noah and his friends had him sufficiently distracted that it didn't last very long.

"We haven't heard any Chinese songs tonight," Ray said, lighting a cigarette. "Winston, why don't you get up there and sing us one?"

"You wouldn't understand it," Winston protested. He had no intention of going up on that stage and making an ass out of himself.

"Doesn't mean we don't want to hear it," Ray objected.

"I'll sing whatever you pick with you," Songmin offered. "I haven't done a song yet."

Before Winston could refuse again, Noah started chanting "Do it! Do it," and the others picked it up. "Goddamn it, fine."

"I'll go put your names down!" Noah all but skipped off to the bar to put their names on the list.

"I think the bartender likes me," Noah said when he returned. "He moved your name to the top of the list."

Ed leered. "Karaoke privileges? How could you possibly resist that?"

"By knowing if he even looks in that guy's direction, Wei would kill him," Winston supplied just as the bartender called his and Songmin's name. *I'm going to get Noah for this*, he thought as he took the stage and lifted the mic.

It didn't take them very long to pick a song—Winston was happy that it was on the shorter side, so his humiliation could end quickly. As the music began Noah, Ed, and Ray let out obnoxiously loud cheers and applause. *You're lucky Wei loves you.* Winston scowled at Noah. As if he could read Winston's thoughts, Noah stuck his tongue out at him like a child.

Winston forced his eyes away from that group, choosing instead to focus on a random place in the bar; it was the only way he'd be able to get through the song. He started singing the song but had to stop, the breath knocked out of him as his eyes fell on a familiar figure at the bar.

Steel, and he wasn't alone. He was with a short guy, and judging by the way the guy kept touching and rubbing Steel's arm, they weren't there as friends. Steel looked up, his eyes locking on Winston's. Something showed in his face, an inner battle of some kind, though Winston could only guess what about, and then Steel turned his shoulder, putting his back to Winston and the stage.

Winston felt Noah's eyes on him and glanced at him, the concern on his face just making the sharp sting in Winston's heart that much worse. He didn't want Noah's pity, didn't want anyone's pity. At that moment, all he wanted was to bury himself in the ground so no one would ever see him again. Instead, he started singing, forcing his eyes to stay locked on an empty table, not daring a look in either Noah or Steel's directions.

He could only fake so much, however, and though the words were coming out, his heart simply wasn't in them.

Thirty-Six

STEEL HATED PATROLLING with Tony, mostly because Tony was old school. He believed that the people of the Eastern District wanted to see more than just a car driving by; they wanted to see the Dragons on the streets, in the neighborhood.

"See how different it feels to be walking around with the people instead of just circling in a car?" Tony said, clapping Steel on the shoulder. "This way we're a part of this place—part of *them*. When we're just driving around we look like we're holding ourselves apart, like we're thinking that we are better than the people here."

"We don't feel that way," Steel protested. "We can just cover more ground in the car. We can protect the people better that way."

"It's not about what we know the point to be, it's about the image that it projects. The people see it a certain way, and for them that's the reality. Just watch the people as we go."

Steel rolled his eyes—making sure Tony couldn't see him; he didn't need to add a lecture about respecting his elders to everything. In the car, he could play music, have something to distract him from his memories.

The previous night haunted him, the sight of Winston on that stage, peering right at him. Even now, hours later, guilt welled up in him. He didn't know why he'd even agreed to go out with that guy, except to help fight off memories of Winston. He had absolutely zero real interest in the guy—though it was quite clear the guy had an interest in Steel. Steel's plan had been to get a couple of drinks, distract himself for an hour or two, and then go home alone, hopefully sufficiently buzzed to fall into a dreamless sleep.

The plan didn't involve Winston being there. Of all the places he could have been, Steel didn't think Winston would go to Aberdeen for a night out on the town. *Maybe he was trying to avoid me.* The idea made Steel more upset than he had any right to be.

And who the hell was that guy Winston was singing with? Just the thought that Winston might be with another man set Steel's blood to boiling. He had no business being angry, no claim on Winston; he'd turned him down, or might as well have. He just hadn't expected to see Winston out and about with a guy so soon.

"What's with you?" Tony demanded, sharp, too-observant eyes trained on Steel's face. "You look like somebody just punched your mother in the face—just an expression," he added, seeing Steel's glare.

"Nothing's wrong," Steel grunted.

"Hungover?" Tony guessed, his disapproval clear in his tone.

Now that you mention it, Steel thought, a twinge at the back of his head, *yes*. He'd needed quite a bit to drink in order to get the memory of Winston's face when their eyes met out of his mind. He wasn't going to say that aloud, though, and he refused to lie to Tony, so he said nothing at all.

"You been smelling like bars and cheap alcohol all the time the past couple of days," Tony went on as they strolled past lines of shops and a few street food vendors in the small neighborhood. It was one of the areas in Dragon's territory that was closest to the Twisted Vipers, and they kept alert as they conversed.

"What I do in my own time is my business," Steel grunted. He didn't want to have this conversation, and he certainly didn't want to have it with Tony—this was the man who'd encouraged Wei to give him a place in the Dragons. Tony had seen his potential and put his faith in him. "Is it getting in the way of Dragon business?"

"Do you think I'd be having this conversation with you if it wasn't? Look, kid, I don't give a fuck if you want to go off and drink yourself into a stupor. That's your business. But when it makes the other Dragons not want to be around you, when it gives you a bad attitude, then I care."

Steel stared ahead, face stone. He didn't show how much Tony's words got to him.

"I have an idea about what's going on," Tony continued, "but it's not my place to get involved. All I want to say is you need to get your shit together before something bad happens. You're lucky it's me telling you this and not Wei. But it's going to come to him, eventually, if you don't knock it off."

Mouth clenched shut, Steel nodded that he understood—and he did, he really did. He needed to keep his head in the game, couldn't let his personal life interfere with his responsibilities to the Dragons and the community they guarded. These people, his fellow Dragons, they meant everything to him.

"Thank you," he muttered, voice rough with emotion.

Tony rested a hand on his shoulder, a brief show of affection. The sound of someone crying out tore through the morning, and Steel and Tony stopped cold, looking around for the source. Steel caught sight of two figures running past the intersection ahead and into an alley, a guy trying to catch up with them.

Steel's eyes widened as he saw it was the guy that Winston had been on stage with singing at the bar in Aberdeen. *What the fuck is he doing here?* On closer inspection, Steel saw the guy's lip was bleeding and he was running slightly doubled over, like he was hurting somewhere.

The guy saw Steel and Tony. He must have recognized them for Dragons, because he hurried to them, eyes imploring, "Help me, please! Those guys just stole my wallet!"

Steel was torn between running up to the guy and demanding to know who he was and what the hell he thought he was doing with Winston and chasing after the thieves. Duty won out, and he took off after the thieves at full speed. He hoped he caught them; he found himself itching for a fight. Beating the shit out of two punk thieves might be just what the doctor ordered to lift his mood.

"Steel," Tony called behind him, but Steel didn't slow down to wait for him; the guys might get away, and then what would he do for fun that morning? The alley the men ran through was narrow, running between a noodle shop and a P C room. Up ahead he thought he caught the sound of voices. Had the two men stopped running? That was pretty stupid of them—not that Steel was complaining.

He slowed down, marching out of the alley into the small courtyard it formed behind several buildings. Along the eastern wall was a narrow alley like the one he emerged from, and along the northern wall was a dumpster. It wasn't just two men that Steel found himself coming face to face with but six. When had their number tripled?

"Looks like we caught one, boys," one of the six guys sneered. Steel glanced from one to the other, weighing them. Most were gangly, probably street kids like he might have been if he hadn't found Winston and his family. Some looked to be packing knives, but none had any weapons more dangerous than that, luckily.

As his eyes scanned the six men, they settled on a familiar face. "You!" It was one of the guys with that thug Rundown, which meant he was a Twisted Viper. Fucking Twisted Vipers in Dragon territory.

"Wait just a fucking minute," the guy from that night hissed, true hatred in his gaze. "This is the fucker who did in Rundown." The air in the small space became instantly charged; the man tensed, ready for a fight.

Well, if it was a fight they want, Steel had no problem giving it to them. "I don't know what the fuck you bastards are doing here, but I'm about to teach you what happens when filth like you comes into Dragon territory." Before Steel could move, one of the six, with a metal bat, stepped forward, swinging his weapon with all his might.

Steel ducked past it but was met on his left by a fist that slammed into his jaw, jarring his teeth and sending sparks flying through his vision. Steel jammed his elbow sideways, clipping the side of the man who threw the punch, but even as he drove him back another came up behind him; Steel heard the scrape of his shoes and the *snip* of a blade locking into place. He spun on his heel, swinging wildly with his arm, causing the approaching knife-wielder to jump back.

A hand gripped his shoulder and a fist slammed into his kidney. Steel tugged away from the hand, only to be shoved to the ground by a fourth assailant. He lashed out with his legs, catching one in the thigh, making the leg buckle. His second target danced away, unharmed.

A fifth man fell on him, and Steel raised his arms to shield his face from the rain of punches he threw down.

"Ping, get offa him," one of them barked. "Hold 'em down. Get his arms." The one called Ping rolled off Steel and moved to take his arms. Steel took advantage of the opportunity and head butted Ping. The punk fell back, howling in pain, and Steel tried to get to his feet. The haft of the metal bat hit his solar plexus, knocking him onto his back once more. The punk held the bat there, the heavy pressure keeping Steel in place and causing his chest to ache. He didn't remove it until Ping had a foot perched firmly on Steel's wrists, pinning them painfully to the ground.

"Where ya goin', *lan ga tsan*? We've got some revenge to get, for Rundown."

"What the fuck are you talking about?" Steel snarled. One of the men kicked him hard in the ribs, knocking the wind out of him.

"You think we don't know? I fucking saw you! I was there, remember? You fuckin' came at my boy Rundown and then that same fuckin' night he gets capped? You think we're fuckin' stupid?" A second kick to his side almost drew a groan of pain from Steel, but he held it in.

He was more troubled by what they said than by the attack. What did they mean about Rundown getting capped? Had there been another victim they just didn't know about?

"Now we're gonna do you, and it's not gonna be as quick as Rundown, neither." Rundown's friend took the switchblade from one of his companions and held it over Steel's head so he could see it clearly, its blade gleaming in the shafts of sunlight that were beginning to pour over the side of the building as the sun climbed toward its noonday zenith.

Where the fuck is Tony?

A gun went off nearby, startling the six men. As if Steel's thought summoned him, Tony was there, pistol pointing at the six men, his face cold and indifferent. It took less than thirty seconds for the Twisted Viper grunts to scatter, darting down the second alley entrance.

"Fucking cowards," Steel spat after then, wincing as he sat up. "Took you fucking long enough," he added to Tony.

"I was right behind you," Tony said, the slightest look of amusement in his eye. "I thought this would be a teachable moment for you. Do you know the lesson?"

"Don't trust an old fuck like you?"

"Close. Don't run off half-cocked alone, when you don't know the situation you're going into. If we were actually at war with the Twisted Vipers, you'd be dead right now. Now get up—we gotta go see Wei."

Thirty-Seven

WINSTON COULDN'T REMEMBER ever seeing Wei so mad. He paced the floor in their meeting place, jaw clenched tight, vein in his forehead throbbing. The Dragons were gathered there, along with Winston, Constance, and Noah.

Winston's eyes kept sliding across the room to where Steel leaned against the wall. His cheek was bruised and swollen, and he favored one side as he stood there, but other than that, he seemed fine, thankfully. He wanted to go over there and see if Steel really was okay, but there was just too much uncertainty between them. He didn't know where they stood, and with everything going on, maybe it wasn't the time.

At least he looked all right.

The door opened and the last of the Dragons joined them.

"I thought this was Dragons only," Walker said the moment he walked through the door and spotted Winston, Constance, and Noah there, his usual sour expression in place. "What are they doing here?"

"Shut up, Walker." Conroy spoke quietly. "Wei asked them to be here, so they're here."

Walker started to say something, but a glimpse at Wei must have made him reconsider because he just scowled harder and walked over to a free space along the wall.

"We've got a problem," Wei said as soon as all of the Dragons were present. "The Twisted Vipers have made another move on us. Earlier today they ambushed Steel in an alley."

"I'm fine," Steel muttered, ducking his head like he was ashamed of what had happened. At that moment, Winston ached to reach out to him and show him some support. Instead, he clenched his hands together tightly and stared at them.

"The *puk gai* were scared off by Tony before they could do any real harm, but that's not the point. The point is the Twisted Vipers have moved into Dragon territory and attacked one of our own."

It was Tony who answered. "They said there was another death last night. Some guy named Rundown."

Winston's eyes flew to Tony. "Did you say Rundown?"

"Do you know the guy?" Wei demanded, eyes raised.

"He's the one who did all the damage to my car, remember? He was one of the drivers in the Dark Streets last night." Winston found it hard to believe that he was dead. He'd seen him less than twenty-four hours ago, and Hong hadn't notified them. There was a chance it wasn't even related to the Dark Streets. And, even more, why did they target Steel? That question swimming in his mind, Winston sat down on the arm of the couch.

"What does this have to do with Steel?" Constance asked, as if she could read her son's mind. "Was it just a random attack on a Dragon?"

"It started out that way, but when they saw Steel, it changed. They think he killed that Rundown guy," Tony explained.

Winston blinked, confused. "But that doesn't make any sense. Why would they connect Steel to this guy's death?"

"That," said Wei with a sidelong glance at Steel, "is a good question."

Steel fidgeted for a moment, and Winston wondered what he hadn't told them. There was no way Winston could believe Steel actually responsible for the death. But then, why did the Twisted Vipers target him directly?

"I may have had a...talk...with that Rundown guy last night," Steel confessed.

"Why would that be?" Winston demanded. He didn't realize he'd gotten to his feet. Anger coursed through his blood. He knew why Steel went there, or at least thought he did. He asked in the hopes that Steel would tell him he was wrong.

Steel couldn't quite meet Winston's eyes, and he knew he was right. "After what happened during the race, I went to see him, let him know he should stop fucking around with you."

Winston groaned, sinking back down on the couch. "You fucking idiot. What the hell did you expect to get from that? I was fine—no harm done, and the car could be repaired. There wasn't any need to go make some big macho tough guy scene."

"He had to know that he can't just fuck with—" Steel stopped, jaw clamping shut before he finished his sentence.

"I always knew you were going to fuck around and cause problems for us," Walker said scathingly. He and Steel didn't get on that well at the best of times.

"Enough." Wei drew attention back to himself. "At this point, it doesn't matter why Steel did what he did." The look on Wei's face told everyone that he and Steel would probably be having a private conversation about that sometime soon. "What matters is Twisted Vipers came onto my turf, *our* turf, and targeted one of our own. I'm declaring no one safe. That's why I asked Noah, Winston, and Constance here. We're going to have to start taking some extra security precautions where they are concerned."

"Great, I really missed not being allowed out of anyone's sight," Noah said lightly, making even Wei smile for a moment.

"Inconveniencing you is a small price to pay for keeping you safe."

Noah's face showed just what he thought about that, but he said no more.

"That's all well and good," Walker said impatiently, "but the more important question is what are we going to do about the Vipers? We can't just let them get away with this. We've got to strike them back."

A cry of agreement went up from some of the Dragons.

"I'm not so sure this was a sanctioned maneuver," Tony said. Of everyone there, he was by far the calmest; the other Dragons, thanks in part to Walker, were all hyped up on their anger. Winston was angry, too—more than angry, actually. The fact that someone had hurt Steel, someone had caused him pain, filled Winston with a rage he hadn't felt for a long time, since the death of his father to be precise. He was also filled with fear at the idea of what this attack might mean.

Walker scoffed at Tony. "Six Twisted Vipers jumped Steel and you don't think it's a sanctioned maneuver? Going senile, Tony?"

"Watch it, Walker," Wei snapped.

"What I'm saying is these guys didn't think they were going to get Steel. If Johnny Hwang were striking back against Steel for killing Rundown, he sure as fuck wouldn't send six cowards who don't know what they're doing. More likely than not they just snuck into our territory with the hopes of catching a random Dragon and earning some cred with the Vipers."

"How are we going to respond?" Chris Ma asked. "We've got to do something."

"Hell yeah we do," said Kevin Shen enthusiastically. Like Jesse, he often acted younger than his twenty-five years. He was overeager and rushed into things without thinking—a lot like Steel, Winston thought darkly. "Let's go show them that they can't pull this shit!"

"Don't you think that's exactly what they want?" Noah asked loudly. He faltered for a moment when eyes turned to him, but didn't back down. "Hwang probably *wants* the Dragons to make the first move. It gives him the legitimacy he wants to attack us."

"You say 'us' like you're actually one of us," said Walker coldly.

"I think Noah's right." Tony threw a harsh look in Walker's direction. "This isn't something we can rush into. What we're talking about here is the potential for open war with the Twisted Vipers."

Wei sighed at that, squeezing the bridge of his nose between his thumb and index finger. The stress of being the leader was showing on him right then. Winston did not envy him the position at the best of times, and now it must be worse than ever.

"I don't want to start a turf war," Wei said at last. "We won't throw the first blow, at least, but I'm not going to sit back while the Vipers pull this kind of shit. We're going to increase patrols, especially in the neighborhood where Steel was jumped."

"So we're just going to do nothing?" Walker demanded. "After what happened to Steel—"

"I'm the idiot who walked into the trap." Steel glared at the ground, shoulders tightened. "That's on me."

"I've made my decision," Wei said firmly. "That doesn't mean we're just sitting back either. Conroy, Chris, Smile, I want you three to go back to where the attack happened. Scour that neighborhood. If you find any more Vipers, I want you to make it very clear what will happen the next time it happens."

A glint came into Conroy's eyes. "Oh, we'll make sure they understand perfectly."

The meeting broke up quickly after that, and Wei crossed to where Winston, Noah, and Constance sat on the couch. "I want the three of you to keep your eyes open, okay? For now, I'd rather you didn't go anywhere on your own."

"Great, another babysitter," Noah said sarcastically.

"If it means you stay alive, then yes, you'll have a babysitter." Wei's voice was gruff but his face softened.

Winston glanced toward Steel in time to see him duck out of the meeting place. He didn't see his face, but Winston knew Steel better than anyone, and he knew he must be having a rough time, walking into a trap like that. The physical pain wouldn't bother him very much, but the fact that he'd been tricked no doubt sat heavily on him.

"I want to help," Winston blurted, turning his eyes back to Wei. "I want to join the patrols."

"You already *are* helping," Wei said, shaking his head. "Focus on the races. The sooner we find out who is behind it and who's sanctioning these murders, the faster things can simmer down here. I hope."

"Okay," Winston said reluctantly. That was all he could do to help the Dragons, but maybe, just maybe, there was something he could do to help Steel. He waited until Wei and his mother were engaged in conversation and hurried out the door, hoping Steel hadn't disappeared.

Thirty-Eight

STEEL HAD NEVER felt like such an idiot than he had standing in that room with his fellow Dragons after he had been an idiot and let himself get trapped by some brainless *jin jang*. He could feel everyone's eyes on him—none of them would look at him directly, no, but they stared when they thought he wasn't looking. Each and every look was a judgment. Either they were blaming him for the mess they were in now or they were shaming him for not being able to handle himself and needing Tony to come running to his rescue.

It was maddening, particularly when he couldn't help but catch the occasional looks Winston threw his way. Those were the worst—that concern when he didn't deserve it—it drove spikes of shame and guilt right through Steel. He didn't deserve to have Winston worrying about him, not after the way he acted.

Steel fled the meeting room as quickly as he could. The coffee shop had been closed for the meeting, so he could at least find a little peace and quiet in there. He entered in through the kitchen and made his way into the front. The lights were off, so the only illumination came in from the streetlights, but that was fine by Steel. He didn't need the lights to make his way around the restaurant; he knew it like the back of his hand. He made his way to the table nearest the counter, slid into the seat, and held his head in his hands.

His jaw ached, and he really wanted a drink, but after what Tony said to him earlier, he thought that maybe he shouldn't. But damn, a beer would taste good—or something stronger, like whisky. Or tequila.

I feel like I've made everything worse, he thought, slumping down until his head was pressed against the table. *First, I completely fuck up my relationship with Winston because I can't control my goddamn cock, and then I can't control my temper and make shit even rougher for Wei and the rest of the Dragons.*

Steel groaned, slamming his fist down on the table. He couldn't have been more of a fuck up.

Get it together, he told himself, forcing his head off the table. *What the hell are you doing, sitting in a dark coffee shop feeling sorry for yourself? That's weak—and you're not a weakling.* He spent his childhood being powerless, and he'd sworn that it would never happen again. Too many people depended on him to be strong.

"Steel?"

Steel tensed at the sound of Winston's voice. The lights in the coffee shop flickered on, and Steel raised his hand to shield his eyes from the sudden halogen glow. Winston stood in the doorway from the kitchen. He looked like he couldn't decide whether or not to approach Steel.

What have I done? Steel was horrified by that change. How had he screwed things up so royally that Winston didn't think he was wanted there? Of course Steel wanted him there—but that was the problem, though, wasn't it? He desperately wanted Winston, but he couldn't give Winston what he deserved. He couldn't be selfish and lock Winston down into something that was beneath him, not when he knew Winston could be much happier without him.

He didn't look too happy, though. Steel didn't want to admit it, but it was true. Winston looked downright miserable and had since he'd admitted what they'd both known for a long time and gotten *Good luck* in return.

Winston apparently made up his mind, walking into the coffee shop and sitting in the chair opposite Steel. "You all right? Your jaw looks like it hurts."

Steel shrugged. "Hurts a bit. It'll be fine by tomorrow."

"Why did you go and get into it with Rundown?" Winston asked, though Steel was sure he knew the answer already.

"Are you kidding? You know what he did. Seeing the car, all that damage, knowing how close you came to being hurt and how it was that *puk gai*'s fault, I couldn't think straight. I was so pissed off. All I knew was that I couldn't let that go. It was stupid, I know that, but I don't regret it. Shit, I'd do it again in a heartbeat."

"Thank you," Winston said suddenly.

For some reason the gratitude made Steel's throat constrict. There was so much left unsaid—like he'd do anything for Winston—but it felt like Winston understood it perfectly. They never did have to say much for their meaning to be understood. "Just—" He stopped for a moment, looking away, a heat rising in his cheeks. "Thank you," Winston finished in a defeated tone.

It was obvious to Steel that Winston wanted to say more but couldn't bring himself to do so. Steel wanted to urge him to speak, to hear the words, but he knew he shouldn't. Winston had said enough. He'd stood in front of him and told Steel exactly what he felt, exactly what Steel wanted to hear, and Steel had rejected him. He couldn't force Winston to go through that again.

Steel couldn't just leave silence hanging there between them, either. "Thank you for being worried about me," he said, trying to keep his voice even and emotionless. "It means more to me than you'll ever know, I think. With everything...with everything that's going on, I can't stop...I just don't...I mean—" He couldn't put it into words, couldn't find the right way to say Winston deserved so much more than Steel. He deserved happiness, and Steel didn't see how he could ever bring that to him. He loved Winston—god, he loved him, but he couldn't trust that. He couldn't think straight, couldn't listen to his heart over the fear that roared through him.

"You don't need to say anything," Winston said, the slightest tremor in his voice and disappointment written across his face. Winston pushed himself to his feet. "I'm glad you're okay," he said before hurrying back out into the kitchen.

Steel watched him go, his eyes lingering on the doorway after he was gone. He couldn't help but feel the only thing that had ever mattered to him in his entire life had just slipped right through his fingers, and he'd let it go without a fight.

Thirty-Nine

WINSTON COULDN'T BRING himself to return upstairs, couldn't face them—particularly his mother—with the emotions he knew were plain on his face. Nor could he remain in the coffee shop, Steel within such easy reach. The urge to go back inside and make his best friend—if they were still best friends—understand the feelings they shared was almost overwhelming, and he wouldn't make a fool of himself like that again.

The only thing he could think to do was get out of there, go somewhere he could at least distract himself from everything he was feeling. He knew that Wei had said not to go anywhere alone, but he couldn't stomach being around the Dragons at that moment.

He didn't have a vehicle, and he thought Wei might actually kill him if he went too far alone—and if Wei didn't, Constance sure as hell would—so he just set off on foot around the area. A little time alone would be good for him, help him get his head on straight.

He knew the neighborhood around Coffee by Constance as well as he knew his own; he'd spent just as much time there as a child as he had at home. He walked the streets with little fear, despite the fact that night had fallen. This was the heart of Dragon territory, and even the Twisted Vipers wouldn't be foolish enough to strike there.

At first he walked simply to do so, no destination in mind. He didn't pay much attention to where he was going, instead trusting his feet to lead him along familiar paths. He came to a corner and was greeted by Hai, a street vendor selling fried chicken skewers. With his sun-worn, carefree face scored by a plethora of laugh lines, Hai always worked the same corner, and he'd built a rapport with the people of the neighborhood—especially the Dragons. His chicken was also delicious thanks to whatever seasoning he used, an ancient family secret, or so he said.

"Winston! A little late for a stroll, ain't it?"

The crossing signal was red, so Winston wasn't opposed to a bit of conversation while he waited, and he always had time for Hai. "I could say the same for you and that cart of yours."

"Bah," Hai said with a big wave of his arm. "It's always a good time for chicken. Actually, I'm just about to pack it in for the day, once I get rid of this last batch." He took a skewer from the fryer and offered it to Winston, steam still rising from the tantalizing morsels of chicken. "It's on the house, of course."

Winston was not one to turn down food, especially free food. He took the skewer gratefully, not waiting for it to cool before biting into the first delicious chunk. It burned his tongue but tasted amazing.

"Don't burn your tongue off, now," Hai scolded. He glanced up. "Sky looks awful cloudy now. I wouldn't be surprised if it rained good and hard tonight."

Winston followed his gaze and frowned. It did look like rain was on the way. "Thanks for the chicken." Winston saluted him with the now meatless skewer stick. The crosswalk light turned green, and he set off across the street, now searching for a place to be inside for a bit in case it did start raining.

He settled for the first establishment he came across—aided in that decision by a smattering of raindrops. The interior of the place looked like it wanted to be a sports bar, with several big TVs suspended behind the counter and in corners, but it lacked that vibe, and instead of sports the televisions were broadcasting some show about celebrity fathers taking care of their babies.

Winston barely paid the show any attention. What was so great about fathers actually taking care of their kids? That's what they were supposed to do, celebrity or not. It was dry inside, at least, and the air was cool, so Winston decided to stay. There were eight people, most of them drinking alone, though there was one pair. Halfway to the bartender, Winston spotted someone he never expected to come across.

"Mimi?"

She looked up, looking as shocked to see him as he was her. Winston was instantly suspicious of Mimi's presence, given her involvement with the Dark Streets and events that had been unfolding in connection to the races. He wondered if Mimi was there to spy on him. It was possible she'd discovered Winston was connected to the Dragons. If the organizers of the races know what he was doing, they could be trying to find out how much he and the Dragons knew.

If she's faking her surprise, she's a good actor, Winston thought, studying her face. Also, she couldn't possibly have known he'd be there. It wasn't that great a place to watch Coffee by Constance from, either; they were nearly four blocks away.

Winston changed directions and made his way to where Mimi sat at one of those really high tables.

"Noisy," she greeted.

Winston cringed. He would never get over that nickname. At least it was only people in the race who used it. Well, people in the race who spoke to him, and that meant just Mimi.

"What are you doing here?" Winston asked cautiously.

Mimi held up a half-empty whisky glass in reply.

"I mean why are you drinking here?"

"What and why are two very different questions," Mimi said, taking another sip from the glass. "I like this place. It's quiet."

"Mind if I sit?"

Mimi shrugged, and Winston climbed onto the stool. This would be as good an opportunity as any to do what Wei had sent him into the races to do in the first place and get some information about the organizers.

"What are you drinking?" Mimi asked.

"Uh, I guess whatever you've got," Winston said. There was a role to play here, and while Winston had to keep his wits about him, forgoing a drink would be an oddity he couldn't afford. Mimi drained her glass, held it up to catch the bartender's attention, and then put up two fingers.

"So Mimi, tell me about yourself." Winston regretted the words immediately; it definitely wasn't the smoothest or most natural start to a conversation, but he'd have to work with it.

Mimi eyed him suspiciously. "Why do you care? And don't say you're into me, because I know you've got a man."

Winston blinked. "I've got a man?"

"Don't play dumb. It won't work. The pissed-off dude who took on Rundown after the last race? You can't tell me he's not your man."

"He's really not." Winston tried not to blush. "He's my best friend."

He could tell Mimi didn't believe a word of it. "No way. No way that guy is just your best friend. Seriously? Well, he wants you. It was clear the way he was pissed off that it wasn't just about friendship. They fucked with someone he loved."

Winston cleared his throat uncomfortably. He didn't have anything to say to that, and he wanted to get Mimi off that topic rapidly. "I'm just curious."

Mimi bit her lower lip for a moment and then sighed. "Well, you are being a gentleman and keeping a girl company while she drinks. Go on and ask away. No promises on answers, though."

Winston decided to try a softball before pitching serious questions. "How long have you been racing?"

"A while. I love cars—I can tell you do, too. Racing just seemed like a good way to make money with something I love. Started out in small races and then worked my way up."

Winston waited for the bartender to hand them their drinks and return behind the bar before asking his next question. "How long have you been in the Dark Streets?"

Mimi shushed Winston, looking around to see if any of the other patrons had heard him. They were all engaged in their own thoughts or conversations or the television show and were paying Winston and Mimi no attention. "You crazy? We don't talk about it out in the open like that."

"Sorry," Winston said quickly, mentally kicking himself. "I wasn't thinking."

"Fucking amateurs." Mimi shook her head. "I've been doing them basically since they started. I might not have been in the first of the races, but got in pretty quick."

"Do you know anything about the people running the show?"

Mimi's face darkened. "We don't ask about that. No one knows anything about them, really. All we ever see are their black sedans and those guys handing out the equipment and details. My guess, though, is that it's some rich fucker just looking to amuse themselves. A few cheap thrills for being involved in something illegal, that sort of thing."

"So you've never met them?" Winston pressed, though he felt like he was going to get nowhere with that angle.

"Didn't I just say that? Why are you asking so many questions about them?"

Winston shrugged, hoping he seemed nonchalant. "I'm just curious, that's all."

Mimi pointed a finger at him in warning. "Asking too many questions can lead to pretty shitty things—like a bullet. Speaking of, did you hear about Rundown?"

"The guy that tried to run me off the mountain? What about him?"

Mimi narrowed her eyes. "You really didn't hear?"

"Hear what?" Winston demanded, faking exasperation.

Mimi bought it; her face softened, and she leaned back. "He's dead. Someone shot him."

"Are you serious?" Winston hoped he sounded surprised enough to be convincing. If he wasn't, Mimi didn't say anything or show signs of being suspicious.

"Actually, he's not the only one," Mimi confessed. She sounded almost afraid when she spoke. "Recently several of the racers have ended up that way."

Winston did a double take, reevaluating his thoughts on Mimi and her involvement. It was a weird topic for Mimi to bring up if she were somehow connected to the murders. It could have been a move to throw him off the scent, but Winston couldn't help but think she was innocent—at least in connection to the deaths and the Dark Streets.

"Do you think that someone involved with the races is doing it?" Winston asked. If Mimi wasn't connected them, she might at least have some idea she could share.

"I can't rule out any of the racers, I guess, but the organizers? Why would they risk losing so much money? The more racers who are killed, the less inclined people are going to be to throw their money in and join the races. Not the smartest business model."

It was true, but that didn't necessarily mean anything. Fiscal security could provide a pretty good cover-up, deflect attention. Unfortunately, it would be impossible to know at this point. The more he thought about it and the more he talked to Mimi, the more convinced he became that the murderer was much more likely to be one of the racers than one of the organizers.

That didn't narrow the field much, but at least it would allow them to put faces to their suspects. There were a lot of them, but it was a start, something he could take back to Wei—maybe even make Wei forget that he'd gone off on his own, despite Wei explicitly saying not to.

Mimi and Winston both fell silent, caught up in their own thoughts—though Winston didn't doubt they were both thinking about the same thing: who in the races could they trust?

Forty

THERE WAS NEVER anything good on television, but having a beer made the bad shows more tolerable. Steel was nearly through his third beer and watching some bullshit show where celebrity dads pretended to give a shit about their kids, acting like they didn't have an entire staff of people hired to take care of them. He could only stand it because of the beers, and he was too lazy to change the channel.

A commercial came on and Steel took the opportunity to finish the rest of his beer and go to the kitchen to get another one. He was almost to the kitchen when his doorbell rang. He considered ignoring it but then decided against it. Part of him thought—hoped—it was Winston coming to see him, though he knew it was unlikely.

Steel opened the door and saw Wei and Conroy standing there, and the temptation to close the door in their faces was overwhelming. It was a terrible idea, though, so he held the door open for them to come in.

"Told ya he'd be drinking," Conroy commented to Wei. "What number is that, Steel?"

"Fuck you, that's what number," Steel shot back, earning laughter from Conroy.

"Well, he's not being friendly, so he's not wasted yet. Any chance we can get some beers?"

Steel wanted to tell Conroy to fuck off, but since he was there with Wei, there wasn't much Steel could do. He completed his journey to the fridge, bringing three beers back with him.

Wei and Conroy were relaxing on his couch, watching his TV like it wasn't strange for them to be there.

"These babies are really fucking cute," Conroy said, holding his hand out for a beer. "Yo, boss, when are you and the missus gonna get a kid?"

"You do know that Noah can't get pregnant, right?" Steel passed Wei his beer and sat down between the two senior Dragons.

"They can adopt," Conroy said in a *duh* voice. "Dumbass."

"Why do these shows always make the dads look like idiots?" Wei asked, pointing to the screen where one of the dads chased his naked kid through the house, trying unsuccessfully to get him ready for bath time.

"Entertainment," Conroy said sagely. "No one wants to watch a guy be an awesome parent—it's boring. It's way more fun to see the guys be idiots."

"I guess," Wei said dubiously. "Noah and I wouldn't have those problems, though. We'd have the parenting thing on lock."

"You'd be great dads," Conroy agreed.

Steel sat between them, the entire situation utterly surreal. He *had* to be dreaming. He wasn't sitting between the two toughest bastards in the Dragons, listening to them critique reality television and talk about being fathers.

"Listen," said Steel when a commercial finally came on. "I'm sure you two didn't come over here to watch *Super Dads* with me. What's going on?"

"Hear that, Wei?" Conroy snickered. "He thinks we're not here to watch *Super Dads*. I don't know about you, but I love this show. Never miss it."

"I'm here 'cause I want to know what the fuck is going on with you," Wei said bluntly. "You're a fucking mess, drinking yourself stupid, catching attitudes with everyone, doing stupid and reckless shit."

"Wei thinks something's up. I just think you need to be medicated," Conroy said.

Steel clenched his fist tightly but held in his temper. The last thing he wanted to do was give Wei more reason to say shit.

"You know you can talk to us," Wei went on. He sounded serious, which surprised Steel. He'd suspected that Noah sent Wei there, but it sounded like he was there because he wanted to be. "If there's something bothering you, I want to know about it. I can't have you running around acting wild and putting others—or yourself—in danger, Steel."

"I'm fine," Steel said, shifting uncomfortably where he sat and focusing on the television, where a commercial had begun for diapers. *What's with this network and babies?*

"Right, you're fine, 'cause you're totally being your normal cheerful self." Conroy's words overflowed with sarcasm. "You gotta know by now that we're not gonna let this go, so you might as well talk to us."

That much Steel knew, at least. These were persistent bastards, he'd give them that. He couldn't bring himself to talk about it, though. It was too personal, and though he trusted these guys with his life, he didn't know if he trusted them with his secrets—especially not where Winston was concerned.

"Relationships, feelings, that shit's complicated," Wei said, as if he could read Steel's mind. "You and Winston are still young, you know. Still making shit unnecessarily difficult."

"Who said anything about Winston?" Steel felt his face reddening despite his words.

Conroy scoffed. "We'd have to be completely oblivious to miss what's going on between you two. We've been calling it for years, man."

Steel drank his beer mechanically, an automatic gesture more than a desire for it. He didn't even taste it on its way down. Had his and Winston's feelings really been that obvious? And he'd thought he'd done a good job of hiding it all.

"Even Noah's picked up on it," Wei added. "And he's known you, what, a month?"

Steel winced. Maybe he *had* been obvious. "It doesn't matter," he said, resting his now empty beer bottle on the coffee table loudly. "All of this is just making everything more complicated for both of us. I'm just going to end up hurting him, and I don't want to do that."

"You seen him lately?" Conroy demanded, quirking one eyebrow up. The facial expressions Conroy made always made Steel think of a movie star. "Does he seem happy to you? Seems to me like you're just making both of you miserable."

Wei nodded his agreement. "You're trying not to hurt him, but that's hurting him. At least if you allowed yourself to actually explore your feelings you might find *some* happiness."

"Who's to say it'll work?" Steel argued. "Who's to say we won't end up breaking up and being miserable anyway?"

Wei shrugged. "That's a possibility, yeah. But the opposite is also a possibility, right? You might end up in love and together for the long haul."

Steel grunted. Wei was right. He'd spent so much energy thinking about all of the things that could go wrong that he'd convinced himself it was a foregone conclusion. But Wei was right—it wasn't. No one could possibly know what the outcome would be, especially if they didn't at least *try*.

"I think he gets it now," Conroy said, smiling. "Now everybody stop talking. *Super Dads* is back on."

Forty-One

STEEL DIDN'T SHUT his eyes at all that night. He lay in his bed, staring up at the ceiling, unable to stop thinking about everything Wei had said. He was right. What was the point of living in fear of what might happen, when all that managed to do was create a situation where that was exactly what happened? He was so afraid of hurting Winston he hadn't thought about the fact that Winston was hurting anyway, and it was his fault.

I'm such a fucking asshole, he thought multiple times that night. The more he thought about it, the worse he felt. He'd taken it upon himself to decide what was best for Winston, without bothering to ask Winston what he wanted.

By the time morning came, Steel knew what he had to do. He had to talk to Winston, make things right with him. But Winston might not want to make things right, if Steel had damaged things so badly between them. *There I go, doing it again.*

He couldn't deny that their friendship was already at a crossroads, and what happened next would determine the role they played in each other's lives. Could he have a life that didn't involve Winston?

No, no he couldn't. Winston was the greatest thing in his life, always had been, and all the other good things in his life were because of Winston. How could he let himself throw that all away? He had become so convinced that he wasn't meant for happiness that he had begun sabotaging himself without even realizing.

Making that choice was the easy part, though. Putting it into action would be a different story. He now had to work up the courage to go talk to Winston. After the way he'd acted, Steel wouldn't be surprised if Winston never wanted to see him again. It would be exactly what he deserved.

Steel and Winston already had a relationship together, one built on a decade of close friendship. They already knew just about everything there was to know about each other. They'd seen each other at their best and their worst. How much could actually acting on their feelings change that? They were best friends now, and wouldn't that continue after it all came out? They'd continue being best friends—best friends who slept together, and it would be better than any friends with benefits arrangement could be.

He messaged Winston a few times that morning and got no response. He wasn't surprised; Winston was notoriously bad about getting back to anyone who sent him a text message. Steel didn't have a car, either—he usually just relied on Winston and his car to get around, since until recently they were pretty much always together.

He messaged as many of the Dragons who had cars as he could think of, but they all gave him a variation of the same answer: they were on patrol. It made sense that Wei had the Dragons who had vehicles out there on patrol, but it still annoyed the hell out of him.

"Damn it," Steel growled after the last guy he could think of told him he couldn't.

He wasn't going to let the lack of wheels stop him, though.

Steel left his place in a hurry, determined to see Winston if it meant he had to walk clear across the island.

His first destination was Winston's house. It wasn't yet noon, so he wouldn't be surprised if Winston was still asleep in his bed. He was definitely a night owl—as was Steel, another way they matched perfectly.

It took him nearly half an hour to walk to Winston's apartment from his own. He had to fight hard to resist running all the way there.

Turned out he didn't really need to worry about that so much; he rang the doorbell several times, knocked on the door, and even tried it to see if it was unlocked, but no one came to the door.

He's probably at the coffee shop, Steel decided. *Wei probably didn't want him staying here alone with everything that's gone on with the Twisted Vipers lately.* It wouldn't be the first time Wei imposed limits for their safety. He remembered the strict rules Wei set regarding Noah when that crazy bastard Leo Tong was fucking with the Dragons. The man took the safety of his people seriously.

Walking from Winston's place to Coffee by Constance took a bit more time. It never seemed that far in the car, but he quickly learned that a vehicle distorted the perception of distance, sometimes a lot.

It took him an hour to get there, and by that time, he was covered in sweat even though he hadn't run. It was September, and fall was approaching, but in Hong Kong summer held on until the bitter end. Steel was grateful for the air-conditioning inside the shop. He stopped just inside the door to catch his wind again, reveling in the cold air blowing on him. The sweat on his body soon made him nice and chilly. It was way better than the heat of the day outside.

"You look like you need a drink," Shelby remarked.

Steel felt a twinge of embarrassment as he approached the counter. This was his first time seeing Shelby since he'd shown up stupid drunk at her house. Thankfully she gave no indication that she remembered the incident. "I can get a drink later," Steel said, though he really wanted one then. "Is your brother around?"

"He left with Wei about an hour ago," Shelby said. Steel could see suspicion in her eyes. She didn't trust him when it came to her brother. That meant that she'd seen things between them, too. He couldn't blame her for wanting to protect Winston. Steel had fucked up and hurt him, and family looked after each other.

Steel deflated a bit. If he'd left with Wei there was no telling where he'd gone or when he'd be back.

"Oh, then I think I'll have that drink after all, Shelby." Steel slumped his way toward a table. "Something cold. I don't care what."

He resolved to stay there in the cafe until Winston got back. He would do nothing else that day until he talked to Winston and set things right between them, or at least tried.

Shelby brought him an iced coffee, but even its caffeine did nothing to combat the exhaustion of staying up all night and then walking all the way there. Add in the smooth, relaxing tone of the jazz playing in the background, and despite his best efforts, Steel fell asleep there at the table.

At some point, Constance woke Steel up—she couldn't have him sleeping in the coffee shop, she said—so he went upstairs to the space above the coffee shop, sprawled out on the couch, and fell asleep again.

The next time he woke up the room was mostly dark. The sound of Wei and Hong arguing drew him back to reality. *What is Hong doing here?*

"You know about it now," Wei was saying impatiently. His tone of voice made it clear that was the final word on the matter. Wei and Hong stood in the middle of the room, facing each other like some sort of standoff was going down.

"I should have been told as soon as he found out," Hong insisted. "This is a police investigation, remember?"

"How could I forget?"

"What's going on?" Steel asked, groggily, looking between the two men.

"Winston got a message about another race," Wei explained, not taking his eyes off Hong. "It's just after night falls, so in an hour or so. Hong doesn't like that we didn't let him know the absolute second Winston got the text."

Steel jumped to his feet. "Where is he?"

"With his car, where else?" Wei answered. Steel didn't wait to hear more; he took off outside, bounding down the stairs. He nearly tripped at the bottom but steadied himself on the rail before continuing.

Winston was bent over the front of his car, the hood up as he examined its inner workings with a critical eye. There wasn't a scratch on the car, not a single sign of damage from his vehicular battle with Rundown. The car looked brand-new.

"Yo, Winston," Steel called in greeting. For a moment, he thought Winston was going to hit his head on the hood he jumped so high in surprise. "I didn't know you were here. I was asleep upstairs."

"I know," Winston said, wiping a bit of grease from his hands with a dirty rag. "Shelby told me you were looking for me."

"Oh." Steel let the words sink in for a moment. "Why didn't you wake me up?"

"You looked like you needed the sleep. Besides, I've been a bit busy here," Winston added with a shrug, gesturing toward the car. "I've got another race. They didn't give us a lot of warning about this one."

"Yeah, I just heard up there," Steel said. Why did he suddenly feel so awkward around Winston?

Steel realized the full weight of what he'd wrought on their friendship.

He was standing there looking like an idiot, saying nothing, while Winston looked at him expectedly. How should he handle this? He didn't know if he trusted himself to say the right thing now.

"I wanted to talk to you," he started, shifting his weight from foot to foot. All of a sudden, he felt like he was a child again who'd just been caught by Constance doing something wrong. "I mean, if it's cool."

Something flickered behind Winston's visage, but it was gone too fast for Steel to identify it. Maybe he'd imagined it, because when Winston spoke it was with the same cool indifference as before. "I'm a little busy. I need to get ready to go to the meeting place for the race." Winston turned back to the car, closing the hood with a loud noise and pushing down on it to make sure it was locked in place.

"I totally understand," Steel said. Though his voice was casual, he knew it sounded too forced, because at that moment he felt like his heart was constricting, being flattened beneath the tires of Winston's car. Something Steel said must have cracked through Winston's inner wall and inspire him to take some pity on Steel; just before he climbed behind the wheel, he called to Steel. "After the race is finished, maybe we could talk."

Steel watched Winston drive off, clinging to the idea that there might be some hope yet. Steel was a Dragon, and Dragons never gave up. He couldn't force Winston to forgive him, but all he needed was for Winston to hear him out. He wouldn't give up as long as he had a shot.

As the taillights disappeared, Steel thought, *Be careful out there.*

Forty-Two

THE MEETING PLACE for this race was a parking lot along a beachfront on the eastern side of the island. It was a well-traveled area, and there were still plenty of cars coming and going. True night had almost fallen, so the race would be beginning soon. Winston couldn't help but be uneasy, what with the extra civilian traffic, the early hour, and the suddenness of the race itself. The Dark Streets were risky enough in the wee hours of the morning with little traffic. Factoring in noninvolved drivers would be a challenge. Maybe that was why the organizers decided to do it.

Pulling into the meeting space, Winston saw right away that there were nowhere near as many cars as there had been at his other two races. Maybe the increasing risk had discouraged some drivers from participating. If that was the case, Winston's task of climbing up the ranks got a little bit easier.

He spotted Mimi's car and pulled his up alongside it. Unlike the last two races, Mimi sat inside the car, looking lost in her thoughts. He thought about honking his horn and wondered if it would be too much. *What they hell, they already call me Noisy.* He honked—just one, short sound—and Mimi startled, turning her head fast enough to give herself whiplash. Winston rolled down his window and Mimi followed suit.

"Low turnout tonight."

Mimi nodded, her gaze still not entirely present. "The early ones don't have as many racers. Good for the rest of us, I guess."

Winston didn't know her well enough to really say, but she seemed almost nervous about this particular race. She didn't seem to have the same confidence she'd had every other time he'd met her. He considered their run-in at the bar. Maybe the events connected to the races was bothering her. He couldn't blame her if that was it; who wouldn't be nervous if they thought there was a chance they'd end up the next victim?

"Is this normal? I mean, a race at this time?"

Mimi shook her head. "I've never been in a race before ten. This is a new one. Probably some new gimmick the organizers are trying to lure in some new racers. They're always looking for ways to get fresh blood—and money—into the races."

That made sense to Winston. The best way to keep the cash flowing would be to get new donations—and considering each new racer added ten thousand dollars, even a few new interested parties could probably be considered a good haul.

The typical black sedan pulled into the parking lot, and Winston's heart began to beat a little faster. Like at the start of his first race, Winston was given a GPS navigator with the final destination already plugged in. It looked like the race was going to take them along the entirety of the eastern coast, coming to an end in the parking lot of a popular observation point. It was ambitious, but he couldn't worry about that right now. He had a job to do, and he'd do it.

Winston and the drivers took their allotted spots. Winston couldn't help noticing all the missing cars and wondering if any of the drivers weren't there because they'd fallen victim to whoever this killer was. Even more frightening, he wondered who amongst the racers was actually the killer.

Having ruled out the organizers—most likely, anyway—that only left his fellow racers. How else could someone know that each of the victims was also part of the races? Considering the illegality of the races themselves, he highly doubted someone was running around bragging about being involved in them.

He thought of Rundown. Then again, maybe some of them were. But not all of them. There was a connection there—there just had to be. He searched through the fog of his mind to touch the thread tying it all together, but was unable to grasp the thin white line at the center. He shook his head free of those thoughts, forcing his attention back to the race itself. He could worry about the who and the why later, when he wasn't about to go driving down a busy road in an illegal street race.

"I can do this," he told himself, saying it aloud in the hopes that hearing it would allay the way his nervous state was slowly escalating. If he didn't get it under control quickly, it would reach near panic before the race began. He'd already proven himself in the previous two races. Now all he needed was confidence.

The air horn that signaled the start of the race sounded and the cars lurched into motion as one. Winston pressed the gas down a second later than the others and very nearly lost his position right out of the gate. He steadied on, though, and the need to merge into traffic out of the parking lot saved him.

As he sped up, he caught sight of Mimi's car ahead, weaving in and out of both lanes as suited her purposes. He realized he was always so far behind in the other races that he had never seen Mimi racing before. She was incredible. He'd never seen anyone handle a car so skillfully outside of the movies. Her vehicle moved through traffic seamlessly, a shark cutting its path through the water.

Winston wished he could drive like that. He had nothing on her skills at handling a car. He wondered how it was possible she didn't get first place every race.

The loud blare of a horn jarred him from his thoughts, and he focused on the road in front of him. It was becoming difficult to tell who the civilians and who the racers were; the cars were blending together, the night turning them into black car-shaped shadows with few distinguishing features.

Winston tried pretending he was just on a normal drive, out and about, nothing out of the ordinary. That didn't work when one of the competitors sped by him, the wind of his passing rocking Winston's car.

He tightened his hands on the steering wheel and concentrated on the race. He was going to show everyone just what he was made of.

Winston pressed his foot down on the pedal, flooring it and enjoying the subtle jolt to the stomach that came with the high speeds he was reaching. It took less than a minute before he saw the taillights of the car that had passed him. He grinned victoriously, ready to maneuver his way around.

He was almost side by side with the car when blue lights filled his vision. The competitor's car veered wildly toward Winston, and he had to jerk the wheel hard to avoid being hit. Police cars poured onto the road from both sides. Winston's heart pounded in his chest loud enough to drown out the police sirens. He slammed on the breaks, tires throwing up smoke as he struggled to maintain control of the car. He finally came to a stop, his front bumper just inches away from the passenger side of a police car.

Forty-Three

THE CHAOS OF the police bust of the Dark Streets race did not die down quickly. Several hours after the trap was sprung, police cars and civilian onlookers still lingered. The racers were all gone by then, but their cars remained, awaiting towing to a police impound lot.

He watched all of this with ambivalence. Some might look on it as an obstacle moving toward his final goal, but he didn't see it that way. Sometimes things came up that would force the flow of events in a certain direction, like a rock redirecting the flow of a stream. One had to be prepared for that; no plan built too rigidly could endure. Allowances must be made for the unexpected.

He enjoyed the unexpected. It made the game that much more fun to win, forcing him to adapt and think on his feet. It kept him sharp, and he was grateful for it.

His cell phone rang. He didn't need to look at the number to know who it was. *Some people*, he thought with disdain, did not appreciate the art that was the unexpected.

"I wondered when you would call," he said once he'd hit the Accept icon.

"*What the hell did you let happen?*" his employer all but screamed into the phone.

"And just what was I supposed to do? Kill an entire battalion of Hong Kong police officers? It was an unfortunate occurrence, but I can hardly be held responsible for it. I believe that blame goes to someone else," he added, the slightest hint of reproach in his voice.

"Well, I hope you know how you're going to fix this," his employer grumbled.

"As a matter of fact, I'd already decided on my next target," he said smugly. "Fear not, I no longer require the races for this to work. Very soon I will be able to deliver everything you've paid me for." *And be done with you*, he added silently. Of all the many employers he'd had in his career, this was without contest the most annoying.

"You'd better hope so," his employer hissed. "I've invested far too much money for this to go to shit because you can't be trusted to do your damn job."

He chose to end the call then, before his employer could run his mouth off and just make him angrier. He stared at his cell phone, contemplating the repercussions of killing his employer. Such actions would give him a bad reputation, unfortunately. No one would hire him if they thought he would simply turn around and kill them—no matter how justified he may think his actions to be.

No, it wasn't his place to decide that. He would just stick to the kills he'd been sanctioned for.

Forty-Four

THERE COULDN'T BE a more miserable feeling than being dragged out of his car and handcuffed by Hong Kong Police. The moment the bands of metal closed around his wrists, his heart leapt into his throat. This was his worst nightmare come to life. The ride to the police station passed in a panicked blur. The entire time he sat in the back of the patrol car—being hauled in with two other racers he didn't know—he felt like he was on the brink of passing out from hyperventilating.

The booking process might have taken hours, but Winston couldn't say for sure; it felt like mere seconds to him. The next thing he truly could remember he was in a holding cell with four other racers they'd managed to arrest. He scanned their faces, unable to see any he recognized. Mimi must have escaped somehow; lucky girl.

Winston tried to sit still, shoulder to shoulder with the others on one of those long benches welded to the wall of the cell, but he couldn't. He gave up, taking instead to pacing the small space of the holding cell, alternating between clockwise and counterclockwise directions. A few guys scowled at him, but no one said anything.

It was a good thing, too. Winston didn't know how he could contain himself if they did; he already felt like he could just scream at any moment, as if a wild animal was trapped in his chest, scratching and clawing to get out. Everything about the place set him off—the bars, the cold gray stone floors, the ugly metallic benches. It reminded him too vividly of the nightmare about his father's murder.

For a moment, everything around him seemed to be tinged red.

I can't stay here, he thought, his steps becoming more frenetic. *I'm going to go crazy if I stay here.*

One of the racers finally had enough of Winston's pacing. "Why don't you sit down already? They'll let us go eventually. Just chill out."

Winston ignored him, barely processing that he'd even spoken much less what he said. He'd progressed to thinking about what was going to happen to him in that place. He hoped the police would let him out because of his role helping on this investigation, but he didn't know how many people knew about that, and he doubted Wei had any pull with the police. A chill ran down his spine when he thought about what had happened to his father in this very place.

Does anyone even know I'm in here?

"Which one of you *puk gai* is Chang?"

Winston stopped cold, turning around at the voice. Hong stood there, a sneer on his face as he took in the racers. Nothing in his eyes gave away that he knew who Winston was. *Typical cop*, Winston thought, disgusted. *Looking down on everyone, judging like he's so high and mighty just because he has a gun and a badge.*

"Well?" Hong barked when no one said anything, and Winston didn't move. "I don't have all fucking day. Where the fuck is Winston Chang?"

Winston didn't have to fake disdain for Hong as he forced himself to walk toward the cell door and a dawdling pace.

"Well," he spat, "here I am. What the fuck do you want?" He heard impressed mutterings behind him, but paid them no heed. He wasn't posing to earn street cred or build his reputation with these people. If that happened, fine, but this was no act.

"We've got a few questions for you, *jin jing*." Hong jerked the cell door open, grabbing Winston by the arm and dragging him out before slamming it back into place behind them. Winston wondered how much Hong was acting as he was manhandled into an area devoid of people. His question was answered by the immediate change in Hong's demeanor when they were alone.

"Are you okay?"

"I'm fine," Winston muttered, jerking his arm free. "Why should you care?"

"I know that this place must—"

"That was a rhetorical question," Winston interrupted coldly. He didn't want to hear anything about his connection to this place, especially not from Hong, of all people. "What the hell happened out there?"

Hong looked like he didn't want to change the subject, and for a moment Winston didn't think he would. "I'm not sure yet. It's being looked into."

"Wow, a whole lot of good you've been," Winston said derisively.

"I'm in talks with my supervisor to get you out of here, but until that happens, you're staying with me."

"No thanks. I'll go back there with the others." Winston tried to step past Hong, but the detective pushed his shoulder back hard. If they hadn't been in the police station, Winston would have punched him right then and there.

"I'm trying to protect you, damn it!"

Winston couldn't help himself; it just burst out, egged on by the situation, where they were and who it was saying those words to him. "Like you protected my father, you mean?"

A strange transformation came over Hong's face then, and Winston thought he would be the one getting hit.

Hong grabbed him from the front of his shirt and tugged him roughly along behind him. "Let me go," Winston growled, trying to pull free of Hong's grip, but he couldn't. "Where are you taking me?"

Hong said nothing until they came to a stop in front of an empty holding cell designed for people who would be there for longer than a night. This one had a toilet and a bed, complete with a flat pillow and thin blanket. He had a sick feeling in his stomach.

"Do you know where you are, Winston?"

Winston felt the blood drain from his face. This place haunted his dreams, though he'd never seen it before. How could Hong bring him here?

"Do you know where you are?"

"Yes," Winston whispered, trembling.

"I'm sorry I brought you here, but I need you to understand something, Winston. You hate me because Wei hates me—"

"No, I hate you because of what you did to my father," Winston growled.

"I didn't do anything to your father, Winston. This is what I want you to understand. Your father was my best friend in the world. He was the only person I loved more than your mother. After what happened to him—"

"After the police killed him, you mean?" Winston shouted, surprised to find that tears were welling up in his eyes.

"Yes, that's what I mean," Hong said. His lack of disagreement startled Winston. He'd expected him to say something to defend his fellow police officers or something, not admit their culpability. "After that happened, I was the one who identified his body. I couldn't let your mother do it, I couldn't put her through that. Seeing him...seeing him the way he was, it destroyed me. I'd lost my best friend in the entire world. He was my brother-in-law, but we basically forgot the 'in-law' part. He was truly like my brother. Almost like what you and Steel have—not quite, but almost. What happened to him right here...I still..." Hong trailed off, his jaw clenching tightly.

When he spoke again, his voice was thicker. "Maybe even worse, though, was the fact that the police did it and got away with it. That's why I joined the police when the Nine Stars were defeated. I tracked down each and every officer responsible for what happened to your father."

"What?" Winston blinked. "You mean you found them?"

Hong nodded, grim satisfaction on his face. "I did, and I made sure each and every one of them paid. I didn't kill them," he added, seeing the look on Winston's face. "But they didn't go in easy, either. I know I didn't clean out the police force, though. I knew the place still stank of corruption, and in some high places, too."

"You mean like Dang," Winston said.

"You guys know that the Dragons have enemies in the police force. I don't want the same thing that happened to your father to happen to Wei or Conroy or Steel—or god forbid, you. From here I can protect you all from the police. You think that I have no loyalty to the Dragons, but in reality, the entire reason I joined was to aid the Dragons—and that's why I stay. There's only so much I can do, but it's something. I keep an eye out for them—for you, for all of you. Maybe it doesn't seem like a lot to you, but it's more than I could do outside."

Winston furrowed his brow, looking away from his uncle. It was so easy to be angry, so easy to hold on to the rage and hurt feelings, but the sincere emotion in Hong's voice when he spoke about Winston's father touched Winston in a way that none of his words before had. It had to be the comparison to himself and Steel; he tried to imagine himself in Hong's shoes, identifying Steel's body. Just the idea of it hurt him more than he could bear.

"I come in here a lot," Hong commented suddenly, reaching out and clutching one of the bars of the door so tightly his knuckles turned white. "It reminds me what I'm fighting for. Sure, Wei and the others may hate me—and it hurts like hell knowing that you, my own nephew, blame me for your father's death—but if I can make sure this doesn't happen again, if I can keep you safe, it's worth it."

The *you* in that last sentence was clearly meant specifically for Winston.

Just like that, something broke inside him, and tears, hot and wet, slid down his cheeks. Winston ducked his head, ashamed to be crying. His shoulder relaxed a bit when he felt Hong's hand on it, a gentle squeeze that spoke volumes.

A voice called out into the echoing corridor that led to the cell, breaking the moment. "Hong, you back here?"

"Yeah," Hong called back. "What is it?"

"The kid you had in the race, he's free to go. His ride's here to get him."

"Got it." Hong cleared his throat. "Well, you go on out. I think it'll be best for everyone involved if the Dragons don't see me right now."

Winston nodded. "Yeah, you're probably right. And oh, uh, thank you. For everything." Winston hurried away before the look on Hong's face brought more tears to his eyes.

Forty-Five

IT TOOK EVERY ounce of self-control Steel had—and Constance controlling the locks on the car—to keep him from storming into the police station and ripping the place apart until he found Winston. Wei had decided that he should go in alone; he didn't want to put Constance in an awkward spot with Hong and didn't want to make a big scene. He only allowed Constance and Steel to accompany him—and Steel only because he'd begged to be included with no sign of stopping until Wei conceded.

Once Wei exited the car—with an admonition to Steel to stay in it—Constance, sitting in the front passenger seat, turned to face Steel, her face serious. Steel knew from the expression that he would probably not like whatever it was she wanted to say to him.

"Why exactly did you beg Wei to bring you here with us?"

"I wanted to be here for Winston. You know as well as I do that this place has got to have him pretty fucked up right now."

"Okay, you've told me what you're doing here, but not *why*."

Steel was a bit confused. He'd answered her question but she wasn't satisfied? "Like I said, I'm here for Wei."

"But why?" Constance pressed. "You haven't really shown an interest in being there for him the past couple of days, you know. Yes," she added, cutting off Steel before he could even speak, "I *have* noticed. It's kind of hard not to when you're either at my house or he's at yours every single night and then suddenly you're not around and he's moping and miserable. I'm pretty sure even Conroy could put that one together."

Steel saw no point in arguing with Constance; not like it would do any good anyway. Even as a kid, he'd never been able to lie to her. It must have been mother's instinct, or something, because Constance just had a way of *knowing*. It bordered on the supernatural, as far as he was concerned.

"Yeah, things have been pretty tense between me and Winston recently, I admit it. But that doesn't mean I don't want to be there for him, especially considering where he's at right now and what he must be feeling. Friends are there for each other when it really matters."

Constance watched his face carefully. "So it's friendship that brought you here."

"Yes—no. I mean, damn it, this is complicated enough already."

"It's been complicated for a long time, Steel. Long enough, I'd say. Wouldn't you?"

"You make it sound like it's easy, Constance," Steel sighed. "But you're right, it has been complicated long enough. That's why I'm here. I want to be there for Winston, show him how important he is to me, show him that I'm ready to step up and be there for him, like he needs me to be."

That had been his intention, but he'd been feeling uncertain about it the entire ride, afraid of what the step might mean for them, still fearful of what the consequences might be. Speaking the words aloud, though, explaining himself to Constance that way, the doubt fell away, leaving only certainty in its place.

He loved Winston, had loved him for as long as he could recall, and that was all that mattered in the end. No matter what he was afraid of, the future was out of his hands. The present, the now, that was his to control, and he would choose to fill his with love and help make sure that Winston's was the same.

Constance held Steel's gaze, her intense eyes searching his. "I hope you mean that, Steel. I don't know if you understand just how much potential there is for you to hurt Winston. If you're going to go for it, go for it. But don't start down that road unless you're serious about it."

"I am serious about it," he assured her. "It might have taken me a long time to figure it out, but this is Winston. How could I not be serious about it?"

"I mean it. Someone else could pull this and he'd be fine, I think. But you...if you start something and then run away, it would destroy him."

Steel wanted to argue with her on that, wanted to tell her that Winston was stronger than she gave him credit for. He couldn't, though, and not because Winston was weak, but because he put his entire heart on the line. As could be plainly seen with the cops and Hong, when Winston hated, he hated with every fiber of his being. The same could be said about love and trust. He put himself—his heart—entirely in Steel's hands, not only because he trusted him but because he loved him, too.

Constance was right. If he started something he couldn't at least see through to whatever its ending was, he'd end up hurting his best friend irreparably. *No pressure, though.*

"Here they come," Constance said, practically leaping out of the car when she spotted Wei and Winston exiting the precinct.

He's okay, Steel thought, relief making his knees weak. *He's okay. Thank whatever god there might be.* Winston looked a little shaken, but he had no signs of injury, and they could get him past whatever emotional pain he was in. His face was tired, but other than that, he looked downright normal.

Steel was slower to get out of the car, unsure what Winston's reaction would be to seeing him. Winston slid into his mother's arms, holding her tightly. They whispered something to each other that Steel did not hear. He did not try to listen, either. He would not intrude on their private moment.

Winston looked up without warning, as if he sensed Steel's approach. Their eyes locked and Steel's steps faltered. He suddenly felt like he was pinned to the spot by the intensity of Winston's gaze.

Steel felt the immensity of the moment, as if the very future hung in the balance, waiting with bated breath to see how Winston would react— and in a way it did.

After thirty seconds that felt like thirty years, Winston stepped out of the protection and safety of Constance's arms, walking toward Steel on unsteady legs. "You came."

"Yeah." He wanted to say more than that, but the words refused to come as his mind was so caught up in his relief that Winston was okay. "I know what being in there must have done to you. I wanted to be here when you got out."

A gamut of emotions ran over Winston's face in a matter of seconds, too fast for Steel to spot them all, though he did see relief there at the last, before he threw his arms around Steel. Steel reacted immediately, sensing what Winston needed. He pulled Winston in close, holding him tightly, letting him press the side of his head into his shoulder.

"You came," he whispered again, squeezing Steel still tighter.

"I always will," Steel murmured into his hair.

"I hate to break up this moment," said Wei—and he sounded sincere, unlike most people when they said something like that. "We should get out of here before we draw too much attention."

"Wei," Constance said, gesturing with her eyes back toward the precinct. Steel looked long enough to see Superintendent Henry Dang, Hong's boss, standing atop the steps of the building, watching them with hawkish eyes.

"Ignore him," Wei instructed.

Steel had already come to that conclusion himself, opening the door to the car and helping usher Winston into the backseat. Despite the fact that Winston and Steel were the only two passengers in the back, Winston stayed in the middle, immediately resting his head on Steel's shoulder when he joined him.

Steel's heart fluttered at the simple action. He caught Constance's eyes in the rearview mirror and gave her the smallest of nods. Yes, this was exactly where he wanted to be.

Forty-Six

EXHAUSTION CLAWED AT Winston the moment he settled into the back of the car. Steel's close proximity put him at ease, but he fought the sleep. He was afraid that if he fell asleep the dreams would come, and he didn't want that. He could only imagine how intense it would be, given he now knew exactly what the place his father died in looked like.

Still, he was grateful to Hong for showing him. It helped him to face it. It helped him start to process the unresolved rage he felt, and that could only be a good thing. He didn't know if he was ready to forgive Hong—it was surprisingly hard to let go of the hatred he'd clung to for so long.

It was a good first step, though, and might help him redirect his anger where it belonged.

Winston didn't realize how close he was to drifting off until Wei's voice jarred him back into full consciousness. "I think Winston should stay at Steel's tonight."

Winston's stomach twisted itself into a knot at the thought of going back to Steel's place.

Constance made it clear she didn't exactly approve. "After everything that's happened?"

"It's a safety precaution," Wei said. "I imagine whoever was behind the killings in the Dark Streets isn't going to like that the races have ended. They might be looking for new targets or go crazy and start trying to finish off racers they can get to."

"Winston won't be any safer at Steel's than at home."

"It's not Winston's safety I'm worried about—not entirely, anyway. It's yours and Shelby's."

"He's right, Mom," Winston chimed in. He couldn't stand the thought of Shelby getting hurt because someone went after him. Constance could take care of herself, he knew that, but Shelby was different. She didn't have the same hard iron in her that her mother had. She needed to be protected. "I won't put Shelby in danger like that. I'm going to Steel's."

"Wei's the boss, so if he says I have to have you there, I guess I can put up with you for a night," Steel replied. The familiar teasing in his voice made Winston's heart feel lighter. It made things seem almost normal.

The closer they drew to Steel's apartment, the more nervous Winston felt. By the time they pulled up in front of it, he was like he was one exposed nerve. He didn't know what to expect from all of this. What did Steel want, exactly? He pushed the thoughts away. He didn't want to think about things too much right now, get too much inside his own head. He'd seen how life had played out when he thought too much, and that just wasn't what he wanted.

Constance twisted in her seat and put a hand on his arm. "Come by the coffee shop first thing in the morning," she instructed. "I'll make you breakfast there."

Winston squeezed Constance's hand tightly. "Will do. I love you, Mom."

"I love you too, sweetie," she said.

Winston followed Steel into the building and up the stairs to the apartment, feeling strangely nervous despite the fact he'd been there more times than he could count.

The familiarity of Steel's apartment comforted Winston, setting him a little more at ease. It seemed almost like things had been before all of this happened, when he and Steel were just friends—or at least when they were just ignoring the sexual tension between them. Letting it go unacknowledged hadn't really helped much, though, in hindsight.

"Thanks for coming to get me," Winston said, turning around to face Steel, who shut the door and locked it behind him. "It really means a lot to me. I didn't think you would, after everything that—after what I said, and what you..." Winston trailed off as Steel stalked toward him, an unusual expression on his face. "What's wrong?"

Steel kissed him, his lips soft and comforting and anything but uncertain. Winston responded slowly, letting Steel set the pace. The last thing he wanted to do was spook Steel. He was content with Steel's lips on his mouth.

Breaking the kiss for a moment, Steel said, "I was so fuckin' worried about you." He kissed Winston again, harder.

"I'm fine, Steel," Winston assured him, clutching tightly onto Steel's back.

"This time," Steel conceded. "But I'm not going to let my chances pass me by again."

"What do you mean?" Winston asked. Steel demonstrated by shoving Winston's shirt up, exposing the hard nubs of his nipples. Winston shivered as Steel ran his thumb over his right nipple, applying pressure, just grazing it.

"Sensitive?" Steel asked, doing it again and watching Winston's face.

"Yes," Winston answered, words trembling.

Steel took that nipple between his thumb and index finger, giving it a firm twist. Winston moaned with the combination of pleasure and pain. The sound must have encouraged Steel; he took the other nipple, twisting both of them gently but firmly.

"You have no idea how long I've wanted this," Steel breathed, leaning down and circling Winston's nipple with his tongue, letting the tip barely touch Winston's skin.

Winston chuckled a bit. "I think I do—holy fuck!" Steel's mouth clamped around his nipple, the perfect combination of tongue and teeth and suction. His knees shook, and he feared they would buckle, but Steel's arm around his waist kept him steady. Winston clung to Steel's shoulder, head thrown back and eyes closed as Steel's lips worked their magic.

Steel switched to the left nipple, trailing kisses across Winston's chest as he did.

Winston's cock ached in his shorts, straining against the material. The fabric of his boxer briefs clung to him, sticky and wet with his precome. His cock needed some sort of relief, and he couldn't free it from his shorts because Steel's body was pressing against him, so he began to grind his cock against Steel's thigh.

Steel stopped what he was doing long enough to smirk up at Winston. "Someone's enjoying themselves."

"I don't think I'm the only one," Winston said, shifting his leg until it came into contact with Steel's own hard cock. "See?"

"Never said I wasn't," Steel responded cheekily. He straightened up, releasing Winston and stepping back from him. The front of both their shorts tented obscenely. "Let's take this to the bedroom."

It wasn't really a suggestion, and Winston followed behind him without thinking about it. He didn't really *need* to think about it; he wanted this more than he wanted anything else. There was no way in hell he'd turn down this chance.

Even if it's a one-time thing.

He wouldn't worry about that right now, though. The future could be dealt with later. Right now he wanted to deal with the present—especially when that present involved Steel rapidly removing his clothing. Within seconds of entering the bedroom, Steel managed to pull off his shirt and step out of his shorts, leaving him with only his boxers on. When he moved, Winston could just catch a glimpse of his hard cock through the front slit.

Winston rushed to catch up, stripping off his shirt and starting on his pants. He pushed his boxer briefs right on down with his pants, not wanting Steel to see exactly how turned on he was.

Steel started toward Winston, moving to get down on his knees, but Winston shook his head. "Uh-uh, not this time. It's my turn." Winston pushed Steel back onto the bed and went to his knees, gripping Steel's boxers by the waistband and pulling them down as he went so Steel's cock pointed right toward his face.

Part of Winston wanted to enjoy it, savor the close-up look with that beautiful erection, but the hornier and more dominant part of Winston just wanted to get things under way. It was no contest which part won out. Winston slid his mouth expertly over Steel's cock, taking great pride in the way Steel slowly said "Fuck yes," in a voice so low it was basically a purr. "Goddamn, man, where'd you learn to do that? On second thought, don't tell me."

Winston set an excruciatingly slow pace, taking his sweet time working the cock over, savoring the feel of every single inch of flesh on his tongue and moving against his lips. Steel wasn't in the mood for slow savoring, though, and he thrust his cock roughly into Winston's mouth until it hit the back of his throat.

Winston coughed, and Steel started to pull back, but Winston pressed forward until he felt Steel's length slip into his throat. Steel let out a low hiss of pleasure. "Sweet fucking god, that's incredible."

Steel's praise motivated Winston, and he set to work, deep throating Steel's cock every time.

Winston didn't know how long he sucked Steel, but eventually Steel stopped him, forcing him off his cock and tilting his chin so Winston was looking into Steel's eyes. "You like my cock?" Steel asked, voice husky. As he spoke, he slapped his cock against Winston's jaw.

"Yes," Winston answered. There was no reason to play coy or hard to get, not when he was on his knees with Steel's cock against his face.

"Good."

Steel stood up, then, hauling Winston to his feet. "Get on the bed. No, on all fours," he corrected when Winston started to lay on his back. Winston complied, getting onto his hands and knees, his lower legs hanging off the side of the bed. Steel gently nudged his thighs farther apart. "Lower the front. Get on your elbows."

Winston followed his instructions again, lowering his front until his face was pressed against the bed and his chest damn near was.

He felt Steel's hands on his ass, and his body tensed in anticipation.

"Relax," Steel instructed, sliding the back of Winston's boxer briefs down as far as they would go, exposing the smooth globes of his ass to the air. Steel pulled his cheeks apart and Winston felt himself redden from embarrassment. This wasn't his first time, but the fact that it was Steel he was with made him feel like it was again.

"Damn, Win, that's one *fuckable* ass." Steel ran his thumb over Winston's hole, making him jump a bit. "Don't worry. I'm going to go easy on you. Unless of course you don't want me to."

At his current angle, Winston couldn't see what was going on behind him so it surprised him when Steel leaned forward and gently nipped at the pale flesh of his ass. Like earlier when he'd moved from one of Winston's nipples to the other, Steel trailed kisses and bites along Winston's ass, though this time he stopped right in the center.

"Mmm, wow," Winston hummed when Steel's tongue began to swirl around his puckered hole. Winston arched his back, spreading his legs until the elastic band of the boxer briefs dug into his thighs painfully. He barely noticed, though; his entire focus was on the pleasure Steel's tongue was giving him.

Steel tongued Winston's hole with enthusiasm, holding the cheeks apart and probing as deep as he could. Winston buried his fingers in the comforter to resist reaching down and jerking himself; he'd been excited for a long while, and he felt like the slightest stimulation could set him off.

Winston heard the sound of a cap being opened, and Steel's tongue disappeared, replaced by the pressure of a finger. Winston forced himself to relax as Steel's finger penetrated the tight ring of his hole, gritting his teeth through the momentary discomfort. Steel's finger curved up inside of him, brushing against the hard bundle of nerves that was his prostate, and the discomfort vanished, replaced by pleasure intense enough to push Winston rapidly toward the edge of orgasm. Only his self-control kept him from plummeting over that edge. Steel inadvertently helped with this by inserting a second finger. The twinge of pain brought Winston back from the precipice.

Steel removed his fingers. Winston glanced over his shoulder and saw Steel rolling a condom down the length of his cock, a bottle of lube tucked under his elbow.

He could not take his eyes off the sight of Steel preparing to enter him. Winston straightened, wriggling his underwear down and off before lying on his back on the bed, getting comfortable on the pillows. His first and maybe only time with Steel wasn't going to be uncomfortable.

Condom on, Steel squirted a liberal amount of lube into his hand and slicked up his latex-sheathed cock. Winston took one of the extra pillows and slid it beneath his lower back for a better angle. He lay there, legs parted, as Steel hurried onto the bed, kneeling between his thighs.

"You ready for this?" Steel asked, putting more lube onto his already slicked-up fingers. Winston nodded—he didn't trust himself to speak—and Steel applied the slick gel to Winston's hole, pushing his middle finger inside a few times, making sure Winston was well prepared.

Steel rubbed the head of his cock against Winston's hole, searching for the right angle to slide inside.

Winston's heart hammered in his chest, anticipation building until he finally felt Steel's cock pressing inside. Steel wasn't small, but he seemed much bigger entering him this way than he had going down Winston's throat. It had been some time, and the burn of Steel's entry drew a small grunt of pain from Winston.

Steel stopped, studying Winston's face. "Are you okay?"

"Don't stop," Winston said. "I'll be fine in a minute. Don't stop."

Steel ignored him, holding still with a little over a third of his length held inside Winston's hole. The pain at last receded, and Winston gave Steel a nod. It was all the encouragement Steel needed; he quickly buried the rest of his length inside the warm heat of Winston's body.

Winston reached up, hooking his fingers behind Steel's neck and pulling him down for a searing kiss. From that point, Winston's memories became a blur of heat and passion: the incredible feeling of

Steel's cock driving inside of him, their lips and tongues clashing again and again, the scent of their sweat and sex. It might have lasted five minutes; it might have lasted fifty—he couldn't tell in the fog of sex. When his orgasm finally came, it ripped through him like lightning, stealing his breath and sending spots of white light dancing before his eyes.

The only indication that Steel was coming was a half-swallowed grunt and the way he went rigid for a moment. When his orgasm passed, Steel withdrew from Winston, collapsing onto his back beside him.

Winston was powerless against his exhaustion as it sapped his strength, tugging at his awareness. He didn't even register the sticky aftermath of his orgasm on his stomach and chest. He heard Steel say something—his focus was too far gone to comprehend what it was—and then he was asleep.

Forty-Seven

STEEL LAY NEXT to Winston, his limbs refusing to move. That had been without a doubt the most intense orgasm he'd ever had, made so by the way his brain constantly reminded him it was Winston's ass fitting snugly around his cock like a glove—like he'd needed the reminder.

He could tell by the sound of Winston's breathing that he was asleep. *Guess I did a good job, then,* he thought with some pride. His body finally started listening to him again, and the first thing he did was reach down and remove the condom before wrapping it in tissue from the bedside table and tossing it into the nearby garbage can. He really wanted to take a shower, but couldn't bother with moving quite that much yet.

Steel turned his head, looking at Winston's face as he slept beside him. Having Winston there at his side just felt right, as if it were what was meant to be. Steel wasn't one for spending the night with lovers; he never felt comfortable enough with any of his sexual partners to do that. To him, sleeping next to each other was somehow more intimate that the act of sex itself. It implied absolute trust, and Steel didn't trust lightly. In fact, the only person he could recall ever sleeping with was Winston.

He trusted Winston, absolutely and without question, always had. He had been so stubborn for so long, but the person who seemed to be destined for him had been there right beside him from the very start. If he thought about his future, he could never see himself with anyone else, no matter how hard he tried. It was always Winston. It had always *been* Winston, but fear of being alone had kept him from seeing it.

He didn't want to be afraid anymore. What was the point of that? Living in fear would do nothing for him, nothing but make him miserable and lonely. Steel was the master of his own fate, and he'd make his own decisions, not let them be made for him.

Mostly recovered from the post-orgasmic lethargy, Steel decided to help get Winston comfortable in the bed. He needed sleep after what he'd been through. Steel wouldn't mind getting to sleep, either, but he was concerned that Winston would have another nightmare, spurred on by being inside the building where his father died. He wanted to be awake and alert if that happened, so he could be there for Winston.

Steel gently rolled Winston's body enough to tug the comforter out from under him so he could cover him up. He tried his hardest not to wake him, but Winston started anyway, blinking at him in surprise. He muttered something that might have been "What's happening?" though Steel couldn't be sure.

"Just go back to sleep," he said in a soft, cajoling tone.

Winston ignored him, sitting up so that Steel could better get the bed prepared for sleep. "Listen," he said, an uncertainty in his voice that gave Steel pause. "About earlier—I know what I said a few days ago, but...but I can't not have you around, Steel. I'll do this however you want—one-night stand, a fuck-buddies arrangement, whatever it is you're wanting."

Steel was surprised. "You're willing to make yourself a fuck buddy just to be close to me?"

Winston looked away. "Yes. I meant what I said that night—I have real feelings for you, but if I can't have that, I can at least have part of you."

"You're so stupid," Steel muttered, pulling Winston into his arms. "I don't want a fuck buddy. I don't want a one-night stand. I want to try this—us. For real."

Winston's gaze shot up, meeting Steel's, his shock clear on his face. Steel wasn't insulted by it, though; he could understand it, based on his behavior the last time they spoke about that particular topic. "Really?"

Steel caressed Winston's cheek with the back of his fingers. "I mean it. I feel the same way you do, Winston. I can't imagine a future for me where you're not in it. I don't *want* a future that you're not a part of. I've been afraid for a long time, afraid that I'm not good enough for you—"

"Steel—"

"No, Winston, let me finish. I was afraid that I wasn't good enough for you, that I couldn't give you what you deserve. I didn't want to hurt you. Now, though, all I can think about is how much it hurts to be apart. I can't promise forever—but I promise that I will do my best to give you forever."

Winston, eyes shining wetly, threw his arms around Steel, ducking his head against Steel's chest. Steel could feel Winston's hot tears against his chest.

"Come on, let's get into bed." Steel settled back on the bed, back against the headboard, pulling Winston into his arms, shifting until they were both in a comfortable place, Winston's back against Steel's front, Steel's arms around his waist, holding him closely. They remained like that until they both fell asleep.

Forty-Eight

WINSTON WOKE UP the next morning in Steel's arms. He couldn't believe the previous night wasn't some fever dream of his, though once Steel was awake, he showed Winston in no uncertain terms just how real last night was. They were so busy that by the time Winston remembered he was supposed to go to Coffee by Constance it was nearly noon.

"Mom is going to kill me," Winston muttered, searching for his cell phone. When he finally found it, the battery was dead. Winston groaned. He would be in for an earful from his mother, no doubt. He borrowed Steel's phone and called his mother.

"I was wondering when you'd be calling," Constance said instead of a hello when she answered.

"My cell phone died," he explained sheepishly. "I was too tired to remember to put it on the charger last night."

"I figured you would be tired. I'll let Wei know you're up, and he'll send someone around to get you."

"Okay," Winston said, surprised he didn't receive a lecture about making sure his phone was charged. Maybe he shouldn't have been; considering the night he'd had, it made sense that Constance would cut him some slack. He didn't expect it to last too long, though. Constance would be back to normal soon enough.

"Wei's going to send someone around to pick us up," Winston informed Steel.

"Hopefully that gives us enough time to take a shower," Steel grinned. "After last night and this morning, I think we need it."

"Me more than you," Winston grumbled. "We definitely need a shower, but we don't have much time, since the coffee shop's not that far from here."

Steel shot Winston a lewd look. "We can take a shower together to save time."

It turned out whoever Wei sent to get them wasn't patient, and as Winston stepped out of the shower, there came a loud knock on the door that persisted.

"I bet it's Jesse," Steel growled, wrapping his towel around his waist and stomping, still dripping water, out and to the front door. "I'm going to kill the little *puk—*"

Steel's sudden silence was disconcerting. Winston followed Steel's example, wrapping the towel around himself and going into the living room. "What the hell are you doing here?" he blurted, seeing Noah standing in the doorway.

"You two both just got out of the shower? Together?" Noah asked shrewdly, looking between the two damp men. "You *finally* stopped being idiots and did it, huh?"

Winston knew he was bright red—he could feel the heat in his face, neck, ears, and even across his chest. He wanted desperately to change the topic, so he said, "Please tell me you didn't drive here."

Noah scoffed. "What? You think Wei would let me drive, even though I have my international driver's license? Chris is in the car waiting. So...tell me! Who was top? Winston, right?"

"Why would you think that Winston was the top?" Steel demanded huffily.

"I don't know, Steel, you look like one of those guys who is super tough by a total bottom in the bedroom," Noah said innocently.

"I'll have you know I was top both times," Steel said hotly.

Noah beamed victoriously. "Aha! So it was two times?"

Winston groaned in embarrassment. "You totally let him trick you, Steel."

Steel scowled at both of them. "We should get dressed so we can go meet Wei."

"Don't try to sneak a quickie in," Noah called behind them.

Steel flipped him off and shut the bedroom door. "He's enjoying this way too much."

"Think it's revenge for the way we teased him about Wei?" Winston asked, slipping into some of the clothes that he kept in Steel's closet.

"Definitely. And I don't think it's going to be stopping any time soon, either."

Winston sighed. "We should have been nicer to him back then."

Once they were both dressed, they followed Noah down to where Chris was waiting in a car Winston had never seen before. He wasn't surprised; the Dragons owned a few auto-body shops around the district—another way the group made money legitimately so they didn't have to resort to illegal means like drugs or gun trafficking. They were always coming across new vehicles that could be gotten at affordable prices.

Thankfully aside from a few smirks thrown their way in the rearview mirror, Noah didn't keep up the teasing while they were in the car, though Winston wasn't getting his hopes up too high. This would be a golden opportunity for Noah to get revenge, and he had no doubt the American wasn't done with them yet.

They reached the coffee shop to find Constance waiting outside. Winston was surprised to see she'd turned the sign on the door to "closed." She hugged him tightly as soon as he was out of the car. "Are you all right?"

"I'm fine, *Mah Ma*. Really, I am."

"I'll bet he's feeling a little more than fine," Noah remarked. "Sorry," he added quickly when Constance gave him a warning glare.

"Are you sure you're okay? After last night?"

"I'm fine," Winston assured her, kissing her forehead. "You don't have to worry about me."

Constance chuckled. "You can't tell a mother not to worry about her child." She sounded emotional and cleared her throat. "Since you're okay, you should head on up and talk to Wei. I'm sure he's going to have a lot of questions."

"I think I have a few answers for him," Hong said, stepping up next to his sister and nephew. His appearance surprised Winston; he hadn't even noticed Hong.

He looked around and spotted his own car across the street. "You got it out of impound?"

"Consider it an apology for the idiots arresting you."

"How are you going to get back to the precinct?" Constance asked.

"Oh, my ride is over at the diner a block over eating his fill of lunch on me, so I'll be fine."

Winston saw Steel tense up, caught his eye, and shook his head subtly. He hadn't forgiven Hong—that sort of thing took time to work through—but he was ready to admit that he might have been wrong about him and at least give him a chance, for his mother's sake. Constance didn't ask much of him, so he could try to give her this.

"Then you should both get upstairs." Constance was clearly nervous that harsh words were going to be exchanged.

"I guess we should," Winston agreed.

Wei, Conroy, and Tony were sitting around the poker table, talking in low voices when Winston, Steel, Noah, and Hong walked in. Conroy glowered at Hong, but said nothing.

Wei, though, seemed to be expecting Hong; he nodded at him neutrally. "What did you find out?"

"Turns out the arrests were ordered by one of the team members. He's a new inspector, so he was looking to make a name for himself, thought this would be the way to do it. He didn't think we were moving fast enough, apparently, and ordered the roadblock. We managed to arrest quite a few of the racers, as you know," he added to Winston. "But we didn't get any hints about who the main organizers or financial backers might be."

"And now whoever they are, they're going to break up shop because they know the police are onto them." Wei sighed.

"They'll suspect we had a man on the inside," Hong agreed. "There's no way we'll be able to get to their leadership now."

The implications of their words sunk into Winston. "Wait, so all of that was for nothing?"

"No, not nothing," Hong said. "We managed to get some of the key racers, people who've been in it for a long time. If we're lucky, at least one of them will know something about the next rung up the chain of command. Not that I'm holding my breath. Dang is furious—I've never seen him so pissed off."

"What's he got to be pissed off about?" Conroy asked. "This bust makes him look good, don't it?"

"You'd think," Hong said. "Seems like he really wanted to bring the whole Dark Streets down, though."

"I wonder what his angle is," Steel mused. "You know the *puk gai* doesn't care about safety or crime in the city. There's got to be something in it for him."

"Think about it," Tony said, as if it were the most obvious thing in the world. "Bringing down the Dark Streets would increase his popularity dramatically, cementing his reputation with the people of the district. It would be a huge win for him."

"I don't really care about Dang and his motivations right now," Wei said. "I'm more concerned with finding the person using the Dark Streets to kill people."

"Maybe it's one of the racers the police arrested," Winston said hopefully.

"It's a possibility, but there's no real way to know for sure."

"Well, until the guy starts killing again," Conroy said with a frown.

"So now we just wait?" Steel asked, incredulous.

"There's not much else we can do at this point," said Hong. His cell phone rang, and he looked at the number and sighed. "Hold on."

Hong stepped away, talking fast into his phone. Winston didn't pay what he was saying much attention at first, thinking instead about all the work he'd put into the Dark Streets only for it to come to an end like this. It hardly seemed fair.

"Wait, there's been a murder where?" Hong asked, the tone of his voice drawing Winston's attention to him. A cop taking that tone of voice could never mean anything good. Hong repeated an address that didn't really mean anything to Winston until he saw the look on Steel's face.

"What's wrong?" he asked Steel, brow furrowing in concern.

"The address Hong just said, that's where Min lived."

Forty-Nine

STEEL COULD THINK of nothing but Yao's young face the entire drive to the apartment the kid shared with his mother. He felt like a horrible person, but he prayed to god the apartment number was wrong, that it wasn't Yao's place.

"What kind of person would hurt a kid?" Winston asked, knuckles tight on the steering wheel.

"There are plenty of people out there who would," Steel said darkly. "I've had personal experience with them, remember?" He'd had his fair share of bruises and scars when Winston met him, and he'd seen them.

"I remember," Winston said softly. "We shouldn't think the worst just yet, though, man. Yao might be fine."

He sees the world differently than I do, Steel thought, watching Winston as he drove. *Winston still believes the world is generally good.* Growing up, Steel had known just how dark the world actually was, a lesson he'd never forgotten. Steel didn't want to be the one to destroy Winston's worldview; it was a good and beautiful thing that Winston could still find good in the world. In fact, his bright attitude was one of the many things Steel loved about Winston, because it was so different from his own.

Steel almost wished Winston wasn't with him; he didn't want this to be the moment Winston's view was shattered if things turned out badly. But once Wei insisted on going, and Steel insisted on accompanying Wei, there had been no chance of leaving Winston behind. So Wei drove Hong, and Winston and Steel followed behind.

The sight of three police cars and an ambulance in front of the apartment building sent Steel's heart right into his throat. He wasn't a praying man, but all he could think was, *Whatever gods are out there, please let Yao be okay. Please.*

"How are we going to get inside past all these police officers?"

Steel didn't say anything; he felt like if he opened his mouth to speak he might throw up. They pulled the car to a stop behind Wei. Steel threw the seat belt off and was out the door before Winston even cut the engine.

"Steel," Wei called out as he hurried past on his way to the building, but Steel ignored him. He had to get inside, had to see for himself what had happened. He burst through the building doors, taking the stairs two or three at a time, weaving his way through residents gathered in the stairwell to discuss this latest excitement.

He reached Yao's floor, and sure enough there were two uniformed cops outside the door to the apartment he'd shared with his now dead brother and mother. Steel couldn't see past them into the apartment.

One of the officers saw Steel and turned, his wide shoulders blocking Steel's view even more. "What the hell do you think you're doing here?"

"I don't have time for this," Steel said, trying to push his way past the two police officers and into the apartment. The officers extended their arms, struggling to hold him back. "Get the fuck out of my way!"

One of the officers shoved Steel back hard, the other drawing his truncheon menacingly.

"Stand down, officers," Hong said from the stairwell. He flashed his badge at the two uniformed cops, who traded looks but didn't move to clear the doorway. "Did you hear me? I said stand down!"

"But, Inspector, this is—"

"Just do what you're told," Hong barked, and the two officers reluctantly stood aside.

Steel hurried past them and stopped cold just inside the doorway. Yao's mother lay on the floor between the couch and the television. The television was broken, lying on the ground. The woman was face up, eyes filmed over. She'd been stabbed multiple times in the chest, by the looks of it. The apartment was a mess, like there'd been a struggle. The most notable thing about the scene, though, was the symbol of the Twisted Vipers, a snake baring its fangs, its body twisted in on itself. It was spray painted on the floor just a few feet from the woman's corpse.

"Wei," Hong said in a low voice, pointing to the mark. "Just like the report said."

Winston stood just inside the door, taking in the scene. "You...you really think the Twisted Vipers did this?"

"Johnny Hwang isn't the kind of man to make threats idly," Wei said grimly. "This certainly looks like the kind of message he would send, too."

Steel searched around the living room, searching for any sign of Yao. He peered over the couch, went into the kitchen and opened every cabinet, every possible hiding place a kid might use—the kind he himself might have used once.

"What are you doing?" Hong asked, but Steel ignored him, going to the door to the one room and throwing it open to check inside. It was barren, but it had a closet, so he went there, opening it and then digging through the clothes for any sign of Yao. The bed was a simple mattress on the floor, so he couldn't be there. "You're contaminating a crime scene," Hong said from the bedroom door.

"There's a little boy who lives here," Steel explained, going back into the living room. "Named Yao. He's about seven. Any sign of him here?"

"The report didn't say anything about a boy," Hong said, frowning. "Just the woman."

"That means he might be okay," Steel said, pulling his phone out of his pocket. He dialed the number to Yao's phone and held the phone to his ear. He was surprised to find that his hands were trembling so much he thought he would drop his cell phone. "Come on, come on," he muttered impatiently, but it went to voicemail. "*Fucking damn it!*"

"Calm down," Winston said, stepping up and squeezing his hand tightly. "If he's out there and okay, we'll find him. I'll help you."

"Whatever you're doing out there, be careful," said Wei, face darkening. "I've got some business to take care of."

Fifty

"HE COULDN'T HAVE gone far if he's on foot," Steel said as Winston followed him out of the apartment building. He had an almost deranged expression on his face. Winston had never seen him like that and wondered what could have brought this on. He must somehow feel like he needed to save Yao, because their situations were similar in many ways.

"Which way do you think he went?"

"I have no idea," Winston said, feeling helpless. "Maybe we should drive around to see if we can find him that way?"

"If we drive around, we might miss him," Steel said. "We need to go on foot. I'll keep calling him." Steel already had the phone to his ear even as he said it. "Sonofabitch! Still voicemail. Why isn't he answering?"

"It's probably on silent," Winston reasoned. "Come on, Steel, we've got to stay calm if we're going to help him, okay?"

Steel nodded, taking several deep, ragged breaths in an attempt to calm himself. Winston could see how important this was to him and knew he would have to be the one to keep a steady head while they searched for him, because Steel couldn't be trusted to right then.

It would be hard to do, when it seemed like the rest of the world was about to fall apart around him. He'd never seen such hatred and anger on Wei's face before, even when Leo Tong and his rogue faction of the Twisted Vipers targeted Noah. There was no doubt in his mind that the business Wei needed to take care of involved preparations for a retaliation against the Twisted Vipers; there was no other recourse available to Wei, not if he wanted to maintain face. If he let this go unanswered after the Vipers left such a blatant message at the scene, he'd be creating an opening for every wannabe triad in the city to come after them.

The threat of a street war had always loomed over them, ever since the Dragons had assumed power with the goal of maintaining peace. It looked like the peace they'd been preserving would be coming to an end sooner rather than later.

Just the thought of it terrified Winston more than he wanted to admit. There would always be casualties in any war, and the idea that he could lose someone important to him—his mom, Shelby, the Dragons who were now like family to him. Steel.

Winston stopped walking. His chest constricted so tightly he might as well have been wrapped up by a boa constrictor. Steel was a Dragon, a warrior, and there was a very real chance that Winston might lose him in whatever conflict might lie ahead.

That wouldn't be fair; he'd only just finally gotten Steel. It was selfish, he knew, but he couldn't change how he felt. If he thought he could manage it, he'd drag Steel away from there. They'd go abroad, maybe Japan or even the United States. Get Noah to show them around. Anything to get Steel away from the fighting.

It was a foolish thought, he knew; Steel's place was with the Dragons, and not even Winston would be able to convince him to turn his back on them in a fight, and in reality, Winston wouldn't want to. The Dragons stood for something, and he was proud of Steel—proud of all of them—for that.

They walked the block, calling out Yao's name in the hopes he would hear them and come out, but he didn't. Every minute that passed made Steel more restless. He was practically bouncing out of his skin and only seemed to calm down when Winston took his hand and held it firmly.

They'd nearly completed the block—Winston could see the apartment building ahead—when Steel stopped walking, tugging Winston around to face him. "What if they took him?"

"What if who took him? The Vipers?"

Steel nodded. "Yeah. What if they took him and that's why he's not answering his phone?"

"Steel, why would the Vipers take Yao? It would have been a better message for them to have killed him, too, if they had him. It would show they were serious and really challenge Wei. I just can't see how kidnapping could fall into their plan here."

"You're right, you're right. Sorry. I just can't stop thinking about that kid and what he might be going through. I told him I'd be his big brother, that I'd protect him."

"Listen to me," Winston said firmly, stepping in front of Steel and taking his face in both hands, holding him steady so their eyes could meet. "This isn't your fault. None of the things that have happened to this kid in his life are your fault, and you can't take them on yourself. I won't let you, okay?"

Steel nodded his head and bit his lower lip. "Thanks, Win."

"That's one thing I'm good for," Winston said with a cheeky grin. "Just one, there are others."

Steel managed a weak smile. "I know a few of the others."

"Should we start searching in the car now? I can drive slow."

"I guess that's the next step, yeah. I thought we would have found him by now."

Just as they reached the car, Steel's cell phone rang. "Holy shit, it's him," Steel said, dropping his phone as he fumbled to answer the call. He managed to catch it, though, and brought it to his ear. "Yao, are you okay? Where are you, *daih dai*?" Steel listened for a moment, nodding. "I know where that is. Stay right there; don't move and don't talk to anyone. I'm on my way."

Steel hung up the phone and set off toward the car at a jog, leaving Winston to follow behind him. "He's about two blocks over at the McDonald's there."

"Huh," Winston said, impressed. "Smart place to pick—people around, not somewhere someone not wanting to be noticed would go. Good kid."

The parking lot was crowded, as usual with McDonald's, but they found a space quickly and hurried into the fast food restaurant. It was easy enough to spot Yao despite the crowd; a lone child at a booth was noticeable. He had an expression on his face that Winston hadn't seen in a long time, not since the night he'd first met Steel.

"You go on over there and talk to him for a minute," Winston said quietly, nudging Steel forward. "I need to do something real quick."

The night he met Steel, he'd brought him food, because even in a ten-year-old's mind, it felt like the right thing to do. After what this kid had been through, Winston thought he could use a little kindness in his life. He ordered two kid's meals, one cheeseburger and one chicken nugget, and carried the tray of food to the booth Yao and Steel now sat in.

"Here you go." He placed the boxes down in front of him. "I figured you could use something to eat; I know I can't sit in a McDonald's for too long and not eat anything."

Yao hesitantly opened the first box, pulling out the burger and a handful of fries, and started eating.

Winston and Steel waited until he had finished the first Happy Meal and started in on the second before they asked questions.

"All right, little man, I need you to tell me what happened," Steel said gently.

"This man came to the door," Yao started, voice trembling a bit. "Mommy let him in. He wasn't very nice. He hurt Mommy and then painted a mark on the ground."

"It was just one man?" Winston asked, raising an eyebrow. He would have guessed a group, two or three, if they were from the Twisted Vipers. "Can you tell me what he looked like?"

Yao dug a cell phone out of his bag. "I took his picture. When he came, I hid, but after he hurt Mommy, I took his picture. He got mad and chased me, but I was too fast for him."

Winston took the phone Yao offered him and went to the photo albums, impressed that Yao had managed to keep his head about himself long enough to get the guy's picture—he was just a kid. The phone was basic, so it was easy to find them right away. There were only three pictures—one of Yao being goofy, one of Yao with his mother—a rare happy moment for the two, no doubt—and the final shot, what must have been an ambush snapshot of a man holding a knife, caught with his mouth slightly agape.

"Holy shit, I recognize this guy!" Winston passed the phone to Steel so he could look at it.

"What? How?"

The features were remarkable in just how unremarkable they were. He thought back to the times he'd seen that face, handing him GPS devices and giving him racing instructions. It was him without a doubt. "He's one of the guys in the Dark Streets. He handed out the equipment and gave racing instructions. He's sure as hell not a Twisted Viper."

"What the hell is going on?"

"I think...I think we're being played," Winston said slowly. "We need to get to the others. Let's take Yao and drop him off at the coffee shop. Mom will know what to do with him."

It wasn't hard for them to convince Yao to go with them—though it wasn't as if he had many options. He rode quietly in the backseat as they made the return journey to Coffee by Constance.

"Shelby said Wei and some of the others already left," Steel said, putting his phone down on his lap. "She didn't know where they were going. Hopefully Constance does."

Winston fidgeted, thinking about the trouble that was barreling toward them. "We really need to stop everything from escalating if we can. This picture should be enough to prove to the Vipers we weren't involved and to prove to Wei and the others that the Vipers didn't do this."

"Even if we manage to do that, it'll only be a temporary fix. You know that, don't you?"

"I do. But however long we can delay this, we should, right?"

Steel's eyes flicked toward Yao in the rearview mirror, and he nodded.

Winston brought the car to a stop at a red light. A loud vibrating noise filled the car, making both Winston and Steel jump. "What the hell is that?"

"I think someone's phone is ringing," Yao said simply.

Winston and Steel both checked their phones; neither of them were ringing.

"Is it you, little guy?"

Yao shook his head.

"Wait, Win, it's coming from in here." Steel opened the glove compartment and pulled out Winston's race phone. "Why would anyone be calling you on this?"

Winston frowned, taking it from him. "I have no idea." He answered it. "Hello?"

"Noisy, that you?

"Mimi?" Winston could hardly believe it. How had she even known which phone number was his? More importantly, she sounded frightened. "Mimi, what's wrong? What's going on?"

"One of the coordinators—Winston, I can't—I need your help. Please, Noisy. I don't know what's going on, but—he says he's going to kill me if you don't come."

"Where? Come where, Mimi?"

"The place where we finished the race down the Peak. Please, hurry." With that, the line went dead.

Winston repeated the conversation for Steel, who adamantly protested Winston going. "No way in hell. There is no way in hell you're going to meet some psychopath. Are you nuts?"

"Someone has to," Winston said impatiently and pulled his car to a stop in front of his mother's coffee shop. "I can't just leave her like this. There's a reason she called me specifically. Whoever this nut job is, he's after me. I can't let Mimi suffer because of me, and you know that."

"You're not going alone," Steel insisted stubbornly. "I'm going with you."

"Someone has to go find Wei and the others and tell them what's going on," Winston reasoned. "If you don't do that, who knows what will get started between the Dragons and the Twisted Vipers. I'll be fine. Don't worry about me."

"Don't be stupid," said Steel affectionately. "Of course I'm going to worry about you. But you're right. You go take care of whoever this Mimi chick is, and I'll stop a war from breaking out."

Winston huffed. "Yours sounds more interesting when you put it that way."

Fifty-One

STEEL EXPLAINED EVERYTHING to Constance as quickly as he could, pausing only long enough for her to bring out one of her delicious baked goods for Yao to enjoy. When he finished, Constance untied her apron and tossed it onto the counter. "Let's go," she said. "I know where Wei asked Hwang to meet him."

"How do you know?" Steel asked, surprised.

"Because it was my idea," she said simply. "Now come on. We don't have a lot of time."

"What are we going to do with the kid?" Steel asked.

"Bring him with us. He'll be safer where Wei and the Dragons are, anyway. Come on, come on. Get a move on."

Steel supposed Constance was right, to a point. But what if despite their efforts fighting did break out? Then Yao would be right in the line of fire. *I'll just have to protect him, then,* he thought fiercely. He'd promised to do that already, and he was a man of his word. He felt somehow responsible for what happened to Yao's mother, and he wouldn't let the kid down again.

"We're taking my car," Constance said, leading them toward her minivan in its usual parking spot across the street from the coffee shop.

"Fine, but I'm driving," Steel said before taking the keys from her. "Just tell me when and where to turn."

They drove in a heavy silence, aside from Constance pointing him in the right direction. They didn't even have the radio on. Listening to the latest pop sensation just didn't seem appropriate for the circumstances. The downside to silence, though, was that it gave Steel ample to think.

Despite the dangerous situation he was driving into, he couldn't stop thinking about Winston and what possible danger *he* was heading toward. Sure, Steel was about to drive into a possible standoff between the Dragons and a dangerous triad, but that was par for the course when you were a Dragon. Winston, though, was on his way to face down a potentially insane serial killer.

No. He thought back to the photo Yao showed them. *Not a serial killer—at least not the kind on American dramas. A hit man.* Everything about the guy screamed professional. There was something big going on behind the scenes here, though Steel couldn't see how it all came together just yet. He didn't need to know all of that, though. All that mattered was the fact that Winston was in danger, and Steel was powerless to help him.

Or was he?

"Hey, Constance, you have Hong's number, right?"

Constance gave him a sidelong glance. "Yeah, why?"

"Will you call him for me? I think he can help Winston."

Constance's eyes widened. "Oh my god, you're right! Why didn't I think of that before?" She dug her phone out of her purse, scrolled to Hong's number, and dialed it. "People don't give you enough credit for your intelligence, Steel," she said, passing the phone to him.

"Thanks...I think."

When Hong answered, Steel once again walked through what they knew now, ending with his and Winston's separate missions. "The thing is," he finished, "I don't know where it is Winston might end up."

"Oh, that won't be a problem," Hong said with surprising assurance. "We bugged his car when he refused to drive one of ours in the Dark Streets."

"For once the police being shifty works in our favor." Steel sighed in relief. "Just find out where he is and get there as fast as you can, Hong. This is the guy who killed the woman in that apartment, and I bet killed all the Dark Streets racers, too."

"I'll protect him, don't worry," Hong said before ending the call.

"You better," Steel muttered, even though the line was dead.

"Turn left up here," Constance instructed, drawing him back to their situation. "We're almost there."

Steel recognized their surroundings. It was an industrial area that fell half into Dragon territory and half into Twisted Viper territory. When Wei and the others had taken the Eastern District from the Nine Stars, they'd made an agreement with the Twisted Vipers to keep the territory neutral—neither group operated inside it. As far as Steel or the Dragons could tell, the Vipers had kept their end of that agreement.

"You picked a smart place, Constance," Steel said, earning a smile.

Steel spotted Conroy's car, along with a few others, parked in front of an old warehouse and turned in, bringing Constance's minivan to a stop beside the car Chris had been driving that morning. "Okay, you stay here with Yao. Hopefully we're not too late."

"I'll look after him, don't worry. Go on and stop this before it gets any uglier than it already is."

Steel exited the minivan and made his way to the door. Before he reached it, two Twisted Viper thugs stepped into his way. Steel recognized both of them from the meeting Hwang had called them to.

"Just where the fuck you think you goin', punk?"

"I don't have time for this shit," Steel said impatiently. What was it with people trying to stop him from getting places he needed to go today? "Just let me in. I need to talk to my boss."

"Yeah, that's not happening," one of them sneered. "You can just get back into your minivan and go back to your baking."

"Should have just gotten out of my way," Steel muttered. He drew his fist back and sucker punched him right in the jaw. He stumbled to the side and Steel shoved him into the second man and stormed into the warehouse. Stacks of old crates lined the walls, but the center was clear. From the looks of it, violence hadn't broken out, but tempers were flaring. Wei stood on one side, Conroy and Tony to either side of him, four more Dragons—Chris, Smile, Jesse, and Walker—behind them. Hwang stood alone, though he did have six Vipers behind him.

"—these allegations," Hwang was shouting. "Did you just call me here to waste my time, Tseng?"

"Your mark was in the house, Hwang," said Wei, steel in his gaze and true heat in his voice. "After our last meeting, am I supposed to just ignore that?"

"Why would I be here if I did it, Tseng? This is just you trying to cover your own asses after you wasted not one but *two* of my men," Hwang spat derisively. "Sure that idiot Rundown was absolutely useless, but he was mine, and that's that."

"The Dragons had nothing to do with that," Steel called loudly, drawing every eye in the room to him. The Vipers with Hwang started toward him, but Hwang held up a hand and they paused.

"Well, if it isn't the very Dragon responsible for the hit on Rundown," Hwang said, lips curving downward in distaste. "Tseng, you really need to teach your people some better manners."

Steel ignored the remark. "I had nothing to do with what happened to Rundown. He was a *puk gai*, sure, and I *should* have done it, but I didn't, just like your people didn't have anything to do with what happened today."

"What are you talking about?" Wei snapped.

"I'm talking about this." Steel pulled the cell phone he had given Yao out of his pocket. "I have a picture of the person responsible for what happened today—and probably for every death in the races."

"Bullshit," Hwang jeered.

"If you'd like, I can show you," Steel said, opening the picture on the phone. He stepped into the center space between the two leaders. Wei and Hwang stepped up to him, both of them studying the picture on the phone.

"Who is that?" Wei asked.

"A hired hitman would be my best guess," Hwang mused. "Which means that whoever hired him intended to frame the Twisted Vipers in this." He glanced at Wei. "It seems someone wants us at odds, Mr. Tseng."

"Whoever they are damn near got their wish."

"How did you come by this photo?" Hwang inquired. The change in his persona was incredible; he'd gone from full of spite and rage to calm and collected. How did anyone manage that?

"A kid also lived in the house. I'd given this phone in case he needed help—that's a long story—and he managed to snap this picture and escape."

Hwang's eyes glinted. "So he might hold more information about this hit man, then? I would very much like to speak to the child."

"No way in hell," Steel said firmly. He probably should have phrased it better, but he simply would not allow a bastard like Johnny Hwang near Yao.

"Steel," Wei said firmly. "If it helps us figure this out, then we'll let Hwang talk to the boy. With us there, of course."

"Wei, he's just a kid, and he watched his mother get murdered," Steel protested. He was surprised that Wei was taking Hwang's side in this.

"I understand that, but this is bigger than that. Someone almost brought us to war with the Twisted Vipers. We're being manipulated by someone, and I want to know who. If It's even slightly possible that the kid overheard or saw something that could help us, then I'm sorry, but we're going to find out."

"Constance isn't going to like this," Steel said, finding a sort of righteous enjoyment in the way Wei flinched at the mention of her name. "He's with her outside in the car."

"All right, Hwang," Wei said to the Twisted Viper leader. "You can talk to the boy—but just you. I don't want your people scaring him."

One of the Twisted Vipers growled, but Hwang just said, "As you insist."

Wei started with Hwang out the door.

"Oh, and Wei," Steel called behind him. "Remind me to fill you in on what's going on with Winston."

Wei frowned. "Something's going on with Winston?"

"Don't worry about it; you handle this. Hong is on Winston," Steel assured him. *At least, I hope he is.*

Fifty-Two

IT TOOK WINSTON nearly thirty minutes to get to the parking lot that had acted as the finish line for the mountain race, thanks to an unusual amount of midday traffic. When he pulled into the parking lot, he spotted nothing out of the ordinary. There were three parked cars and no sign of a black town car. It took him three passes around the lot to realize that one of the three cars belonged to Mimi.

Winston pulled into the spot beside that car and got out. A look into the passenger seat revealed one of those GPS systems that were used in the races along with a note. Winston tried the door; it was unlocked. He grabbed the note and scanned it quickly.

Take the GPS and go to the indicated destination. Leave your cell phone—both the race phone and your personal phone—behind.

Winston sighed. He should have known it would be something like this. It felt like a game, a way for this guy to manipulate and play with him. This guy had Mimi, though, and Winston couldn't in good conscience let him harm her, not when it was clear that it was Winston he wanted. Mimi was a bystander in this—she wasn't innocent, considering her role in illegal street racing, but she didn't deserve to be brought into what appeared to be a power struggle between some unknown individual and the Dragons.

Winston took the GPS and left his phones on the seat. He wanted to contact Wei and the others, but who knew if he even could at this point? For all Winston knew, Steel was too late and the fighting had already broken out. He couldn't think about that right then, though. He had his own duty to see to, just like Steel had his.

Please, Steel, be okay.

Winston got back into the car and activated the GPS. The route it highlighted would take him along numerous back streets and avoided any major thoroughfares. The final destination looked to be—unsurprisingly, given where Winston had found himself going in the various races—a parking garage in the Eastern District. Tactically speaking, it seemed like a pretty sound idea, using a parking garage; there was usually only one way in and one way out, so this guy would definitely have the advantage.

Winston was afraid, and he wasn't ashamed to admit it. His had dad once told him that fear was the best way to get the true measure of a man. "It's not about whether he's afraid or not," he'd said, "but about how he responds to that fear. Does he let the fear direct him, or does he overcome it?"

Winston wouldn't let his fear direct him, not this time. There was someone's life at stake.

Now that he knew where his destination was he elected *not* to follow the path the GPS had laid out. What if this killer had picked a long roundabout way of getting there to buy time for himself? Winston wanted to get there as quickly as possible, and hopefully in doing so gain a bit of an advantage for himself. He needed *something* to even the field, even if it was only a bit.

The parking garage was empty, its sign turned off. Winston wondered if they were doing any repairs on it. There was no attendant on duty at the entrance, but the guardrail was up, so Winston drove in cautiously. He didn't catch sight of Mimi or the killer or a black town car on the first level, so he continued up to the second. Again he found nothing.

On the third level, he saw the car in the parking spot farthest from him, but didn't see Mimi or anyone else. He brought the car to a stop next to the Lincoln and climbed out hesitantly, eyes peeled and ears straining for any sign of movement. He slowly approached the town car, trying to peer inside through its darkly tinted windows.

"Thank you for coming so quickly," a male voice called, words echoing loudly in the empty parking garage. Winston wheeled around and saw the man from the races, the man from Yao's photo. How had he gotten behind him? However he'd done it, he was now blocking Winston's exit. He had one arm tightly around Mimi's neck, and in the other hand he gripped a revolver. "Not that I expected anything less from one of the legendary Dragons of the Eastern District."

Mimi's eyes widened, and she gasped in shock.

"Oh, did you not know he was one of the Dragons? I knew it all along. In fact, his involvement with the Dark Streets was entirely my doing."

"Well, I hate to disappoint you, but I'm no Dragon. Friend of a Dragon, sure, but not one myself."

The man scowled. "Don't lie to me! I've followed you, I know you're connected to the Dragons, just like I've known you've been spying on the races for the police."

"Spying?" Mimi repeated, eyes narrowing. "That bust was your fault!"

"Nope, actually it wasn't; that wasn't the plan. Who *are* you, anyway?"

"Does it matter? Though I guess since I have the pleasure of knowing both of your names, it would only be polite. And I'm going to kill you, anyway. You can call me Mr. Yang. Now, we might as well all get comfy, yes?" He released Mimi then and shoved her toward Winston.

"Why are you doing this?" Mimi demanded, real fear causing a tremble in her voice.

"You're asking why? What a ridiculous question. Because it's what I was paid to do, of course."

Winston snorted derisively. "Figures. You're nothing more than some hired goon, running around doing what he's told."

Mr. Yang bared his teeth at that. "Careful now, you'll hurt my feelings, boy. I'd hate to have to take out any perceived slights on your lovely sister when I'm done with you."

Winston stiffened, clenching his fists tightly. Who the fuck did this guy think he was, threatening his sister like that?

"So you someone hired you to pit the Twisted Vipers and Dragons against each other? Why?"

"I don't ask questions," Mr. Yang said with a wave of his hand. "But surely you've realized that your precious Dragons have enemies, Mr. Chang? Enemies that would love to see the streets pour blood if it meant an end to them."

"And lucky for them there's people like you willing to do anything for money," Winston said coldly.

"If not me, someone else would do it," Mr. Yang said. "It's the way of the world, boy."

"Your plan isn't going to work," Winston said, desperate to keep Mr. Yang talking and *not* shooting. "There's not going to be any turf war—at least not today. We know it was you who killed the woman and left the Twisted Viper symbol behind."

Mr. Yang shook his head deprecatingly. "You think you've won because you managed to delay me? You think it's as easy as that? Look at the world around you. It's time you stopped thinking like a child and saw the world as an adult. The fight is inevitable. What you've put off today will come in the end. It is unstoppable!"

Mimi suddenly let out a choked scream and took off running on shaking legs toward a door not too far from them that was marked "stairs." She didn't make it more than a few feet before Mr. Yang leveled his gun on her and pulled the trigger. The loudness of the shot was magnified by the parking garage's acoustics, and it left Winston's ears ringing. The bullet caught Mimi in the right shoulder, and her body arched back as she fell to the hard concrete floor.

Winston had never seen someone shot before; it was horrifying, but he was unable to turn away. Nothing prepared someone for seeing it in real life, not television or movies, not video games. Winston could feel the moment being burned into the memory tracks of his brain. He doubted he would ever be able to forget the sight of blood and flesh splattering, the sound of Mimi's body being struck, or the sound of the gun ringing in his ears long after the shot was fired.

Winston's heart raced dangerously fast; he felt like he was going to have a heart attack. He saw his opening as Mr. Yang walked to stand over Mimi's fallen form, gun in hand and finger prone on the trigger. There was no way he'd be able to get past him without getting shot; it was a long run down the ramp with no cover.

He needed another plan.

What he really needed was a weapon, but he didn't carry any on him. He'd have to reconsider that, if he lived through this. He felt around in his pockets, hopeful he'd find *something* he could use. When his fingers closed around his car keys, he got an idea. Most of the upgrades he'd done to his car had been for looks, but he'd had an auto starter added for convenience, so he didn't have to sit in a freezing cold car and wait for the heater to kick in during the winter.

Maybe he could get the upper hand on this guy with surprise. It was really the only chance he had, so he decided to go for it. He moved quickly but quietly toward Mr. Yang, left hand behind his back as he clutched his keys, his thumb touching the auto start button. He wanted to make sure he was as close as he could be before he hit that button.

Finally he could wait no longer; he was within arm's reach of Mr. Yang. He pressed the button with his thumb, waiting on the balls of his feet. The sound of his car's engine roaring to life was loud in the parking garage and it had the desired effect. Mr. Yang jerked around, face surprised and somewhat fearful. Winston shoved him hard as soon as he turned, sending him sprawling onto his back, his head hitting the concrete hard and the gun sliding several feet away.

Winston hurried to Mimi, relieved to see that she was still breathing and semiconscious. "Oh god," he muttered, catching sight of all of the blood. He didn't know what to do; did he leave her there, face down on the cold ground, or did he move her? Could he injure her further by moving her? "Don't worry, I'll go get help for you, okay? It's going to be all right."

He heard Mr. Yang start to stir, and Winston rose, taking off running as fast as his feet could carry him down the ramp toward what he hoped would be safety.

"You can't escape your fate, Mr. Chang," Mr. Yang called behind him. He heard another gunshot, sounding like an explosion in his ears and felt shards from the splintered concrete from where the bullet hit the ground just behind him pelt the back of his legs.

I'm going to die. The thought struck him with the force of a meteor, but it left him strangely...calm. He thought facing his death would be more terrifying, but he truly felt no fear. He didn't want to die, but if it was his fate, like Mr. Yang supposed, then he would meet it honorably and without hesitation. Though not his only regret, his biggest was that he didn't get to spend more time with Steel as a couple.

The thought of Steel spurred fresh energy into him, and he gained speed. All he needed to do was turn the corner and he'd be safe, he knew it.

The gun went off again just as he turned the corner; he heard the sound of the bullet striking the concrete, possibly right where he'd been moments before. But it didn't matter because he could see the exit. His lungs and legs felt as if they were on fire, but he could see the way out, and safety. Someone out there would have a cell phone, and he could call for help for Mimi.

"Winston!"

Winston couldn't believe what he saw and heard at first, assuming instead that it was some sort of manifestation of his mind to comfort him before his death. There was no way Hong and what might have been a small army of police officers were there. How could they be? No one knew he would be there.

"Don't shoot," hallucination-Hong called out to the other officers. "Don't shoot, that's my nephew!"

Oh my god, he's real. They're all real. It was a miracle. Winston kept running, right up until Hong's arms came around him. Hong was saying something to him, but the blood rushing in his ears drowned out his words. When he finally came to, he heard lots of shouting and realized that Hong had his gun drawn.

Winston looked back the way he'd come. There stood Mr. Yang, taking in the sight of the police officers, his face unreadable.

"Lower your weapon," Hong warned. Mr. Yang held both hands out in a sign of surrender. He began to bend down, presumably to put his gun down, when yet another gunshot rang out. Winston jumped, confused, as Mr. Yang's head snapped back and his body crumpled to the ground like a rag doll.

"What the fuck, Leung?" Hong shouted at a man next to him. This Leung guy, too, was dressed in a suit like Hong, so Winston assumed he was also an inspector.

"He had a gun," Leung said simply, not a trace of emotion in his voice. He ignored Hong's hot, angry glare and walked over to where Mr. Yang's body lay.

"Are you okay?" Hong asked, redirecting his attention to Winston.

"I'm okay, I think," Winston said. "How did you—?"

"Find you? Steel called me, told me about your message. We had a tracker planted in your car for the races—I'll have it removed today, don't worry—so we tracked you here."

There weren't words for the emotions Winston was feeling at that moment. "Thank you," he said, knowing that didn't do him justice and hoping Hong understood. Suddenly he remembered Mimi. "We need an ambulance quickly," he said.

"We'll take care of it," Hong said immediately. He called for the medics to come in. They'd apparently been waiting behind the police.

"Level three," Winston called to them as they hurried off.

"Come on," Hong said gently. "Let's get you back to your mother."

Winston nodded, letting himself be led off to Hong's car.

Fifty-Three

WINSTON FIDGETED IN the backseat of his car, wondering where it was they were taking him. He'd been working on his car in the usual place behind the coffee shop when Wei, Conroy, Tony, and Steel had ambushed him, Tony and Steel shepherding him into the backseat while Conroy took the wheel and Wei took the passenger seat.

"Why won't anyone tell me where the fuck we're going?"

"You're too goddamn impatient," Conroy said, glaring at him through the rearview mirror. "You'll know when we get there."

"In the old Hong Kong gangster films that would mean you're leading me to a spot to dump my body."

Wei chuckled. "Good thing I'm not like those Dragonheads, yeah?"

Winston didn't know if he should be reassured by the remark. He hated when the guys acted so secretive.

Steel reached down and grasped Winston's hand, caressing the back of it with his thumb reassuringly. "I guess now we know how Noah felt when we dragged him off to the night market." He smiled fondly at the memory. Noah had been so antsy, anxious to know where they were going, and hadn't liked getting told to wait and see. Being in his shoes, Winston was starting to see why it had been a dick move on their part.

"I'll keep that in mind. No more surprise trips through the city."

"Where's your sense of adventure?" Conroy asked. "That ended up being great for Noah, and you'll like where we're taking you, too."

"We'll see," Winston muttered.

The building Conroy stopped in front of had no sign over the door and the windows were heavily curtained. There was no indication of life that Winston could see. He wondered if it was a pit stop, but everyone piled out of the car, so he did, too, his confusion not abated.

"Where is this place? I've never seen it before." Winston looked around. The building was located in a sort of cul-de-sac in the heart of the Eastern District. It stood alone, no other businesses in sight around it.

"Just come on," Conroy said impatiently.

Winston sighed and followed the three Dragons up the stairs and into the building. He found himself standing in a dimly lit waiting room of sorts, several three-ring binders lying around. A curtain separated the space from a room behind it, though Winston couldn't see what lay beyond.

A tiny bell over the door rang as they walked in, and someone appeared from behind the curtain. He was a rail-thin, elderly man, with an almost stereotypical appearance. A white mustache tapered down thinly, almost to his chin, and he had an equally long goatee, though it was speckled with bits of darker black hair.

"Wei, you're here!" His voice was dry as old paper, but hearty, strong. He held his bony arms out, and Wei hugged him like a father. "I thought you were going to be late, but you barely made it on time." The old man glanced at the clock on the wall before turning his attention to Winston. "This is him?"

"Yes, Ping. This is Winston." Wei rested a hand on the man's shoulder, like he was introducing his grandfather. "Winston, this is Old Man Ping. He's the best tattoo artist in all of Hong Kong."

"Bah." Ping batted Wei's hand away. "Not hard to be the best in this city. Best in all of China—now that's how you praise a man."

"He's humble, too," Tony said with an uncharacteristic grin. Ping responded with a very un-grandfather-like gesture.

Where the hell did they bring me? "This guy is a tattoo artist?" Winston asked Steel slowly, starting to understand.

Steel's answering smile affirmed his idea. "He's the man who puts the ink on all of the Dragons. Wei won't trust anyone else for the job."

Winston's eyes widened. He almost didn't dare believe what he was hearing. He'd been waiting for so long; were they really about to give him everything he wanted? "This better not be some sick game," he warned, pointing a suddenly shaking finger at Steel and then Wei, Tony, and Conroy in turn.

"It's no game," Wei assured him. "This has been a long time coming. Winston Chang, you've put your life on the line for the Dragons, helped us in more ways than I can say. You've proven yourself a true brother to each and every one of us. As a testament to that, I'm making you one of my lieutenants. Welcome to the inner circle. As a sign of my trust in you, you've been brought here to receive your Dragon tattoo. You know this isn't something we do lightly."

Winston felt a heady rush of emotions, so many and so rapidly that he could not put a name to them. The swell of emotions made his eyes sting. He blinked back the tears, embarrassed by them. He would not show himself to be weak in front of the most important men in the Dragons—the men he respected more than anyone else.

"I almost cried, too," Steel confided, sliding his arm around Winston's waist, the touch providing him support. "No shame in it. It's an important moment for you."

Winston squeezed Steel appreciatively.

Wei walked up to him, putting a hand on his shoulder. "You know where you want the tattoo?"

Winston didn't have to pause to think. He'd thought about this enough times over the last five years. He knew exactly where he wanted the tattoo. He held his right arm out, palm up, indicating the expanse between his wrist and elbow. "Right here." He wanted to be able to see it all the time, a constant reminder of what he was a part of.

Ping came to him then, bony fingers lifting his wrist and examining his arm. "This will be no problem. Come along. Have you considered a design?"

Winston looked back over his shoulder at Steel one last time. Steel gave him a reassuring smile and a wink before he disappeared behind the curtain, taking the first step into his new brotherhood.

Epilogue

HENRY DANG SAT behind his desk, feeling weary in a way he hadn't before. He'd never actually felt his fifty-two years before, but that night he felt every one of them, and then some. He was on pins and needles, waiting to find out what had gone down with the man responsible for the recent rash of deaths. He should have known it would turn to chaos—what didn't with the damned Dragons involved?

The Dragons had become a thorn in Dang's side from the beginning. They acted high and mighty, but to Dang, they were even worse than the Nine Stars had been. At least the Nine Stars knew what they were; the Dragons seemed to think that they were more than just street punks with delusions of grandeur.

It had been too much to hope for them to be removed from the picture. Now he merely waited to see exactly what the damage was.

He cleared his throat as someone knocked at his office door. "Come in."

Inspector Hong entered, followed by one of his uniformed officers, Leung. Leung met Dang's eyes for the briefest of moments and offered the slightest of nods, his face passive. Hong, the troublemaker, noticed none of it.

"The man responsible for the murders was found," Hong began without preamble.

"I'm aware of that," Dang waved his hand in a *Go on* motion.

"He was apprehended after having critically injuring one of the other racers in a parking garage near Aberdeen. She'll survive, the doctors think, which is lucky."

Dang stiffened a bit, but kept any tension clear of his voice. "So you have him in custody, then?"

Hong frowned, glancing at Leung accusingly. "Not exactly, no. Officer Leung here shot and killed him before he could be questioned."

"With all due respect to Inspector Hong, the man was chasing a second potential victim—who happens to be the inspector's nephew," he added pointedly, "with a gun. I made the right choice to conserve lives."

"You shot to kill purposefully," Hong accused.

For fuck's sake, Dang wanted to groan aloud. Hong was entirely too *good* for the job. He kept that behind the facade of dutiful superintendent, though, instead saying, "Hard choices must be made, Inspector. As difficult as it might be to accept, it sounds as if Officer Leung made the best choice he could make in the situation. Lives were at stake."

"He was—"

"I've said what I'm going to say on the matter, Inspector. You both may go. And Inspector," Dang called before Hong exited the office. "Go home and be with your family. This must have been traumatizing for your nephew."

Hong gritted his teeth as if he had something he wanted to say, but in the end merely nodded and managed to mutter a "Thank you," before leaving.

The door to his office again closed, and Dang relaxed in his chair. Things hadn't worked out the way he'd hoped, but Leung's fast thinking had kept everything from going pear-shaped. *I'll have to keep an eye on that Leung. He's got good potential.*

Dang's cell phone rang, cutting his musing short. A glance at the display chilled him, like ice water pouring through his veins. He took several deep breaths to calm his nerves before he slid his thumb across the screen to answer it.

"Hello?" He heard the shaking in his own voice and felt the sharp bite of shame at it. He was a superintendent of the Hong Kong police; a phone call shouldn't leave him quaking in his boots.

But Johnny Hwang didn't make casual phone calls. Hwang was a dangerous man, and Dang knew he'd have fallout from him if everything went to hell. He just hadn't expected the fallout to come so soon.

"Superintendent Dang, how nice to speak to you." Johnny Hwang's voice was smooth and warm, like a nice brandy, but Dang wasn't fooled for a moment. "I have a feeling you were expecting this phone call, though."

"What makes you say that?" Dang asked, hating himself for beginning to sweat. At least Hwang hadn't come in person.

"Cut the shit, Dang." Just like that, the warmth was gone from Hwang's voice, replaced by a cold, brutal hardness that made him so effective as the leader of the second largest piece of territory on the island. "You know I don't like playing games."

"Of course."

He didn't come himself, Dang reminded himself. *If Hwang wanted me dead, he'd come to do it himself. No, this is a reprimand, that's it. He didn't come himself.*

"We both know what you did."

"The Dragons have been a pain in both of our asses for—"

"Shut up," Hwang snarled, and Dang fell silent. Hatred boiled up inside him, hatred for Hwang and the men like him, the thugs who thought they owned the goddamn city. He had to tread lightly, though. Hwang was a brute, but he was a clever brute, and that made him dangerous. "You'll know when I'm done, Dang. I know you underestimate me—that's a mistake. I know what you were thinking— pit the Dragons and the Twisted Vipers against one another, shake loose Tseng's grip on the Eastern District. That's why some of my own are dead now, right?"

"We both benefit," Dang said carefully. "I'm rid of that troublesome *puk gai* and you get to expand your territory. Isn't that what you want?"

"Of course it's what I want," Hwang snapped. "That doesn't mean I want you to get me there. I have my own plans for Wei Tseng and the fucking Dragons, Dang. They will be taken care of, and I will take great pleasure in being the one to put that dog Tseng down myself. I don't want any more interference on your part, Dang. I won't ignore it again. Do I make myself clear?"

"Perfectly."

With that, the line went dead, Hwang was done with him.

Dang didn't realize how tightly he'd been gripping his cell phone until he released his grip and his fingers ached. Wei Tseng was his top priority, but he'd need to get Hwang shortly after. He propped his elbows on his desk and rested his chin in his hand as his brain went to work spinning more plots and plans.

Dramatis Personae

A glossary of the characters in the world of *Hong Kong Nights*.

The Dragons

Wei Tseng—30 years old, the leader of the Dragons
Conroy Wong—28 years old, second in command of the Dragons
Tony Lau—53 years old, friend and advisor to Wei
Chris Ma—29 years old, a Dragon
Jesse Zhang—27 years old, a Dragon
Kevin Shen—22 years old, a Dragon
Smile Kang—33 years old, a Dragon
Steel—24 years old, a Dragon
Walker Teng—29 years old, a Dragon

The Cops

Allen Hong—32 years old, an inspector, brother of Constance Chang, former friend of Wei
Henry Dang—47 years old, Superintendent of the Eastern District, corrupt
Inspector Leung—34 years old, one of Dang's

Others

Constance Chang—41 years old, sister of Allen Hong, mother of Winston Chang, owner of Coffee by Constance
Shelby Chang—17 years old, sister of Winston Chang, daughter of Constance Chang
Winston Chang—20 years old, brother of Shelby Chang, son of Constance Chang, has been best friends with Steel for ten years, wants to be a Dragon
Mimi—31 years old, a racer in the Dark Streets who befriends Winston
Noah Potter—27 years old, American, lover of Wei
Songmin Choi—26 years old, friend half Korean, half Hong Konger, friend of Noah Potter

Glossary of Cantonese Words and Phrases

This is a list of the Cantonese phrases used throughout the book. It is by no means comprehensive, nor do I include tonal markings for ease of reading in the book itself. There are a lot of online resources for studying Cantonese if you are interested.

Da fei gei—Jerk off (literally translates as shooting airplanes)
Daih dai—Little brother
Dim Sum—Dim sum
Diu—Fuck (exclamation)
Diu lei—Fuck you!
Diu lei lo mo chau hai—Fuck your mother's stinky vagina*
Dzu pa—Ugly girl (literally translates as porkchop)
Fai di laa—Hurry up!
Fo Wo—Hot Pot
Ga tsan—Asshole
Gong dzau tin ha mou dik, dzou dzau mou lan wai lik—All talk, no action.
Gwei—White, foreign. (literally means ghost)
Gweilo—White guy, foreigner
Gwei mui—White girl
Ham sap lou—Horny bastard
Hanzi—Chinese characters
Hou sei la lei—Drop dead, go to hell
Jai—Son
Jin jang—Low-life (pariah)
Joutau—Good night
Lan—Dick (body part)
Mah ma—Mom
Mei gwok—America
Mh goi—Thank you (for a service)
Ong lan gau—Dumb fuck
puk gai—asshole, bastard
Sau seng—Shut up

Sei—Damn (adjective)
sei bat po—Damn bitch
Sei gei lou—Fag (derogatory, obviously)
sei yan tau—Jerk
Shaojiu—Chinese sorghum-based alcohol
Sik si la lei—Go to hell
Siu ze—Lady, a polite address for a woman you don't know
Yan you—Slug
Yau mo gau lan chou—You fucking kidding me?
Zhou—Clumsy

*This is pretty much the worst insult you could possibly say to someone; it *will* get you attacked if you use it with a Cantonese-speaking person or on the streets of Hong Kong; this isn't even something you could say to your friends, jokingly.

About the Author

J. C. Long is an American expat living in Japan, though he's also lived stints in Seoul, South Korea—no, he's not an army brat; he's an English teacher. He is also quite passionate about Welsh corgis and is convinced that anyone who does not like them is evil incarnate. His dramatic streak comes from his lifelong involvement in theatre. After living in several countries aside from the United States, J. C. is convinced that love is love, no matter where you are, and he is determined to write stories that demonstrate exactly that. J. C. Long's favorite things in the world are pictures of corgis, writing, and Korean food (not in that order...okay, in that order). J. C. spends his time when not writing by thinking about writing, coming up with new characters, attending Big Bang concerts, and wishing he was writing. The best way to get him to write faster is to motivate him with corgi pictures. Yes, that is a veiled hint.

Email: jclongauthor@gmail.com
Facebook: https://www.facebook.com/authorjclong
Twitter: @j_c_long_author
Website: http://www.jclong.org/

Also by J.C. Long

Unzipped Shorts
New Year's Even Unzipped
Unzipping 7D

Hong Kong Nights Series
A Matter of Duty

Gabe Maxfield Mysteries
Mai Tais and Murder